Also by Manda Collins

Good Dukes Wear Black

Manda Collins

St. Martin's Paperbacks

This is a work of fiction. All of the characters, organizations, and events portrayed in this novel are either products of the author's imagination or are used fictitiously.

GOOD DUKES WEAR BLACK

Copyright © 2016 by Manda Collins.

For information address St. Martin's Press, 175 Fifth Avenue, New York, NY 10010.

ISBN: 978-1-250-06108-9

Our books may be purchased in bulk for promotional, educational, or business use. Please contact your local bookseller or the Macmillan Corporate and Premium Sales Department at 1-800-221-7945, ext. 5442, or by e-mail at MacmillanSpecialMarkets@macmillan.com.

Printed in the United States of America

St. Martin's Paperbacks edition / April 2016

St. Martin's Paperbacks are published by St. Martin's Press, 175 Fifth Avenue, New York, NY 10010.

10 9 8 7 6 5 4 3 2 1

For Heath and Joanna—all my love.
May your journey together be filled with happiness.

Acknowledgments

As always, I'd like to thank the Hollys: my wonderful, supportive, ninja agent Holly Root and my kind, insightful, magician editor Holly Ingraham. Thanks also to my SMP publicist, Amy Goppert, marketing guru, Erin Cox, and the art department who once again has given me a magnificent cover. My friends at Kiss & Thrill: Rachel, Lena, Amy, Sharon, Krista, Gwen, Diana, and Sharon. My support network: Julianne, Terri, Santa, Janga, Lindsey, and PJ. My sister and the menagerie for keeping the home fires burning. And last but not least, the wonderful readers who make this the best, most rewarding job in the world.

One

The club members were acquitting themselves rather well among polite society, thought Piers Hamilton, Duke of Trent, the latest president of the Lords of Anarchy, as he surveyed them mingling with the highest sticklers of the *ton*.

Especially considering that the last party the Lords of Anarchy had hosted was an actual orgy.

The duke, known to his intimates as Trent, was the latest in a quick succession of leaders of the aforementioned driving club, which, on top of being known for its fast races and drunken debauchery, had also been helmed in the past couple of years by men who turned out to be somewhat less than scrupulous about some laws.

The one against murder, for instance.

So when the few remaining members with a conscience had approached him about becoming president, Trent had been hesitant. But he liked a challenge. And his years as an officer in His Majesty's army had shown him that even the most undisciplined of men could be molded into good soldiers. Thus he'd accepted the position with an eye toward reining in the wildest elements of the membership and giving the rest of them a club they could be proud of.

Now, watching the newest members of the club dancing with perfectly respectable ladies in the ballroom of his London residence, Trent was hopeful that there would be no more bad behavior from the Lords of Anarchy. At least not under his watch.

"Trent," said Lord Frederick Lisle, clapping his old friend on the shoulder, "you've done yourself proud with your first entertainment as the duke. I wouldn't have guessed a man with so little patience for socializing would manage it, but you proved me wrong."

Before he could retort, they were joined by the recently wed Earl of Mainwaring, who was the third in their circle since their schooldays. "You know you're supposed to dance with them," he said dryly, with a nod in the direction of a pair of young ladies who whispered furiously behind their fans while casting longing looks in Trent's direction.

As the three men watched, a young gentleman with laughably high shirt points and hair that had been pomaded and teased until it added three inches of height to his willowy frame approached the bevy and bowed deeply. Words were exchanged, eyelashes fluttered, and soon the young man was leading out the prettier of the two onto the dance floor. The other, her courage waning with the departure of her friend, turned her attention to the partygoers on her other side.

"Who was that strange creature?" Mainwaring asked, raising his quizzing glass to get a closer look at the bold young gentleman. "I don't think I've seen shirt points that high since—"

"You were that age?" Freddy finished with a laugh. "I seem to recall you were rather fond of the pomade as well."

"No more than you," Mainwaring retorted with a frown, turning his glass upon his friend. "And if we are paying calls in Memory Lane, then by all means let us discuss the time you so knotted your neck cloth your valet had to cut you out of it?"

"It's a very complicated knot," Freddy said with injured dignity. "Which you would know if you ever tried it yourself."

"Before you come to blows over your youthful fashion choices," Trent said mildly, "to answer your original question, Mainwaring, that 'creature' as you call him is my cousin Waldo Hamilton, who also happens to be my heir."

He watched with amusement as his friends blinked and glanced once more at Waldo, who was mincing through the steps of a country dance, careful not to hold the lady so close that she mussed his cravat.

"My condolences," Freddy said with a wince.

"Perhaps he'll get better with age?" Mainwaring asked, his voice rising with the question in a manner that indicated he didn't quite think so.

"He is seven-and-twenty years old," Trent said

dryly. "If he hasn't grown out of the taste for that fashion by now I fear it's too late."

"I now see how truly lucky I am to be the youngest son," Freddy said sincerely. "No need to worry about the line of succession so no mixing with family members like that."

"One of the benefits certainly," Mainwaring said with a nod. "My heir isn't the sharpest stickpin in the jewel box but he's at least . . ."

"Sensible? Able to dress himself without ending up looking like a caricature of a Parisian hairdresser?" Trent shook his head. "As you can see, gentlemen, I cannot allow the dukedom to go into Waldo's hands. He'd likely invest all the income from the home farms in pomade and the tenants would starve to death."

"He's not that bad, surely," Freddy said encouragingly. "Perhaps he has hidden depths."

"Wait until you've had a conversation with the fellow before you make that judgment," Trent said grimly. "And even if he were to become sensible overnight, I still have to think about the succession. Just because it is my duty."

"You and your duty," Mainwaring said with a roll of his eyes. "One of these days you'll realize that sometimes life is about doing what you want. Not just what you're required to do by duty."

"And sometimes duty and wanting blend together," Trent said with a speaking look. "Or do you deny that you wed Hermione because of both and not one or the other?"

"It's true," his friend said without rancor. "In my case the two overlapped. But I can tell you that even if I weren't duty-bound to marry her, I'd have found a way to make it happen regardless. Because I wanted her."

Trent knew that his friend's situation had been more complicated than he currently made it out to be. And he was happy that both Freddy and Mainwaring had found ladies to whom they could pledge their hearts as well as all their worldly goods. But he wasn't sure such a match was something that he could find for himself. For one thing he knew that with a dukedom at stake he was likely to be besieged with all manner of young ladies who were eager to become his duchess, whether she cared for him as a person or not. And for another, he hadn't the sort of charm Freddy wielded, or the effortless manners that Mainwaring possessed. He was, beneath all the polish of his title, a soldier at heart. And though he'd wooed his share of women with his red coat and a smile, without the uniform he was just another gentleman. At least that's how he felt. No matter how many times he was called *your grace*.

"Of course you would have," Freddy said with a nod. "And I have no doubt that Trent will be able to find someone just as we have. It's just a matter of, you know, talking to ladies. Dancing with them."

"What kind of host doesn't dance at his own ball?" Mainwaring asked with a speaking look at his friend. "You know that the more ladies you interact with, the sooner you'll find someone to prevent that awful twit from—"

"Ah, Waldo," interrupted Trent, as his cousin, now that the dance was finished, approached them with the young lady he'd so lately squired still on his arm. "I hope you are enjoying yourself."

"May I present Miss Clementina Sutpin, cousin?" Waldo asked with a bow. "She could speak of nothing but you throughout our dance. Miss Sutpin, this is my cousin, the Duke of Trent. And as we discussed, I am his heir."

The chit's eyes widened at her escort's words. "I'm sure I didn't . . . that is to say, I never . . ."

Trent dared not look at Freddy or Mainwaring lest he see their undoubtedly droll expressions.

"Miss Sutpin," he said, bowing over the young lady's hand, which trembled a little. "A pleasure to meet you. I hope you're having a pleasant time."

Before she could reply, Waldo spoke up. "Of course she is, Duke. And she's quite happy to meet you and your friends as well. These two fine fellows, my dear, are Lord Frederick Lisle, the fifth son of the Duke of Pemberton, and the Earl of Mainwaring."

The girl's cheeks colored at Waldo's words. "It is a pleasure to meet you, your grace," she said. Then turning to Freddy and Mainwaring, she added, "And you too, my lords." Removing her hand from Waldo's arm, though he looked as if he'd like to snatch it back, she continued, "If you gentlemen will excuse me, I need to find my next dance partner."

And before Waldo could ensnare her once more, she hurried off.

"A well enough looking chit if you discount the nose," Waldo said to the three men in an undertone. "I'd best be off to find my next partner as well. My thanks for the invitation, cousin. A fine gathering of suitable young ladies here."

As he too took his leave, the three men exchanged speaking looks.

"I can see why you are determined to marry soon," Freddy said baldly. "He's an appalling fellow."

"And I had thought the cravat and pomade were the worst of it," Mainwaring said, sounding a bit stunned. "But his manner is the worst by far."

"A definite incentive to find some suitable young lady and get her with child," Trent agreed, wishing he had a glass of claret to wash away the bad taste. "Can you imagine what sort of progeny he'd foist upon the world?"

Both Freddy and Mainwaring shuddered.

"I thought I'd find the three of you together," came a lady's voice from behind them. Turning, Trent saw Freddy's wife, Leonora, slipping up beside her husband. "Though you should all be doing your duty by dancing with the wallflowers."

"I might have done so," Freddy told her with a wink, "but Mainwaring and I had to stay by Trent here and give him some tips. I hear rag manners run in his family."

"Freddy," Leonora chided, "don't tease. There's nothing wrong with Trent's social graces. He simply isn't as much of a butterfly as you are. Which is not altogether a bad thing."

"Butterfly, eh?" Freddy frowned at his wife. "And here I thought I'd settled down with one beautiful flower in particular. I promise I'll sip nectar from no other, my dear. Which means no wallflowers. But Trent is free to flit among them."

"Yes, Trent," Mainwaring said archly, "why don't you go find some winsome wallflower to bestow your . . . er—"

This line of metaphor could get ribald quickly, Trent thought wryly, interrupting his friend before he went too far. "I do not need permission from either of you to dance. I simply wanted to ensure that things were going smoothly."

"It's not as if you're the only man in the room on the lookout for a wife, Trent," Leonora said, interpreting his diffidence as shyness. "Besides, I don't think the horde of mothers with marriageable daughters are paying attention to our conversation just now. Not when that particular argument is taking place."

Following the direction of her gaze, he saw that there was indeed a quarrel going on.

One of the newest club members, and a fellow army veteran, George Grayson, was engaged in a heated discussion with a blond lady Trent assumed was the fellow's wife. They were standing just to the side of the doorway leading into the main hall, so only this side of the room was privy to their conversation.

"I asked you not to see that fellow anymore,

Maggie," growled Grayson, gripping his wife's arm tightly.

"Let go of me, George," she hissed. "You're drunk. And you're embarrassing me."

"You're embarrassing yourself," Grayson said bluntly. "Chasing after a man so far below you."

"If anyone is bringing embarrassment on this family," she retorted hotly, finally pulling away, "it's you. Thank you for ruining the first night's entertainment I've had in months. I'm going home now."

As they looked on, Maggie Grayson stalked toward the cloakroom and away from the assembled company while her husband stared after her, his jaw set, his expression bleak.

Excusing himself to his guests, Trent threaded his way through the crowd that, now that the show was over, had turned away again.

When he reached Grayson's side, he laid a calming hand on the other man's arm. When Grayson turned with a growl, Trent held up his hands. "Easy, old man, I'm just here to see if there is aught I can do to help."

His response delayed a bit by the amount of alcohol he'd consumed, Grayson looked thunderous, but when he finally realized who it was who dared speak, his shoulders slumped. "Sh-sh-sorry, your g-grace," he slurred. "Fight with m'wife, don't y'know. D-damned headstrong woman."

"Refusing to cut a man who poses no threat to her husband does not make Maggie headstrong, Mr. Grayson," interjected an angry young woman who approached the drunk man from the other side. "She has done nothing wrong yet you continue to accuse her. You'll ruin both of them before you're through. Not to mention your marriage."

Trent was well acquainted with Miss Ophelia Dauntry, who as a dear friend of both Leonora Lisle and the Countess of Mainwaring was often in attendance at the same small parties of those couples as he was. Even so, he hadn't really expected her to be the sort who would accost a man in an open ballroom for mistreating his wife.

Grayson, it would seem, also knew Miss Dauntry. "Psh, you're just as bad as she is. Hoydens with no self-control, the pair of you."

Realizing that he needed to get Grayson out of the room as quickly as possible, Trent took the man by the arm and marched him past Miss Dauntry toward the same hallway through which Mrs. Grayson had just departed.

"Where're we goin'?" Grayson demanded blearily. "Got t' find m'wife."

"After you've sobered up a little, I think," Trent told the other man.

Miss Ophelia Dauntry followed as closely behind the Duke of Trent and George Grayson as she could without calling attention to herself.

If her mother got wind of her confrontation of Maggie's husband in the Duke of Trent's ballroom, she'd have a conniption fit for certain. But hopefully, Mrs. Dauntry was safely tucked away in the card room losing what was left of her pin money for the month. Safe in the knowledge that her younger daughter was betrothed to the Marquess of Kinston, Ophelia's mother would surely not trouble herself over the behavior of her elder daughter just yet.

At least not until she recalled that she wished for Ophelia to be settled as well as, or better than, Mariah.

Like George Grayson, Mrs. Dauntry didn't approve of the editor of the *Ladies' Gazette* one bit. But rather than fearing Edwin Carrington had designs on Mrs. George Grayson's virtue, Mrs. Dauntry thought his eye was on her daughter Ophelia.

And a newspaper editor was as far below a marquess in rank as a pauper was below a prince.

It mattered not that Ophelia had no interest in Edwin as a husband or anything other than as editor of her short essays for the paper. As Mrs. Dauntry saw things, every unmarried man who came into contact with one of her daughters had designs on them. Especially those who had something to gain from the hypothetical match.

Poor Edwin, Ophelia thought as she kept the top of Trent's head in sight. He likely had no idea what a bone of contention he'd proved to be for his two most popular contributors.

It soon became obvious that Trent was leading Grayson to one of the private family rooms of the large town house. She was aware of the impropriety of her course of action even as she continued to follow them, but she could see no other option.

George Grayson was not only going to ruin his

wife's reputation among the *ton*, but he was also going to expose her identity as the author of one of the most popular columns with the ladies of the *ton*. "Ask a Reigning Toast" was an advice column to which the most desperate of society ladies turned when they needed advice on how to climb the ranks of the social ladder. And it had turned the *Ladies' Gazette* into a best seller among the ladies of both the *beau monde* and those who aspired to enter it.

Since the success of Maggie's column also ensured the success of Ophelia's own, lesser known column about needlework, she had a vested interest in keeping Maggie's going.

That meant stopping George Grayson from revealing his wife's identity as well as convincing him to leave her to her own devices.

"I suggest you turn around and go back to the ballroom, Miss Dauntry," Trent called to her over his shoulder as they neared the door to his study. "I appreciate your need to fight for your friend, but I will manage Grayson from here."

But she hadn't followed them this far just to turn around and go back to the dancing.

"I can appreciate your concern, your grace," Ophelia said, rushing forward and slipping into the room just when Trent would have closed the door. "But I must speak privately with Mr. Grayson."

"Don't have nothin' to say to ye," that man said from where he'd collapsed into a wing chair. "Damned nuisance. Convincing m'wife to take up w' that newspaperman."

Glaring at Ophelia in exasperation, Trent sighed deeply and gestured for her to take the seat near Grayson's. "If you insist on being here, then you'd best get on with it before your mother comes searching for you."

For a moment, Ophelia was flustered. She hadn't thought Trent paid her the least bit of attention. Certainly not enough to note her mother's intentions for her. While they were often in company together, she knew that as a duke and a devilishly handsome one at that, what with his broad shoulders and gleaming dark hair with a tendency to curl if it was left too long, he had no reason to take notice of her at all.

"Do not look so surprised," he said in answer to her wide eyes. "You are an unmarried young lady out in London society. It's hardly a great leap of logic to guess that your mother has aspirations for you to marry well."

She closed her mouth, abashed. Of course he'd guessed. It was foolish of her to think he'd been paying close attention to her and her family. He had much better things to do.

"Well," she said once she'd regained her control. "I think we are safe for a bit since she's in the card room at the moment. And even if she were not, I would risk bringing her wrath down on me in order to speak to Mr. Grayson."

"Why," Trent, asked, glancing to where Grayson sat scowling at a fray in his shirt cuff as if it had personally done him a wrong. "You've already scolded the fellow for his mistreatment of his wife. I should think that was a conversation best had when he's sober enough to remember it."

He had a point there, she thought. Still, she had to try to get through to Grayson now so that he wouldn't speak out again tonight.

Not bothering to respond to Trent, she turned to her friend's husband.

"Mr. Grayson," she said in a too-loud voice that she knew sounded silly but hoped would seep into his drink-addled brain. "I must remind you not to speak about Maggie's position with The *Ladies' Gazette* in public. She's asked you again and again. You must respect her wishes. Unless you wish to ruin her."

Grayson made a rude noise in the back of his throat. "Secret," he muttered. "On'y secret I know of is Carrington's lecher . . . ism. Should call the bastard out for it."

As if realizing what a brilliant idea that was, he attempted to stand. But Trent was there with a staying hand on the other man's shoulder. "Not just now, old fellow. Carrington isn't here. And besides, you promised you'd give me your advice about that bay mare I'm thinking of buying."

Even as he held his friend back from rising, Trent glared at Ophelia and jerked his head in the direction of the door. "Why don't we have a drink and we'll talk," he told Grayson.

Despite Trent's very obvious desire for her to leave the room, Ophelia pressed on. "I must have your word, Mr. Grayson, that you will stop making a spectacle of your wife. Her position with the *La-dies' Gazette* is sensitive and should not be talked about so openly in public."

"What's so dashed important about hiding Mrs. Grayson's involvement with the newspaper?" Trent demanded in a low voice that Grayson wouldn't hear. "It's not as if she's writing screeds against the government or scandalous stories. If I re-call correctly, her column deals with social niceties. It's hardly the sort of thing to cause scandal."

"It isn't," she explained patiently, "but there is still the fact that by calling attention to Maggie's role with the newspaper, and what's worse, accus-ing her of infidelity with poor Mr. Carrington, it becomes a threat to everyone at the paper."

A look of disappointment flashed across Trent's face. "So it's really your own reputation you're hop-ing to save," he said with a scowl. "I might have known."

"It's important to me," she said, holding her head high, not daring to let him see how much his derision stung. "And I won't apologize for trying to protect both mine and Maggie's positions. No one else will do so."

Their heated discussion was interrupted then by a loud snore. Looking up, Ophelia saw that George Grayson had leaned back in his chair and, his mouth hanging open, was snoring loudly.

"It would seem you've been on a fool's errand, Miss Dauntry," Trent told her with a barely sup-pressed grin. "You'll simply have to wait until another time."

Her hands on her hips, Ophelia scowled at both men. "I should have known this would be pointless. Maggie has tried and tried to convince him that her work for the paper is perfectly innocent, but he refuses to believe her. And he'll doubtless be waking up tomorrow with no recollection of tonight's contretemps. Typical."

"I think perhaps if you understood just what it is that drives Grayson to drink so deeply," Trent said pointedly, "then you would have a bit more compassion for the man. He's had a difficult time of it since the war."

"So have you," she retorted, "but I don't see you shouting at your wife in ballrooms and accusing an innocent man of debauchery."

"If I had a wife," he said, not giving an inch, "I might. Until you've walked a mile in another man's shoes you can have no idea of what presses him to behave as he does."

Ophelia sighed. She'd heard other such excuses for the bad behavior of both former soldiers and errant husbands, but there was no denying the fact that they were responsible for their own bad behavior. Not some long-ago war experience or being coddled too much as little children. Even so, she wasn't prepared to argue the matter with Trent, who, even if he was pig-headed was the dear friend of her own friend's husband. She would keep the peace for Leonora's sake.

"I thank you for the advice, your grace," she said to Trent as she took one last look at the still-sleeping Grayson. "Now I suppose I'd better get back before my mother returns from the card room."

"I'd offer to escort you," Trent responded with a short bow, "but I don't think you'd wish for the scandal that would ensue from such an arrival after several minutes' absence any more than I would."

Now that was a dreadful thought. Ophelia shivered a little. "No, no, I quite agree. I'll go back on my own, thank you very much. Good evening, your grace."

"Good night, Miss Dauntry," she heard him call to her as she shut the door to his study behind her.

Really, she thought as she headed back to the ballroom, it was too bad that Trent was so high in the instep. For he was as handsome a man as she'd ever met.

Fortunately, Ophelia had long ago resigned herself to the fact that handsome men, for all that they might be pleasant to look at, were rarely worth the trouble.

Just look at what poor Maggie had had to endure at the hands of George Grayson.

No, she thought, stepping back into the crowded ballroom, she was quite happy not to let her mother see her in the Duke of Trent's company.

She valued her freedom far too much to dangle after a man like that.

Two

"This is excellent prose, Miss Dauntry."

Ophelia couldn't stop her smile of satisfaction at the compliment from her editor, Mr. Edwin Carrington. She'd worked hard on her piece for this week's *Ladies' Gazette* and was pleased to know he had noticed.

"Thank you, Mr. Carrington," she said from the doorway of his office in the cramped quarters of the newspaper. "I thought my readers might appreciate hearing about my own trouble mastering the French knot. It can be quite difficult for a beginner."

"And that's just the sort of personal touch I appreciate about your columns, Miss Dauntry." His smile was genuine, though Ophelia could tell that he was ready to get to the next in the stack of stories on his cluttered desk. Running a newspaper wasn't an easy business and Ophelia knew from her time with the *Gazette* that Edwin gave it his full attention.

Before he could dismiss her, however, she broached the topic that had actually brought her to her editor's office. "Did you have a chance to look at my piece about the orphan problem in the East End? I know it's not the sort of thing we normally print, but I thought perhaps . . ."

His sigh at her words told Ophelia all she needed to know.

"It's not that your story is bad, Miss Dauntry," he said, his gray eyes kind as he gathered another set of pages. "It's just that the *Ladies' Gazette* isn't that sort of paper. I've tried to tell both you and Mrs. Grayson as much, but you both keep coming to me with these kind of pieces. I greatly fear that I will lose both of you to one of the larger London papers soon."

Before she could respond, Ophelia felt her friend Maggie Grayson step up beside her. Both ladies moved farther into the office to stand side by side in front of Mr. Carrington's desk.

"But we could make it that sort of paper, could we not, Mr. Carrington?" Maggie asked with a reassuring squeeze of Ophelia's arm. "It's just a matter of a piece here and there about more serious issues. Ladies do not wish to always be wrapped in cotton wool, you know. And I believe they would appreciate hearing about things that are happening right here in their very own city. Some of them have very deep pockets indeed and might dip into them to help some of those unfortunates who live in those parts of London the genteel usually avoid."

Mr. Carrington's handsome face twisted with

genuine unhappiness. "I do understand what you both are saying," he said, running a hand through his light brown hair. "But I have to think about the bank balance. And unfortunately, our advertisers do not like change. Perhaps sometime later we can revisit the issue, but for now, I'm afraid the answer is still no. Besides, I believe in that asylum story you've been begging me to publish, Mrs. Grayson, you are very clear about the ties between one asylum in particular and the Lords of Anarchy."

Maggie's gaze sharpened.

This was the first Ophelia had heard about the link between the Lords of Anarchy and an asylum. Had Maggie refrained from mentioning it because of Ophelia's connection with Trent? Why would she when her own husband was a member?

Her thoughts were interrupted, however, by her friend's reply to their editor. "I do understand that you would refrain from drawing the wrath of a group like the Lords of Anarchy, Mr. Carrington. I believe they have any number of powerful men counted among their number. But sometimes it is necessary to cross powerful people in order to get the truth out in the open."

"It's not so much fear, Mrs. Grayson," Carrington replied, "though I am quite abashed that you would think me such a coward—as knowing where our audience lies. We appeal to ladies who are looking for a bit of escape from the realities you both speak about in these stories I've rejected. They do not wish to hear about filthy urchins without enough food in their bellies. Nor do they look to the *Ladies'*

Gazette for descriptions of what it's like to be held against one's will in a madhouse. They come to us for gentle commentary from trusted friends—you two—that they can rely upon to help them with their needlework, or to divert them with a bit of gossip. I am sorry, but the answer is still, it must be, no."

His refusal hung in the air for a moment before Ophelia felt compelled to speak up.

"Thank you for reading the piece anyway, Mr. Carrington," she said, reaching out to take the sheets she'd carefully copied from her draft the evening before.

"Now, I wish you will both drop this formal business and call me Edwin," he said with a smile that was a bit sunnier. "We're like a family here. At least I feel as if we are. Perhaps you both feel differently."

It was something he'd brought up before, but despite her admiration for her editor, Ophelia wasn't quite ready to drop the level of formality between them. Edwin Carrington was a handsome single man. And he was her employer. She needed that last bit of distance between them, if only for her own sake.

Maggie, on the other hand, felt no such compunction. "Very well, Edwin," she said with a bright smile. "Now I believe we will leave you to your work. Ophelia and I promised ourselves we'd go hat shopping after we turned in our stories. And I've got my eye on a very pretty bonnet in the shop down the street."

"Good morning, then, ladies," he said as they turned to leave.

"Good morning, Mr. Carrington," Ophelia said over her shoulder.

She heard his sigh as she and Maggie shut his office door behind them.

Once they were on the street, she spoke up. "Do you think it's a good idea to become so familiar with Mr. Carrington, Maggie? Especially after your husband's accusations?"

But Maggie threaded her arm through Ophelia's and made a noise that sounded remarkably like a snort.

"You let me worry about my husband, my dear," she said firmly. "I hardly think allowing Edwin to call me Maggie will lead to any sort of romantic liaison. We are friends. Just as you and I are friends. It would be absurd if you made me address you by your title all the time."

"Not in my mother's circles," Ophelia said wryly. She knew just what was expected of her as the eldest daughter of a gentleman, but she really did wish that she could go through life with the same ease of manner as Maggie did. Despite the fact that her father-in-law was a baron, Maggie was never high in the instep or worried about her own consequence. "She is already unhappy enough that I've chosen to write for a newspaper. I can only imagine the sort of fuss she'd kick up if she knew Mr. Carrington was encouraging me to address him as Edwin. She'd likely see it as an assault on my virtue and demand that I stop writing for the paper at once."

"Well, what she does not know won't harm her," Maggie said firmly. "Now, let's concentrate on that delicious little chip bonnet you've got your eye on. I for one have had enough grimness to last a lifetime after all my research about madness and asylums."

"I hate that you've done all that work only to have Edwin refuse to publish your story," Ophelia said, still focused on the paper.

"Never you fear, Miss Dauntry," her friend said as she opened the door of Watson's Haberdashery. "I have other options. And you do too. But now, let us focus on something pretty."

Soon the two ladies were discussing the merits of green ribbon versus red, and silk versus grosgrain. Ophelia had gone to the other side of the shop to look at a pretty hat decorated with violets when she heard a male voice from where Maggie had been standing.

"I'm afraid you'll need to come with us, madam."

Though he didn't say her name, Ophelia knew instinctively that the man was speaking to Maggie.

"What's this about?" she heard Maggie ask, and turning she saw that the other lady was flanked on either side by two enormous men who were clearly not gentlemen.

Setting aside the bonnet she'd been contemplating, Ophelia hurried across the shop to where the hulking men had each taken one of Maggie's arms.

"Everything has been arranged, madam," said the larger of the two men in a placating tone. "We're going to take you to a place where you can get a nice long rest."

"What's the meaning of this?" Ophelia asked sharply as she arrived at her friend's side.

"I'm sure I don't know," Maggie said, her eyes wide with worry, even as she tried unsuccessfully to pull away. "Unhand me, please, sir. At once."

"Can't do that, ma'am," said the shorter fellow. "You're Mrs. Margaret Grayson, correct?"

Exchanging a troubled look with Ophelia, Maggie nodded. "I am, but that still doesn't give you the right—"

"Here," the larger man said, pulling a much-folded page from somewhere within the folds of his coat. "Right here it says we're to take you to the Hayes Clinic." He pointed at the page with a beefy finger.

At the mention of the Hayes Clinic, Ophelia's stomach dropped. She knew all too well that the inhabitants of Dr. Archibald Hayes's hospital for the mentally unstable were made to suffer. Maggie herself had related the horror stories to her as she researched them for her story about madhouses.

Surely that was no coincidence.

Ophelia knew instinctively that Maggie was in real danger.

"May I see your writ, please?" Ophelia asked the nearest of the two attendants, hoping her brisk tone would cow them for a moment.

Wordlessly the man handed the page to her, which she read aloud. " 'By direction of Mr. George

Grayson, I hereby authorize the bearers to take charge of Mrs. Margaret Grayson, she being insane and a danger to herself and others, and convey her to the Hayes Clinic'. Signed by A. L. Hayes, M.D."

On hearing the words, Maggie's eyes widened and she paled. "George did this?"

Ophelia's heart broke for her. But she knew where the real blame for this debacle lay—with the Lords of Anarchy. Trent might have said he was going to root out the bad elements of the club, but his support for Grayson last night had shown he wasn't serious. If public shaming of his wife hadn't gotten Grayson kicked out, why should he fear having her kidnapped would have consequences for his membership?

Whether he knew what his men were up to or not, Trent was the club's leader. He was responsible.

He might be the close friend of Leonora's and Hermione's husbands, but Ophelia knew better than to trust him. Not when Maggie's life was on the line. And not when the Lords of Anarchy had shown themselves to be open to violence and even murder in the past.

Leopards, she knew from experience, didn't change their spots.

Stepping in front of her friend, Ophelia drew herself up to her taller-than-the-average-lady height. "Insane?" she asked them, adopting the air of a dowager duchess facing a defiant underling. "Mrs. Grayson is no more insane than the man in the moon. Leave her be this instant."

"Can't do it, miss," said the man nearest her. "Orders is orders and if this here paper says Dr. Hayes says she's insane, then she's insane."

"Let me see that paper, then," said Mr. Watson, the owner of the haberdashery, who along with his clerks had been watching the scene with wide-eyed interest. With a shrug the beefy attendant took the paper from Ophelia and handed it to the shop owner.

Putting on his spectacles, Watson scanned the paper and looked up apologetically at the women. "It does look official, Mrs. Grayson. Though I don't think you look any madder than Miss Dauntry does."

"See here, miss," said the talkative attendant, "we've got our orders and if we don't get back before too long we're going to get in trouble. We'll take good care of your friend."

Even as he said the words, the other fellow had gone behind Ophelia, and by the time she turned, he'd already put her friend's wrists in irons.

"Unhand me," Maggie said, trying and failing to pull away. "This is absurd! My husband would never do this! Go see him if you don't believe me!"

"Wait," Ophelia said, alarmed at how quickly they'd got round her. "You can't do this. It isn't right!"

But the two men ignored her pleas and began marching Maggie toward the door, where a crowd of gawkers had gathered to watch the show.

"Why don't you help me stop them?" Ophelia demanded to them. "Can't you see she's being taken against her will? That writ could be a forgery for all we know."

"No offense, miss," said a man dressed in a military uniform near the door, "I don't know the two of you from Adam's cat. Maybe this lady is insane. I've heard of Dr. Hayes and he's a Harley Street specialist. Happens he knows what he's talking about."

Even as he said the words, Ophelia felt the hopelessness of her argument. These men didn't know them. And clearly logic wouldn't sway them.

As the men hauled Maggie toward the door, her friend cried out, "Find my notes, Ophelia. There must be something in them that will settle this."

But even if she did find something in the notes, Ophelia knew that if she allowed the men to take Maggie it would be that much more difficult to get her away from them later.

Desperate, she grabbed hold of one of the kidnappers, and pulled with all her might. But to her frustration, he only flung her off like a giant swatting a fly. In fact, he threw her back with such force that she flew into a shelf where an elaborate display of ladies' boots had been stacked, which tumbled down as she hit it. The heel of one boot caught her in the forehead.

"My notes," Maggie called as the men shoved her through the door and out into the street beyond. "And contact George. He can't have approved of this."

Even as the shop clerks helped her to her feet Ophelia watched in frustration as the two men thrust Maggie into their waiting carriage and sped off.

Trent let out a grunt of exertion as he parried a thrust from his opponent's foil. Lunging forward, he took advantage of George Grayson's crow of excitement at putting Trent on the defensive to riposte and slip his weapon into the other man's unguarded shoulder.

"A hit!" shouted one of the men who looked on as both Trent and Grayson lowered their swords and caught their breath. "Point to Trent!"

"That's the end of the match, your grace," said Bamford, Trent's valet, who had also served as his batman during the war. "Not too shabby for a duke, if you don't mind my saying so."

Trent handed his foil to a waiting footman and, using his shirtsleeve, wiped the sweat from his brow. In normal circumstances, he knew such a gesture would be looked at askance by those who sought to call attention to his humble beginnings, but he knew his present company wouldn't care one way or the other.

"He's the best man with a saber I ever saw," Grayson said without rancor, "duke or no."

Never comfortable with praise, Trent pretended he hadn't heard the other man's words. Being good with a weapon of war had served him well on the Continent, but it wasn't something that was valued in peacetime. And it was hardly the sort of thing he could boast about with his friends over a drink at the club.

Since Grayson had remained all but unconscious in Trent's study for most of the evening the night before, Trent had simply had the footmen carry him into one of the many empty guest rooms in the town house. The Lords of Anarchy, intent on building back the sense of camaraderie that had been lost with yet another loss of leadership, had planned to gather the morning after Trent's celebratory ball for some competitive swordplay.

Though the art of the sword fight had fallen out of favor of late, as sporting men, the club members were keen to partake of any activity that might let them prove their superiority to one another. Not to mention the fact that Trent had convinced the great Angelo to personally work with them over the course of the day. The younger members who were a bit too green to command the sword master's attention in his own establishment were quite eager to meet the man himself in the relative privacy of Trent's now-empty long gallery.

As he watched the next two opponents take their positions, Trent scanned the chamber he'd transformed into a fencing salon. Many of the men there had served with Trent as officers in the campaign to defeat Bonaparte. And though they had left the battlefield alive—some just barely—their time since the war had passed with varying degrees of success.

He'd already managed to convince many of them to join the Lords of Anarchy. It had been a bout of nostalgia for army days that had made him agree to take the position as president. The duties of the dukedom were challenging in their own way, but listening to his fellow peers drone on in the House of Lords was not nearly as satisfying as cheering on his fellow club members as they sped along a narrow lane in their curricles.

It had surprised him how much he enjoyed the feeling of the wind on his face and the challenge of handling the reins. He'd realized he'd not felt so alive since leaving Belgium.

And the club had needed him. After the two past presidents had used their leadership positions to embroil the club in illegal activities and all forms of debauchery, the Lords of Anarchy needed to mend their reputation. Who better than a decorated veteran and a duke to do the job?

So far so good, Trent thought with satisfaction as he watched the sparring.

"A good match," said Grayson, interrupting Trent's thoughts.

Glancing over at the other man, Trent saw that he looked better than he had the night before.

"I wanted to thank you for allowing me to sleep it off here last night, your grace." Grayson looked ill at ease, but sincere. "I would have been just as happy if you'd tossed me into a cab and sent me on my way, but I cannot deny that I was likely safer here in one of your guest chambers than I'd have been out there in the street. I made an ass of myself, and I'm damned sorry for it."

Trent shrugged. "The least I could do. Though I

think perhaps it's your wife you should be making your apologies to. That was quite a row you two had."

At the mention of Maggie, Grayson grimaced. "I don't remember everything I said last night but I know I was unforgivably rude to her." He shook his head slowly, as if doing so more vigorously would hurt him. "I wish I knew how best to handle her. Ever since she took up with that bloody newspaper, she's been damn near impossible to control."

"I rather thought one was supposed to control one's horses rather than one's wife," Trent said mildly. He wondered if Ophelia's complaints about Grayson last night had had basis in truth after all. "Perhaps you should just allow her to continue with it. If it is something she feels strongly about."

"I don't think I'd mind it so much if it didn't seem as if that fellow Carrington were constantly nosing after her," Grayson complained. "God knows she's got little enough reason to spend her days being condescended to in my father's house."

"Can't imagine that's been easy," Trent sympathized.

The man's father, Sir Michael Grayson, was overbearing to say the least. Trent had heard that he'd objected vociferously to George's marriage to Maggie despite her rather large dowry. Her father was a country squire with little pretensions to nobility and that wasn't quite what the elder Grayson had wished for his son. And unfortunately, since their marriage the couple had been forced to live under Sir Michael's roof.

"It isn't," Grayson said with a rueful smile. "But the small estate in Cornwall that he is letting us live in is still in disrepair and the refurbishment is taking longer than any of us intended. Maggie keeps busy with her writing, but I often find myself at loose ends. And one can only stand so many hours reading the papers at White's."

And it surely didn't help matters that Maggie had become involved in the rather less than respectable newspaper business.

Having seen how the vultures of the press preyed upon the weak and vulnerable with his own father, Trent had little respect for the profession. Leonora, Freddy's wife, wrote columns about ideas, but so-called reporters were obsessed with plastering the pages of the daily scandal sheets with rumor and innuendo. It was, in his opinion, a profession with little more dignity than the common rat catcher.

He'd hardly tell Grayson that, however. And from what Ophelia had said, Maggie Grayson seemed to have more in common with Leonora than the men who'd hounded his father.

"Which newspaper does your wife write for again?" he asked, thinking he'd find one and perhaps just see what it was Ophelia had been so passionate about last night.

"The *Ladies' Gazette*," said Grayson reluctantly. Though Trent noticed a hint of pride as he continued. "She writes about society goings-on and the like. It could be silly what with some of the things people get up to, but she always manages to make it entertaining. She's got a way with words, my Maggie."

Perhaps there was some hope for the couple after all, Trent reflected, hiding a smile. "If I happen upon a copy I'll look for her column, then," he said with a nod. "Not my usual style but I'm curious now."

"I'll send you one round," said Grayson with a nod. "I might not trust that editor Carrington, but Maggie's pieces in it are good."

They were quiet for a moment as they turned their attention back to fencing.

"Marriage suits you then?" Trent said. It hadn't seemed likely when the man was shouting at his bride, but now, he seemed like any other husband taking pride in his wife. "Despite your arguments?"

Though he'd just seen two of his closest friends marry ladies they were utterly besotted with, his own parents had been example enough of what could go wrong when two people with nothing in common were pressed into a match. His father had been a devil-may-care, spendthrift younger son of a duke, while his mother was a parsimonious Scot with a sharp mind and even sharper tongue. And when his father was involved in a scandal with the wife of a prominent general, both Trent and his mother had suffered the consequences.

What had been a distant, if amicable, marriage had turned into outright acrimony. And his father had died not too many years later in the bed of his latest mistress.

With that for an example, Trent considered it a

miracle that he was even contemplating the institution at all. But he knew his duty to his family, even if his father had not. And he was quite certain he could manage the thing without bringing shame on the Trent name or any children who might be born of the union.

"Thinking about the state yourself, eh?" asked Grayson perceptively. "I have to admit that it's not easy. Especially when your bride is as stubborn as mine. But Maggie and I rub along well enough together. When we're not fighting about the paper, of course. And when we don't there's always the club."

This last he said with a wink that let Trent know his friend wasn't completely serious. He supposed that was part of the trouble with seeking advice from friends on the subject. Marriage, it seemed, was one of those journeys that one couldn't quite understand until one was in one himself.

But he would have to simply grit his teeth and choose someone soon. Because he wasn't getting any younger. And he wanted to secure the succession before his cousin Waldo got too comfortable in his position as the heir.

"It's not all bad," Grayson said, mistaking Trent's silence for trepidation. "And being a duke you'll have your pick of the lot, won't you? So you'll be able to make your own decision without the kind of parental input I had to endure."

"Was your father not happy with your choice then?" Trent was momentarily distracted from his own matrimonial intentions. He'd heard Sir Michael was ambitious. And he could imagine that having his only son marry a lady journalist hadn't made the man entirely happy.

"Not at all," Grayson responded with a scowl. "But once we were married there was nothing he could do about it. But he cut up rough at first. If we'd not already consummated the thing, I suspect he'd have demanded an annulment."

Trent blanched. He supposed he should be grateful that he was the head of the family and could make his own decisions without fear of an overbearing parent attempting to gainsay those decisions.

"But it's all water under the bridge," Grayson assured him. "And now we're all together in the same house and get along without too much fuss."

"And will there be fuss about what happened last night?"

Grayson winced. "I hope not. I expect I will have to throw myself on Maggie's mercy and hope she will forgive me. I'm afraid I embarrassed the entire family last night, but most especially my wife."

With no experience of handling irate wives, Trent let the man's words hang in the air. He rather expected it would take a great deal of effort for Grayson to smooth last night's events over.

Better Grayson than him, he thought with a shudder.

They lapsed into companionable silence to watch the next pair of fencers cross swords. Though Trent couldn't shake the feeling that there was something dark lurking beneath Grayson's assurances.

A moment later, however, Trent felt a presence behind him. Brow raised, he turned to see the butler, Wolfe. Leading him away from his guests into a side parlor, he waited to see what had the man in such a huff.

"I beg your pardon, your grace," the regal man said with stiff dignity, "but there is a . . . person at the front door who insists on seeing you. I tried to send her to the tradesman's entrance, but she assures me that the two of you are acquainted. And that she is a lady, though she has no maid."

Trent reached to take the card Wolfe extended.

Miss Ophelia Dauntry.

What the devil?

Surely she wasn't here to rip up at Grayson on her friend's behalf again. It was bad enough she'd risked her reputation by doing it the night before. But really, though his mother was in residence, it was still not quite the done thing for her to call upon him at his home.

Still, if she'd bucked convention enough to call upon a single gentleman at his home, then she must have reason enough. Recalling that business with the Countess of Mainwaring and the Lords of Anarchy a few weeks ago, he strode down the gallery toward the staircase. It might very well be that there was some emergency that had prompted Miss Dauntry's unexpected visit.

"Where did you put her, Wolfe?" he asked the butler, who hurried along behind him.

"I . . . that is to say . . ." The butler stuttered as he tried to keep up with his master. "I left her on the doorstep."

Reaching the bottom of the grand staircase,

Trent turned and glared at him. "What do you mean you left her on the doorstep? Is that how you treat a guest?"

Wolfe swallowed, then recalling his own elevated status, he stood up straight. "She might have been anyone, your grace. And you have not seen what a state she is in. I am not in the habit of admitting just anyone into this house. It would not be fitting."

"What's not fitting is you leaving my acquaintance on the front stoop like a country beggar," Trent snapped. "Go about your business. And have Mrs. Pierce send some tea and biscuits to the front drawing room."

He didn't know much about entertaining ladies, but if his time with Ophelia's friends Mrs. Freddy Lisle and the Countess of Mainwaring was any indication, they consumed lots of tea and biscuits.

Wrenching open the front door himself, he blinked to adjust his eyes to the sunlight and saw Miss Ophelia Dauntry was indeed standing there.

Or perhaps swaying there would be a better turn of phrase.

"Your grace," she said, lowering her handkerchief from where she'd been dabbing at her forehead. "I apologize for the intrusion, but . . ."

And he realized several things simultaneously.

First, that she did indeed look disheveled. Her gown was dusty and torn on the sleeve, and her hat, which must once have been quite pretty, was crushed and hanging down her back by the ribbons.

Next, that she was swaying because she was, in

no uncertain terms, about to succumb to a very splendid faint.

And third, and most disturbing of all, the reason she had been dabbing at her forehead was that there was quite a large cut there, which was bleeding profusely. As he well knew head wounds were apt to do.

All of these things flitted through his mind even as he watched the intrepid Miss Ophelia Dauntry begin to crumple.

Then he did what any gentleman worth his salt would do.

He caught her.

Three

Ophelia returned to awareness slowly. Inhaling the delicious scent of bay rum, she snuggled in a moment before she realized there was something very wrong with this situation.

Her memory of that morning's contretemps came flooding back, and just as her eyes flew open she realized she was clasped against a hard, sweaty, male chest.

Desperate to get away, she cried out, "No!" and shoved both hands against her captor. Recalling a lesson in fighting off an attacker from a male cousin, she twisted in the hopes of getting her legs low enough to kick him in between the legs, but the man who held her proved too strong.

"Be still," he said, wrestling to regain control of her. "Miss Dauntry, be still."

The voice was familiar to her, but in her frenzy to get away, the speaker's identity did not dawn on her. Knowing that if she did as he asked she would likely be taken away to the madhouse just as her friend had been, she raked her fingernails over his exposed neck and was rewarded by a curse.

"Damn it, you hellcat, will you stop?"

And unfortunately, that was when she realized to whom the voice belonged.

The Duke of Trent, who she was unhappy to see was glaring down at her even as he carried her through an opulent drawing room.

"Yes," he said, as if in response to her silent question. "It's me. Trent."

Before she could apologize he lowered her to an overstuffed settee and stepped back, his hands on his hips as he surveyed her from head to toe.

And she took the opportunity to look back.

The duke was not dressed for company that was of a certainty.

He was in his shirtsleeves, and he wore buckskin breeches but no boots. It was obvious he'd been engaging in some sort of exertions for his dark hair, which he kept shorter than was fashionable, was glistening with sweat. Ophelia had always thought him to be an intimidating man, but she'd never guessed just how much more so he would be in dishabille. Through the fine lawn of his shirt she was able to see the contours of his muscled chest and the hard strength of his arms.

She felt a blush rise in her cheeks at the memory of being clasped in those arms.

But a glance at his angry gray eyes was enough to banish the memory.

"Here," he said curtly, handing her a pristine

white handkerchief. "Your head is still bleeding. It is likely the reason you fainted."

At the mention of it, her wound suddenly began to sting like fire. Wordlessly she took the cloth from his hands and raised it where she could feel the trickle of blood.

"May I?" he asked quietly, indicating that he would like to approach her.

Mortified at her behavior earlier, Ophelia nodded and sat quietly while he examined the cut.

She had known coming to Trent for help would be difficult but it hadn't occurred to her that she'd so thoroughly manage to embarrass herself.

"I don't think you'll need stitches," he said curtly, his face uncomfortably close to hers, "but it definitely needs to be cleaned. I'll have someone send for the doctor."

His mention of the doctor brought her out of her momentary fog.

"No," she said quickly, recalling her purpose in coming here. "We don't have time. And besides, I came here for answers. Not medical treatment."

But she made no move to rise, because even as she said the words she knew that she was in no condition to do so. Her legs were shaky and she wasn't even standing on them yet.

Trent dropped to a crouch beside the sofa, and as if he sensed her despondency, he gentled his voice. "What in the dev . . . heavens happened to you? Were you in an accident? Did someone strike you?"

And to her horror, Ophelia felt tears spring into

her eyes. She might have been able to withstand brusqueness. But Trent's concern was too much for her flayed nerves.

Taking a deep breath, she regained her composure and related the story of what had just happened in Watson's hat shop.

"I made them show me their writ," she said after she'd finished, "and it looked quite official."

"And who did that to your head?" Trent asked, still frowning. "And tore your gown?"

She didn't miss the way he scanned her, as if trying to determine whether she'd been injured in ways that weren't visible to the naked eye. Despite their brief acquaintance, she sensed he was angry at the notion and only waited for her confirmation to set off after the culprit.

For someone like Ophelia who had grown up in a household of women, such protectiveness was utterly foreign. And, if she were honest, a bit heartening.

But, she reminded herself, he was the leader of the Lords of Anarchy. And likely knew already why Maggie had been taken.

Attempting to sit up and adjust her clothing into a better semblance of order, she downplayed what had happened. "I foolishly attempted to latch onto one of the men's arms and was flung into one of Mr. Watson's shelves for my troubles," Ophelia said. "I assure you I'm quite well now."

"I don't call fainting in my doorway from loss of blood quite well, Miss Dauntry," said Trent, his mouth tight with anger. "And I don't tolerate men who commit violence against women. No matter the provocation."

He was still close enough that Ophelia could see the tiny lines fanning out from the corners of his eyes. As if he'd spent a great deal of time squinting at the sun. Or glaring at foolish ladies, she thought, realizing what he'd just said.

"I hardly call trying to rescue my friend provocative behavior, your grace," she said, sitting up straighter, ignoring the throb of the cut on her forehead. "They had no right to take her away. No matter what that piece of paper they waved around said. And certainly not with the assortment of implements they had on hand. Two strong men had no need of rope and manacles to subdue her."

Trent's dark brows drew together. "And did they use them?"

"Of course," Ophelia said with a scowl. "Well, the manacles at any rate. And when she fought back, they used their fists. That is when I attempted to intervene. I couldn't stand by and just let them take her away. Even if no one else was willing to do something, I was."

He was silent for a moment, as if imagining the scene for himself.

"And if you are so opposed to violence against women," she said, her voice sounding strident to her own ears, "then perhaps you can tell me why the Lords of Anarchy are connected to Dr. Hayes and his clinic in the first place. And why George Grayson, a member of your club, would have his own wife taken there. If it's because of the article

Maggie was writing, you will be happy to know that our editor, Mr. Carrington, had chosen not to publish it. So George Grayson's little stunt was pointless."

As she spoke, Ophelia saw Trent's brows draw together and his smooth jaw clench. He opened his mouth to respond, but before he could speak, however, a kitchen maid entered carrying a tray of tea and a platter of assorted biscuits.

As if suddenly aware of how close he was to her, Trent rose from his position beside the settee and took a seat in the chair opposite. The only hint of his impatience was the slight tightening of his lips as they watched the maid set out the tea and cups and plates on the small side table.

When she was gone, he leaned forward. Not waiting to see if Ophelia was able to, Trent himself set about pouring for both of them and despite her objection put two spoons of sugar in her tea. "You've had a shock," was all he said as he handed it to her, then set a plate piled high with biscuits before her.

As she began to sip, he rose and tugged on the bellpull. When a footman responded, he requested a small basin of warm water, basilicum powder, and bandages.

When he was seated again, the duke said, "Your wound seems to have stopped bleeding for now, but I'll take a closer look at it once you've had time to calm down."

Ophelia waited for his response to her accusation like a prisoner awaiting a sentencing.

Finally, when he made no move to address her words, she snapped, "I realize that you think something like this is beneath your notice, but I am quite prepared to take this story to my editor. I feel sure that he will wish to let all of London know just how the Lords of Anarchy treat those who cross them."

But if she was hoping to provoke a confession from him, she was sorely mistaken.

To her annoyance, he merely raised one dark brow and tilted his head. As if trying to figure her out.

"I can assure you, Miss Dauntry," he said, setting his teacup gently down on its saucer, "that I have no knowledge of any ties between the Lords of Anarchy and this Dr. Hayes. Or his clinic for that matter. You must understand that I've only been the president for a few weeks. And as you know, the previous leadership was . . . ah . . ."

"Shot dead by Lord Freddy Lisle?" she finished for him. "Do not look so alarmed. It's not as if Leonora didn't tell me the whole story."

"It just isn't something that I would think suitable talk for a lady," he said with a shrug. "Though it sounds as if you and your friend Maggie know quite a bit about the goings-on of the Lords of Anarchy. Perhaps more than I do, which I don't mind telling you is troubling."

"Because it's so unladylike?" she asked sweetly. Really, she was quite tired of being told not to worry her pretty little head over serious subjects. It wasn't as if she were incapable of understanding what went on in the world.

"Because I'm the president of the damned club and I know nothing of this business," he snapped. Then immediately apologized. "I beg your pardon. It's just that this club has been a nuisance since the moment I decided to take leadership of it."

"Then why do you stay with it?" she asked, curious.

"Because it's only been a few weeks," he said with a shrug. "And I have hopes that the new members I've recruited will have an impact on the way the club behaves as a general rule. That will take time, however. And your friend, it would appear, doesn't have much of it before she is subsumed into the bowels of this Hayes Clinic."

"No, she doesn't," Ophelia said, reminded that there was more to this than just her own petty annoyance with Trent. "I was so useless to her," she said once she'd set her cup down. "I might as well have been a small child for all the help I rendered her."

"You can hardly blame yourself for being unable to thwart two large men with experience and tools at their disposal," Trent said, brushing biscuit crumbs from his hands. "I'd have been more astonished if you'd succeeded. But that doesn't mean that you were useless. You've a good eye for detail. And I have little doubt you can describe them both accurately."

When the maid arrived with the warm water and bandages, Trent rose to take them from her, and moved to sit beside Ophelia on the sofa.

"To distract yourself," he said matter-of-factly, "perhaps you can tell me about them now."

And while her heart beat fiercely in her chest at the nearness of him coupled with the instinct to flinch every time he neared the wound on her forehead, Ophelia described them. "One was quite large. Like a prizefighter. His hair was light brown and long, held back with a bit of leather. His clothing was surprisingly well made. I'd have expected someone employed in such a position to be impoverished, but judging from the shine on his boots, I don't think he was."

"Go on," Trent said as he gently probed the edges of the cut with his fingers.

Ophelia closed her eyes, both to picture the men in her mind's eye, but also to avoid staring at the duke's strong jaw. "The other was shorter, but also wider. And his boots were not as fine as his friend's. And he smelled of onions."

Once he was finished wiping away the blood, she felt him sprinkle the basilicum powder over the cut. "And what precisely did this writ they presented say?"

She thought back, picturing the flourished script as it had appeared on the page. " 'By direction of Mr. George Grayson, I hereby authorize the bearers to take charge of Mrs. Margaret Grayson, she being insane and a danger to herself and others, and convey her to the Hayes Clinic.' Signed by A. L. Hayes, M.D."

Before she had even finished, Trent pulled away

from her. Ophelia opened her eyes to see him scowling. "What is it?"

"You never said your friend's married name," he said, rising to stride over to the bellpull once again.

"So you will refuse to help me because George Grayson is a member of the Lords of Anarchy?" she asked, drawing the obvious conclusion. "I might have known you'd side with him."

"Miss Dauntry."

"I mean, it should hardly be surprising to me at this point in my life, considering just how many times I've seen men stick togeth—"

"Miss Dauntry!"

At his sharp tone, Ophelia's eyes widened. "What is it?" she demanded, her arms akimbo. "Do you wish to tell me to take myself off now that you've learned just who is my friend's husband?"

But if she meant to get a rise from him, she was to be disappointed.

His eyes flashed, but more from impatience than anger, she noted.

"George Grayson is at the present moment upstairs in the long gallery."

"What do you mean 'gone'?" Trent demanded when Bamfield came in response to his master's summons.

What had begun as a simple day of honest exertion for Trent and the former soldiers had turned into something out of a gothic novel, what with wives being taken up for lunacy and husbands disappearing into thin air.

Ophelia, he was quick to notice, did not look surprised to hear that George Grayson had fled. In fact, with her freshly bandaged wound and worried eyes, she looked as if Bonaparte himself arriving in their midst would not faze her.

"Just that, yer grace," said Bamfield with a shake of his weather-beaten head. "He must have slipped out as soon as you came downstairs. He wasn't crossing swords so I wasn't paying him any attention. But when Reynolds brought up your request for Grayson, we all realized he'd been gone for some time." The former batman looked concerned. "If'n I'd known ye were after keeping an eye on him, I'd have done it, make no mistake. But as it was, he slipped the net with none of us the wiser."

"Not your fault, man," said Trent with a frown, dismissing him.

Where the devil had Grayson gone off to? Clearly he'd known that his wife was going to be taken up this morning. Which was odd. He certainly hadn't spoken like a man about to be rid of a troublesome wife. Far from it. He'd seemed like a man frustrated with but still in love with his bride.

There was definitely something not quite right with this situation.

But how could Grayson possibly have known that Ophelia would come to him for counsel? Especially when Trent himself—and even Ophelia, he'd wager—had had no idea she'd do so?

As if reading his thoughts, Ophelia said, "Doesn't the long gallery look out over the drive? Perhaps

George saw me approaching? As Maggie's friend and colleague, I am well known to him."

Trent hadn't seen her approach because his attention had been on the fencing match before him, but it was possible that Grayson had, he supposed. And when Trent had been called downstairs he could have taken off in order to avoid a confrontation with Ophelia.

But he wasn't ready to admit as much to her yet.

"Perhaps," he said, fingering the small scar on his jaw, where a bayonet had grazed him in France. "But it makes no sense to me that Grayson would do such a thing. He was remorseful about the scene last night at the ball. He even planned to apologize to her this afternoon."

"As well he should," she said tartly. "He was dreadful last night."

"Which he admitted," Trent said thoughtfully. "I simply cannot believe the man I spoke with just a half hour ago could possibly have arranged for his wife to be taken to a madhouse. He's not that good at lying for one."

"I suppose it's possible that the order came from someone else," Ophelia said, pinching the bridge of her nose, as if it pained her.

Noting her action grimly, Trent focused on her words. "Who else would do such a thing?"

"Well," Ophelia said with a frown, "just that Maggie told me that her father-in-law did not approve of her low rank. And he didn't think Maggie's association with the paper was appropriate for the wife of a baronet's son. They had many arguments about it while George was away, and I think Sir Michael had hoped that George's return would mean that she would be brought to heel at last."

"And I'm guessing because of last evening's scene that George was not as successful at that task as his father would have wished?" Trent asked.

"No," Ophelia said with a shake of her head. "In fact, Maggie told me that he professed himself to be quite proud of her, though he had begun to grow suspicious of Mr. Carrington's relationship with her. He's the editor."

Surely jealousy would make Grayson keep his wife close to his side, not cause an even bigger scandal by having her locked away.

If anything, if he were jealous, he'd go after Carrington and not his wife.

"I cannot imagine dinner conversation in their home is conducive to digestion," Trent said wryly.

Ophelia laughed. "Hardly." Then, the moment of levity passed. "We both saw what passed between Maggie and Mr. Grayson last night. It was a heated argument. But surely if he were expecting to be rid of her today he'd not have caused a scene. If anything he'd have been looking forward to her comeuppance."

"You make a good point," Trent said, smoothing his hair absently. "I agree that George doesn't seem to be responsible for your friend's abduction. But why would he run away this morning?"

"Perhaps he overheard me speaking about what happened and he went to search for her on his own?" Ophelia's eyes seemed hopeful, but Trent was not so sanguine. If George wanted to find his wife why would he not have asked for Trent's help? He was a duke, after all, and his title was able to open many doors that remained closed to others.

"Perhaps," he said aloud. "Though if Maggie has been a source of embarassment for her father-in-law, I suspect he is the source of Maggie's capture."

He knew a little of Sir Michael Grayson, and that was not all good.

"I think you might be right," she said, her pretty eyes troubled. "Sir Michael's greatest point of anger with Maggie was his fear of her bringing embarrassment upon the family. Last night's debacle might have been the last straw if it got back to him."

Trent felt the shift as she turned her pleading gaze on him. "Will you help me find her? I cannot possibly sit by while my dear friend is subjected to God knows what in some asylum. It would be horrible for someone not in her right mind, but perfectly sane and sober, it would be a waking nightmare. And I have a feeling they will take someone of your rank and power much more seriously than they will me."

He was silent for a moment, thinking of just how little he wished to become embroiled in the situation Miss Dauntry had brought to his door. And yet, as the president of the Lords of Anarchy, he did have an obligation to find out more about the clubs' ties—if any—to Dr. Archibald Hayes. Aside from the fact that George Grayson might have traded on that association to have his own wife taken up, there was also the fact that it was damned suspicious for a club devoted to sport to be linked with a madhouse. The implications of the various ways in which that connection might be misused was enough to make Trent's head pound with tension.

"Please, your grace," Ophelia said, obviously mistaking his silence for denial. "You must surely see how wrong it is to lock away someone who is not ill. But if not for that reason, then do it to find out for yourself just how this was planned and carried out, and whether it will have any bearing on the club's reputation."

Clearly she was not above using his own conscience against him, Trent reflected wryly. "Fine," he said with a brisk nod. "I will look into the matter. For all the reasons you've listed, and one of my own."

"Which is?" she asked.

"Because you asked me. And a gentleman tries to accomodate a lady when it is at all possible."

For a moment, Trent thought she would argue, but perhaps because she was still a bit woozy, Ophelia contented herself with a smile so bright he was momentarily knocked off-kilter himself.

He was accustomed to seeing Miss Dauntry as one of a trio of ladies whom he'd mentally labeled "off-limits"—mostly because he associated her with his friends' wives, who were her own dear friends. It had become as much a reflex as anything else. But suddenly he was reminded of the decision he'd come to last night, that it was time for him to begin looking for a wife of his own. With her shining dark hair and blue eyes, she would make a lovely duchess. But it was her determination and loyalty that had impressed him the most today.

He could do far worse than to marry a woman like Miss Ophelia Dauntry.

The memory of holding her against him earlier suddenly flashed through him. As if his body was reminding him that he'd rather liked the feel of her in his arms.

"Thank you so much, your grace," Ophelia said, apparently unaware of the direction of his thoughts. "I cannot tell you how grateful I am."

"I will just go upstairs and make myself presentable for the visit to the Grayson town house," he said, feeling his color rise as if he were a green lad again as he stood. "And then I'll be off. You must make yourself comfortable until I return."

"But I thought I would go with you," Ophelia said, her smile turning into a frown. "I'm a frequent visitor there and even if they weren't expecting Maggie to return they would not be surprised for me to stop by."

"Absolutely not," Trent said reflexively. "You are unwell."

Seeing a mulish expression on her lovely face, he softened his tone. He must recall that she wasn't one of his soldiers to be ordered about. "Stay here and I promise I will relay everything I learn to you as soon as I return."

But he could feel her glare on his back as he left the room.

Clearly he had much to learn when it came to dealing with ladies.

This one in particular.

Four

I might have known you'd ignore me," grumbled Trent as he spied Ophelia waiting for him in his curricle. "You are in no condition to make the journey to the end of the drive, let alone to the Grayson house."

"That is not for you to decide," Ophelia said firmly, trying not to notice the brush of his hip against hers as he took the seat beside her. "I do not expect you to fight my battles for me. I simply wished for your assistance. There is a difference, you know."

She could all but feel the power radiating from him, especially when his strength was combined with the perfectly tailored attire of his station. From the top of his cropped, expensively cut, dark hair to the toes of his shining black Hessians he was every inch the duke. And there was something both compelling and, to her shame, exciting about being so close to him.

This trip wasn't about exploring her attraction

to Trent, it was about saving Maggie, she told herself.

Perhaps realizing that argument was futile, he didn't respond to her, only took the reins from the groom and set the horses in motion.

Which, in turn, set Ophelia's head to pounding. Though she'd die before admitting as much to Trent.

"How is it that you are acquainted with Mrs. Grayson?" he said, distracting her from her aches.

"We both write for the *Ladies' Gazette*," Ophelia responded through gritted teeth. "Her column is quite popular, but not with her family, I don't think."

"Her own family or her husband's?" He reached a protective arm across her as the curricle sped around a sharp corner.

"Her husband's," Ophelia said. "I got the feeling that the Graysons were not particularly pleased with her for it."

"I spoke a bit with George Grayson about her this morning," Trent said. "He seemed to be sanguine about her writing."

"That's true," Ophelia agreed. "I believe George, though sometimes annoyed that it kept her away from home, was supportive. Sir Michael, George's father, is the one who frowns on it. He's quite a stickler, I think. They argued about it, I believe."

"When was this?" Trent asked, turning to look at her, his blue eyes sharp.

"Earlier this week, I believe." Ophelia tried to recall just what Maggie had said about the row, but she was having difficulty concentrating at the moment. She gave a frustrated sigh.

Perhaps sensing that she was in pain, Trent was silent after that. Soon they were turning in to Bruton Street where the Grayson town house was located.

"I think it would be best if you let me speak to them," Trent said as they came to a stop before the house. "Perhaps you could see her maid. Make up some tale about taking some of Maggie's things to her."

"But I want to speak to George and convince him to confront Dr. Hayes," Ophelia said, annoyed at his attempt to shove her off into the domestic realm. "And I'd like to talk to Sir Michael as well. George's name might have been on that writ, but it was Sir Michael's idea. I know it."

"And you think they will simply do as you ask?" Trent asked in a reasonable tone that made her want to box his ears. "George isn't likely to admit his reasoning to you. And I doubt Sir Michael will even dignify your accusations with a response. I've dealt with such men before. They respond only to other men they see as being on their level or higher. And like it or not, as a duke I am higher."

Ophelia glared at him. Hating that he was making logical sense.

"I also know George Grayson better than you do," he added gently. "Let me speak to him as a friend. He's much more likely to open up to me than he is to you."

She pressed her fingers to her pounding head.

"Fine," she huffed out. "I will talk to Hopkins, her maid. But remember that I am relying on you. If we bungle this I fear Maggie will be trapped there indefinitely."

"I give you my word, Miss Dauntry," Trent said, dipping his head so that he could meet her eye. "I will get the information you need."

Knowing that would have to do, she nodded.

Once they'd descended from the curricle, Trent offered her his arm as they climbed the few steps to the door of the Grayson town house.

Their knock was answered by a very dignified butler, Thompson, who upon learning who Trent was, became much more welcoming.

"We are indeed fortunate to welcome you, your grace," Thompson gushed.

"I need to speak with Sir Michael at once," Trent informed him before he could go on. "As well as Mr. George Grayson if he is here."

If Thompson was annoyed by the interruption, like any good butler, he did not show it and merely gave a bow and ushered them into the drawing room.

"I will have Sir Michael summoned at once, your grace."

Ophelia should have been annoyed that the man ignored her so completely, but who was a mere miss when there was a duke to be offered obeisance?

When the door closed behind him, she turned to Trent. "The house doesn't seem to be particularly upset given that one of its inhabitants was taken to the madhouse this morning."

Turning from his inspection of a particularly ugly painting of a long-dead Grayson spaniel, Trent shook his head. "It's likely most of them haven't heard of it yet. I suspect there will be a great deal of gossip about it below stairs once word gets out."

Just then, Sir Michael strode into the room, looking flushed. Perhaps he was not as happy to drop whatever it was he had been doing to answer the duke's summons as Thompson had given them to believe.

"Your grace," he said to Trent. Then turning to Ophelia he gave a condescending nod. "Miss Dauntry, I was not aware you were acquainted with his grace."

And why should he be? she wondered, mentally rolling her eyes. Before she could respond, however, Trent spoke up.

"She is hardly required to give a list of her acquaintances when she pays calls, Sir Michael," he said with a raised brow. "Miss Dauntry came to me after your daughter-in-law was taken up by two gentlemen at the behest of Dr. Archibald Hayes. She herself was injured in the process and needed medical attention."

Sir Michael's eyes widened. "Miss Dauntry, I am sorry to hear about your injuries. But what's this about Margaret? I don't understand."

"Perhaps Miss Dauntry can go speak with Mrs. Grayson's maid while we discuss the matter," Trent said smoothly. "I would not wish her to be upset further. And I believe she is familiar with the location of Mrs. Grayson's rooms from previous visits."

Nodding, Sir Michael indicated the door. Ophelia, despite her annoyance at the suggestion that she was too weak to handle their discussion, hurried from the room.

"I wonder at your agreeing to become involved in this, your grace. It is a family matter," Sir Michael said stiffly, indicating that Trent should take the wing chair opposite his own. "And really, it is none of Miss Dauntry's concern."

Though there was nothing outwardly unwelcoming, Trent got the sense that the man would have been far more agreeable had Trent not arrived with Ophelia on his arm.

Ignoring Sir Michael's chilly demeanor, Trent got down to business. "Miss Dauntry is a friend, and could have been gravely injured by Dr. Hayes's men. And as a close friend of your daughter-in-law's she wished to take some of Mrs. Grayson's things to her to make her more comfortable. And as your son was at my home while this unfortunate incident occurred I came to offer what assistance I could to him. He slipped away without letting me know he was leaving, you see. Is he here?"

If possible, the baronet's manner became even more glacial.

"As I said, Trent, it's a family matter," said Sir Michael, ignoring the question about George's whereabouts, instead saying, "My son did not consult me, but I cannot say that I am surprised that he sought help from Dr. Hayes. Margaret has been quite unruly of late."

"So unruly that he would have her locked away for it?" Trent tilted his head. Having one's spouse locked away in a madhouse was not something to be taken lightly. Yet George had shown no indications earlier that morning that any such thing was on his mind. "That seems a bit extreme."

"I am not privy to George's reasoning," Sir Michael snapped. "He is a man grown and makes his own decisions."

"Do you perhaps know where he is now, sir?" Trent watched closely to see what his reaction would be. But the older man didn't flinch.

"As far as I know he is at his club. But he might have gone to attend to his wife in Dr. Hayes's facility since you say she's been taken there. I really do not keep close watch on his comings and goings, your grace."

The baronet's tone suggested that he would not have told Trent even if he did know where George was.

"I see," Trent said thoughtfully. It was impossible to say whether Sir Michael was merely covering for his son or if he himself had something to do with Maggie's situation.

"Just so," said Sir Michael, his teeth clenched. "Now, if you really don't mind."

But Trent wasn't ready to leave yet.

"I really do find it extraordinary that your son would have his wife taken away against her will in manacles," he said, leaning back in his chair and crossing one booted foot over his knee. "Most families would take great pains to keep the embarrassment of such a thing out of the public eye. But Hayes's men accosted her in a hat shop of all places. In front of any number of witnesses. Especially someone with social standing, like you, for instance."

"I don't see what business it is of yours, Trent," Sir Michael snapped, finally losing his poorly leashed temper. He stood and waited for Trent to do so as well. When his guest did not rise, he made a growling noise in the back of his throat.

"What do you want from me?" he demanded, clearly out of patience. "I only learned of it a short while ago. And yes, I would have much preferred that George go about the business in a more discreet manner. Is that what you wished to hear?"

Striding to a table on the far side of the room, he unstoppered a decanter of brandy and poured himself a generous glass.

Not caring that his host hadn't offered him a drink, Trent watched him as he walked back over and resumed his seat.

"I told him it was a mistake to marry her almost as soon as he informed me of the match," Sir Michael said, taking a drink. "She's a good enough chit, I suppose. But clearly has her own opinions. And isn't afraid to voice them."

Not unlike another lady of Trent's acquaintance then. It was no surprise that Mrs. Grayson and Ophelia were friends.

"But having opinions is not generally the sort of thing that makes one a candidate for Bedlam,"

Trent said carefully, not wanting to stop the flow of words now that Sir Michael was talking.

"No," his host agreed. "And to be honest, I don't know what my son was thinking to have her taken up like that. I knew they were having problems, but the girl isn't mad. Just a bit high-strung. And so I would have told him if he'd consulted me about it. But he didn't."

"So, you had no notion that she was going to be taken up today?" Trent asked. So much for Ophelia's theory that it had been Sir Michael behind Maggie's predicament.

"I said as much, didn't I?" Sir Michael asked, shaking his head. "Do you think I wished for my family to become a byword in town? That I'd want it known hither and yon that a member of my family has been sent to an asylum? This isn't the sort of thing a man in my position brags about, Trent."

"And what of Grayson?" Trent asked him, ignoring the sarcasm. "Do you truly not know his whereabouts?"

"I have no idea where he is," Sir Michael said with a sigh. "As far as I knew he was still at your meeting of the Lords of Anarchy—a ludicrous name, by the way, for a group of well-bred gentlemen. He should be home anytime now. I daresay he's gone to visit his wife in that place. Or to see Dr. Hayes."

This was not what Trent had wished to hear. When Ophelia had informed him that it was George's name on the writ, he'd hoped that it was a mistake. It was one thing for a husband to take his wife to see a physician against her wishes. Sometimes one needed outside coercion to get the help one needed. But even if she had been behaving with signs of madness—and it sounded from what both Ophelia and Sir Michael said that Maggie had not—it would take a great deal of cause to make a man have his wife sent to the madhouse. And Trent found it hard to believe that a man like George, who had visited such places with Trent to see some of their former comrades-in-arms, would ever do such a thing.

"When your son returns," he said aloud, "I would like you to send for me."

Sir Michael nodded. "I will. Though I can make no promises. There is something about this whole business that I find troublesome. Aside from the harm it will do to our reputation, I cannot believe my son would have Margaret locked away without cause. No matter how strong-willed she might be, she is not mad."

"Let us hope that our fears are unfounded, then," Trent said with a grim smile.

As they both rose, Sir Michael asked, "If you don't mind my asking, your grace, what is your interest in all of this? I know you said you are acquainted with Miss Dauntry, and I know you are friendly with my son, but that is hardly enough to make a man of your stature become involved in such a mess."

Not a bad question, Trent thought wryly. Still, he felt he owed the older man some explanation. "I dislike injustice," he said simply. "And I trust Miss

Dauntry's judgment. If she says that her friend isn't mad, then I believe her.

"And," he added as they approached the door, "I would not wish my worst enemy in an asylum. Especially not if he had his wits about him."

Five

After consulting the butler, Ophelia made her way upstairs to Maggie's rooms where her maid, Miss Hopkins, was said to be.

Finding Maggie's sitting room empty, she took the opportunity to search for something that might tell her more about what had happened to her friend. Situated between the dressing rooms of George and Maggie Grayson, the little room where Maggie spent most of her free time was a cozy little chamber, with a pair of comfortable chairs before the fire, and a writing desk facing the window.

After listening for movement from the adjoining rooms, Ophelia hastened to the desk and began opening drawers, searching for any document or letter that might give a clue as to why she'd been taken up by Dr. Hayes's men.

It felt wrong to be prying into her friend's personal papers like this, but there was a need. And she hoped that if their situations were reversed, her own friends would not cavil at searching her own belongings in order to save her.

The first drawer held a number of pages written in Maggie's neat copperplate script. They appeared to be drafts of articles meant for publication in the *Ladies' Gazette*, covering everything from *ton* gossip to the latest fashions from France.

Ophelia knew from her own time writing for the *Gazette* that one's assignments varied from month to month, and sometimes with one's own interests. Because Maggie was trying to write more serious pieces—against the wishes of their editor, Mr. Carrington—she'd spent some time researching the conditions in the various private asylums that had begun cropping up across the nation as the public institutions grew overcrowded. And she'd also looked into the unwed-mother problem. Of the pages she looked at now, one was a profile of a home for unwed mothers in London, one detailed the true plight of babies who through no fault of their own ended up in the poorhouse, and a third told the story of a mother and her two children as they tried to escape from a vengeful husband and father.

Were these the notes that Maggie had told her to look for? Gathering them up into a pile, Ophelia folded them and hid them in her reticule.

As for the articles themselves, it was clear from the letters attached to them that Maggie hadn't attempted to convince Mr. Carrington to publish these.

But why? It was true that he hadn't been particularly encouraging to them about leaving their lighter fare behind, but both Maggie and Ophelia had agreed that they would keep at him until he either gave in to their persuasion, or sent them to another newspaper with his blessing. Neither of them was comfortable approaching someone else without Mr. Carrington's blessing, since a word from him could blackball them from the newspaper business altogether.

A look in the next drawer proved answer enough.

Letter upon letter reviled *M. Grayson* for purveying "filth and gossip," "rank untruths," and "dirty secrets" in the pages of a respectable publication like the *Ladies' Gazette.* Clearly Maggie and Ophelia weren't the only ones who wished the *Gazette* would focus on something besides gossip.

Could it have been one of these letter writers who convinced George to have Maggie sent away? Someone who felt strongly enough about the content of Maggie's columns would be able to paint quite a picture of her wrongdoings. And perhaps George had grown tired of his wife reporting on the latest *on dits* from his own peers. It can't have made life easy for him socially.

Not wanting to leave the letters for George or his father to find, Ophelia stuffed them into her reticule as well.

She was just turning away from the desk when the door leading into Maggie's bedchamber opened, revealing a plain woman who had obviously been weeping.

"Oh, miss, it's that awful," the normally taciturn

Miss Hopkins said, her eyes bright with tears. "Mrs. Grayson won't be able to sleep a wink in that dreadful place. Who could be so wicked as to have her taken up like that?"

Touched by the girl's obvious affection for her mistress, Ophelia led Hopkins to a chair near the fire.

"That is just what I intend to learn, Hopkins," she said to the other woman. "Has there been any indication that your mistress was having any trouble with anyone? Letters that upset her? Or perhaps more fights than usual with her husband?"

But the maid shook her head. "There were complaints, of course. But Mrs. Grayson didn't pay them any mind. She said that was the cost one paid for writing for a public paper. She didn't take them seriously."

Just because Maggie hadn't felt threatened by them didn't mean that the letter writers hadn't posed a threat, Ophelia thought grimly.

"Has she had any unusual visitors of late? Perhaps someone who upset her?"

At that, the maid looked down at her hands for a moment. "There was one lady who paid a call a few weeks ago."

When she didn't continue, Ophelia pressed her. "And what about this particular lady made her stand out?"

Hopkins pursed her lips. Then, as if she'd made a decision about something, she said, "This lady— Miss Altheston, her card said—was as fidgety as a chicken in a room full of cats. She was quite pretty, and when I brought Mrs. Grayson her card, my mistress stared at it for a full minute before she bid me to bring her in. Like she was trying to decide if it was worth it."

"Worth what?" Ophelia asked.

"I'm not sure I know, miss," said Hopkins. "But it was clear that her first instinct was to send her away. Why she decided to let her in anyway, I don't know. But they were closeted together for nearly a quarter of an hour."

"And when she left?" Ophelia had at first thought the young lady might be the subject of a story, but now she wasn't so sure. The way the two had interacted sounded personal.

"Yes, but not before my mistress had the carriage called around for her. And had the coachman take her back to wherever it was that she came from."

"You didn't ask the coachman about it?" Ophelia found it hard to believe that the maid, who was so forceful in other matters, would have let the matter pass without at least attempting to find out.

"Oh, I asked him," Hopkins said sourly. "But he wouldn't tell me. Said the mistress told him to keep it to himself."

That the coachman had chosen to remain loyal was unusual, but not unheard of. And Maggie had inspired loyalty in her other servants as well.

"And what did Maggie do then?"

"She went back to whatever she'd been doing before. And we never spoke of it again."

Ophelia shook her head. She wished Maggie were here to ask about the mysterious Miss Altheston.

But then again, if she were here there would be no need to ask.

Setting aside the mysterious Miss Altheston for the moment, Ophelia asked Miss Hopkins one final question. "I know you do not wish to speak ill against your master or mistress, Hopkins, but what about Mr. Grayson? Have there been any more arguments than usual between them? Or something that you may have overheard that might shed light on why he would have her sent away?"

But Hopkins shook her head mournfully. "I've tried and tried to remember if there's been anything that I might have seen that would show that Mr. Grayson was thinking of such a thing, but there's nothing. If anything, it seems like they've been getting along better than ever."

Which had been Ophelia's assessment as well—with the exception of the fight at Trent's ball.

Can that have only been last night? It felt like a lifetime ago.

"I thank you for your candor, Hopkins," she told the maid aloud. "I am going to try my best to find out what happened to your mistress. If it is necessary, can I come to you again, to ask for assistance?"

The maid nodded vigorously. "She's a good mistress. And she doesn't deserve to be locked away in a place like that. As soon as you can get her out of there—or if you learn they'll allow me in to tend her—let me know. I'll do whatever I can to make her comfortable."

With a grim nod at the maid, Ophelia said, "I'm sure she'll appreciate your loyalty, Hopkins."

When Ophelia met Trent again in the entryway, she would have spoken but for his subtle shake of the head.

Silently they left the house, and as Trent handed her into the curricle, Ophelia schooled herself against her visceral response to his touch. How could she possibly feel this degree of attraction for someone she barely knew? It was absurd.

Then there was the fact that though he seemed to be as keen on finding Maggie as she was, he was the leader of the Lords of Anarchy, who despite Trent's denials surely had something to do with her friend's incarceration.

"I didn't want whatever it is you were going to say to be overheard by anyone in the house," he said once he'd taken the reins in hand and they were on their way. "Something is definitely amiss in that household and I do not yet know who we can trust there."

"So you agree with me that it is Sir Michael who is responsible for Maggie's removal?"

"I didn't say that," Trent said with a glance in her direction. "I do believe that Sir Michael isn't overly fond of Mrs. Grayson, but his surprise at what happened in the hat shop seemed genuine. And he certainly disliked the fact that it was carried out in such a public place. If he were going to have your friend confined to an asylum he'd have made quite sure it happened away from the watchful eye of polite society."

"So that leads us back to the Lords of Anarchy then," she said. She might find Trent disarmingly attractive, but she refused to tiptoe around his connection with the driving club.

"What precisely is it you suspect the club of having done?" he asked with a raised brow. "I can assure you that since I've become its leader the membership has engaged in nothing more sinister than a group drive to Brighton and a fencing tournament this morning."

"Perhaps that is just what you want me to believe so that I do not alert the authorities to your club's ties to Dr. Hayes."

Trent had just steered them into the traffic on Bruton Street, but with a curse, he pulled the horses to a stop just a few doors down from the Grayson town house. Once they were at a standstill, he turned to face her.

"Miss Dauntry," Trent said through gritted teeth, "if you truly believe that I or any other members of the Lords of Anarchy are in cahoots with this Dr. Hayes, then I would suggest that you allow me to drive you home at once so that you are not subjected to the same sort of treatment as your friend. Because not only would your allowing me to drive you through town be dangerous, it would also be foolish. And I do not believe, despite your putting your trust in me this morning, you to be foolish."

As he spoke, Trent lowered his head so that they

were face-to-face. He was so close, in fact, that she could smell the sandalwood of his cologne. Her heartbeat quickened, though out of genuine fear or something more dangerous, she couldn't have said.

And once she'd comprehended his words, she realized he had a point. If she did truly believe he and his club were responsible for Maggie's predicament, then it would be foolhardy for her to put herself so fully in his power.

"When you put it like that," she said in a resigned tone, looking down to avoid his too-knowing gaze, "then I suppose it doesn't make sense for me to be here with you."

"No, it does not," he said with a shake of his head. "I do not know how many times I must assure you that I had nothing to do with this business, but I will not do so again. And if we are to work together, then I must ask you to stop suggesting it."

He turned to look out over the horses, then, and Ophelia heaved a sigh of relief.

"I do not mind telling you that it's been difficult enough to take on the leadership of the club given the crimes of its previous presidents," he said conversationally as he once again steered the curricle onto the street, "but thus far you are the only one who has accused me personally of being up to no good. If you were a man I'd have called you out."

Ophelia blinked. She hadn't considered her accusations in that light. She'd only thought to prod him into some sort of admission. Mostly because she felt as if he were a good enough man that he would do the right thing eventually.

"I suppose it is a good thing I am not a man, then," she quipped, hoping to lighten the mood. But if anything that only seemed to annoy him more.

"You certainly are not," he said with a scowl as he prodded the horses to more speed.

An awkward silence lingered between them as Ophelia considered how to get the conversation back on track.

But Trent spoke up first. "Now, back to the Grayson household. I do not believe Sir Michael had anything to do with his daughter-in-law's removal to the asylum. Did you learn anything from Mrs. Grayson's maid?"

Grateful to get back to business, Ophelia spoke up. "Not from Hopkins, but I did find some curious things in Maggie's desk."

Quickly, she told him about the anonymous letters criticizing Maggie's columns, as well as her notes for the articles about asylums and poorhouses.

"So, we've only to contact every anonymous letter writer, every asylum, and every poorhouse in the greater London area," Trent said with a sigh. "That should be no trouble at all."

"I think we can safely confine ourselves to one asylum in particular for the time being," Ophelia said dryly. "Especially since it is the only one we know has a connection with Maggie. And besides that, I did have Hopkins pack a few of Maggie's belongings for me to take to her."

"Then by all means," Trent said, "let us take

ourselves to the Hayes clinic. I have a mind to meet this Dr. Hayes, at any rate. It seems to me that it must take a very confident man indeed to send someone to the madhouse on the basis of only a loved one's word. Because unless your friend consulted him and did not tell you, that is precisely what happened."

"Not unless she did so in an effort to interview him for her article about madhouses," Ophelia said firmly. "And I saw nothing in her notes that indicated such a meeting had taken place."

"I do wish we'd found George at his father's house," Trent said, and from this angle, Ophelia saw that his jaw was clenched. He must feel his friend's role in this affair troubling, she thought.

"Perhaps his signature was forged," she offered, for the first time considering that Maggie's husband might indeed be entirely blameless in the matter.

"Perhaps," Trent agreed, turning to glance at her in thanks. "But his disappearance this morning from my home, coupled with the fight with his wife last night, seems to point in the opposite direction."

"Then I hope for your sake he is innocent," Ophelia said.

Six

The Hayes Clinic was located in a relatively secluded area of Richmond on Thames, far enough away from any nearby residences that it was afforded some degree of privacy from its neighbors.

As Trent steered the curricle up the long drive, Ophelia gazed toward the large edifice at the end, curious for a glimpse of the place where Maggie was being held. But from her vantage point she could see only grass and trees and what appeared to be the sort of bucolic scene one would expect in the countryside.

"What have you heard about the Hayes Clinic?" Trent asked as they passed through the sheltering trees.

"Very little," she replied with a sigh. There had been only a mention of the Hayes Clinic in Maggie's notes and nothing that would give her any indication of what sort of reputation it had. She'd never heard tell of a particularly happy asylum, but surely they weren't all horrible.

For Maggie's sake she hoped this one wasn't.

"I've visited a few former officers at such places in the past few years," he said, his jaw tight. "They are not uniformly horrific. Perhaps none are what we would wish them to be, but some at least attempt to keep their . . . inhabitants busy with industry and occupation."

"What does that mean precisely?" Ophelia asked. "Industry and occupation?"

"Just that they aren't locked away in solitary rooms, left to their own devices," Trent said. "I believe every occupant has a task in the running of the household—at least those with the ability to take them on do."

"Enforced labor then," she said grimly, trying to imagine what it must be like for Maggie to be locked away against her will. Expected to carry out some rudimentary household chore along with her other inmates—all the while knowing she didn't really belong. It must be hellish.

"I suppose it is, yes," Trent said with a nod. "Though that needn't be a bad thing necessarily."

But Ophelia could hear the strained optimism in his voice. Clearly he was trying to sound cheerful for her sake. What must he have seen at the asylums he'd visited? she wondered. Suddenly she was glad that she hadn't ventured here alone.

When Trent pulled the curricle to a stop, a groom stepped forward to take the reins. So the place must be accustomed to receiving daily visitors then, Ophelia thought with some relief.

This time when Trent reached up to lift her from

the carriage, Ophelia steeled herself against the odd exhilaration. And soon she was on his arm as they approached the very ordinary front door of what appeared to be a medium-sized country house, with a brick façade and cheerful windows overlooking the front drive.

"The Duke of Trent and Miss Ophelia Dauntry to see Mrs. George Grayson," Trent told the mobcapped nurse who answered their knock.

"I'm afraid there's no visitors without you speaking to the doctor first," she said with a quick curtsy. Opening the door wide, she gestured for them to follow her inside. She led them to a small antechamber that was plainly but cozily furnished, with a comfortable-looking sofa and a few wingback chairs and a fire burning in the fireplace.

When the door closed behind their guide, Ophelia began to pace. The walls were not particularly thick and they were able to hear the sounds of conversation, shouting, moans, and singing from various locations throughout the house. Since the nurse hadn't seemed to think there was anything untoward going on, Ophelia had to assume that the cacophony was a regular occurrence in the house. Closing her eyes, she tried to imagine just what it would be like to know she wouldn't be able to leave when their visit was done. It was not a pleasant thought.

"I wonder if the men who took your friend this morning are here," Trent said, from where he stood looking out the window. "I should like to have a word with them."

"So should I," Ophelia said, shuddering, unable

to forget the hulking brutes who had overpowered Maggie. "Especially the one who gave me this bruise. Not to mention what they must have done to poor Maggie."

Manacles were surely not very comfortable.

The door opened then and they both turned to see a tall, thin man dressed in a finely tailored suit of black.

"Your grace, Miss Dauntry," he said with a deep bow. "I am Dr. Charles Gideon. To what do we owe the honor of your visit?"

"We should like to pay a call on one of your patients, sir," Ophelia said before Trent could speak up. "Mrs. George Grayson. She was taken up by two of your men at the behest of Dr. Archibald Hayes this morning. Against her will, I might add."

At the mention of Maggie, she thought she saw a flash of alarm cross his countenance, but it just as quickly disappeared beneath a mask of cloying solicitude.

"My dear Miss Dauntry, I'm afraid that I cannot allow that at this early stage in your friend's treatment," he said with a sympathetic grimace. "It is imperative that she be kept as calm as possible for her own health. You understand."

"And a visit from a friend could cause her to become upset?" Trent asked, and to Ophelia's surprise, raising a quizzing glass to his eye in a display of ducal hauteur. "I should think seeing Miss Dauntry would have the opposite effect. Especially since Mrs. Grayson was not showing any obvious signs of lunacy at the time when she was apprehended. Were I taken away against my will by two strange men, I'd be quite upset indeed. A familiar face would be most welcome."

Having never seen Trent in this mien, Ophelia watched in awe as Dr. Gideon's eyes widened.

It would not do to anger a duke.

Still, he did not relent. "You must let me be the judge of that, your grace," Dr. Gideon said with an apologetic smile. "I am after all the man with years of medical training in the treatment of the lunatic. And Mrs. Grayson is a very ill lady."

"If she is so ill," Ophelia countered, "then why were there no signs of that illness in the weeks prior to her confinement this morning? I've spent nearly every day in her company and found nothing untoward about her behavior."

"It is often thus," Gideon said with a wave of dismissal, as if he'd no time for such nonsense. "There is often a period where only those who live in the same house with the lunatic are witness to the true madness. Mrs. Grayson's actions before her husband were enough to have him consult with Dr. Hayes about the matter, and that is sufficient to prove her illness."

"But Dr. Hayes never even met with my friend before he ordered her to be taken up," Ophelia argued. "How could he possibly know whether she is ill or not?"

"Miss Dauntry, I cannot explain to you the mind of Dr. Hayes," said Gideon with a frown. "But I can assure you that I myself have examined your friend. She had to be sedated, naturally, considering how overset she was by this morning's exertions, but she will be well enough in a few weeks for you to see her and I'm sure—"

"A few weeks?" Ophelia demanded, shocked by his pronouncement. "That is unacceptable! I demand to see for myself that my friend is well. And I will not leave this place before I do."

"Your grace," Gideon said, appealing to Trent. "Surely you can reason with Miss Dauntry. Her concern for her friend is admirable, but in my medical opinion it would be highly detrimental to Mrs. Grayson's well-being. She cannot be upset at this critical time."

"And yet," Trent said, stepping up beside Ophelia, "I too cannot understand why you are so insistent upon preventing Miss Dauntry from assuring herself that Mrs. Grayson is safe, at least. It seems perfectly reasonable to me that if you fear Mrs. Grayson will be overset by seeing her friend, that it could be arranged for Miss Dauntry to simply peek in on her. She is, after all, sedated and I cannot imagine that whatever drug you administered is so weak that the mere presence of her friend in the room will cause a relapse."

Gideon did not like being contradicted. That was certain from the way his mouth puckered at Trent's suggestion. "I have explained my position to you, your grace. I do not know how I can be clearer on the matter. Now, if you will excuse me, I have many patients to see before I can leave for the day."

But before he could cross to the door, Trent

stretched out a hand and clasped the physician by the shoulder.

Ophelia almost laughed at the doctor's audible gasp. He was quite willing for his own men to lay their hands on innocent women, but he didn't like being accosted himself. What a hypocrite, she thought.

"Not just yet, sir," Trent said, turning the man bodily to face them again. "I would like to ask you a few more questions about your patient."

"What?" Gideon demanded, not bothering to address Trent properly.

But Trent's next question caught even Ophelia off guard.

"What color is Mrs. Grayson's hair?" he asked casually, almost as if he were wondering about the time.

To Ophelia's surprise, the doctor's eyes widened in shock. It was an odd question, but surely didn't warrant the alarmed response.

"I . . ." Gideon's mouth opened and closed like a fish coming to the surface of a lake. "What kind of question is that?"

"An easy enough one to answer for a man who has spent the day treating Mrs. Grayson, I should think," said Trent grimly.

"It was . . . that is to say, I didn't . . ." Gideon struggled to find the right words, but Ophelia could tell from his discomfort that he clearly had no notion of the correct response.

"Perhaps she was wearing a mobcap?" Trent asked. "So you could not see her hair? Is that it?"

Grasping at the lifeline, Gideon nodded, his Adam's apple bobbing up and down as he swallowed repeatedly. "Yes," he choked out. "That's it. A mobcap."

But any relief he felt was quickly dispelled when Trent grabbed him by the neck cloth and raised him a few inches from the floor. "No, that's not it," he growled. "Because you haven't seen Mrs. Grayson today, have you?"

Ophelia gasped. Of course! No wonder the man didn't want to let Ophelia see Maggie. He couldn't because she wasn't even here.

"Where is she?" she asked, stepping up beside Trent to stare into the doctor's terrified gaze. "What have you done with her?"

Clearly no longer able to keep up the pretense of being in control, Gideon shook his head. "I don't know. Honestly, I don't know where she is. I received a note from Dr. Hayes saying that if anyone came asking for her I was to tell them she was unable to have visitors. That's it. I don't know anything else."

"Surely he told you more than that," Ophelia said, scowling. "You're partners in this endeavor, aren't you?"

But Gideon shook his head vigorously. "No, I'm just the physician in residence here. I come every day and look after things. Dr. Hayes is the man in charge. He owns the clinic. He oversees all of the treatment. I just do what he asks. I promise."

Realizing that the man was telling the truth, Trent set him back down. While Gideon rubbed at his neck where Trent's hand had been, Ophelia asked, "When did you receive this note you spoke of?"

"Around ten?" he said, frowning. "He said to expect someone today or tomorrow. And that I was under no circumstances to reveal that Mrs. Grayson wasn't here."

"She was taken up at nine-thirty this morning," Ophelia told Trent grimly. "Hayes was setting the stage for what would happen after she was taken up."

"Where might he have taken her?" Trent asked, glaring at the doctor. "Does he have another place where he keeps difficult patients? Or some other institution where he might have taken her?"

"I don't know," Gideon declared. "Truly. I only know what he tells me and that isn't a great deal. He pays me well to keep my mouth shut."

"And so will I," Trent said, reaching into his pocket to retrieve his purse. Quickly, he shook out a handful of guineas into the man's outstretched hand. "Tell your master that we came here today, but not that you divulged the fact that Mrs. Grayson isn't here. Will you do that?"

"Yes, your grace," the doctor said, pocketing the coins. "I give you my word."

"If I hear you've divulged the truth to Hayes there will be the devil to pay," Trent said, his tone as sharp as glass.

When Ophelia took one last look back at Gideon as they left the room, she saw him collapse onto the overstuffed sofa, looking miserable.

*   *   *

"Where is she?" she asked under her breath after she and Trent were seated in the curricle.

"I wish I knew, Miss Dauntry," he replied, signaling for the horses to move. "I truly wish I knew."

"Perhaps we should search out Dr. Hayes in his Harley Street offices?"

Ophelia knew that she had imposed upon Trent's goodwill for the better part of the day, but she was desperate to find Maggie. And like it or not, his status opened doors that she as a mere lady could not.

But his silence following her question told her more than a response would have.

"Very well, then," she said stiffly. "I will go myself if you will just drop me back at the offices of the *Ladies' Gazette* so that I can solicit the assistance of the editor."

"Do not be foolish, Miss Dauntry," he responded gruffly, as he turned to give her a brief glance before returning his attention to the horses. "I did not say I would not accompany you. But I do think it might be best to stop our search for now. It is growing late and I daresay Dr. Hayes has left his office for the day. Why do we not resume our quest in the morning?"

"I am not being foolish, your grace," she snapped. "I do not wish Maggie to be forced to spend the night in whatever place Dr. Hayes has confined her. She must be terrified. And if there is some way that I can relieve that and find her, then I will."

Trent muttered a curse, and pulled the horses to

a stop. "Miss Dauntry," he began, "Ophelia. I do not wish to discourage you, but there is something havey-cavey about this business. If it were as simple as your friend being put in an asylum, I would agree with you that all it would need is a visit to Dr. Hayes to see her freed. But if, as I suspect, there is more to it than that, it might serve us better to have a bit of strategy in place before we confront the good doctor."

Ophelia scanned his face, looking for any small sign that might reveal him to be lying. But all she could read there was sincerity and perhaps a bit of frustration at her mistrust. Well, it wasn't as if they were the best of friends, she thought with equal frustration. Before today she'd never spent any time alone with him at all.

Still, Leonora seemed to trust him, and so did Hermione. And she trusted them.

With a sound of frustration, she looked away and said, "All right. You may have a point." And as much as she loathed to admit it, it was getting late, and since they didn't know where Maggie was at this point, they would likely need to do a bit of investigation to discover her whereabouts. "My mother is likely wondering where I've got to by now as well."

She looked down at her gloved hands clasped together in her lap. And to her shame, they blurred as her eyes filled with unshed tears.

Trent touched her lightly on the arm, then reached down to cover her clasped hands in his own large one.

"We will find her, Miss Dauntry," he said quietly, his voice strong and clear, and she wondered if this was the sort of confidence he'd instilled in his troops. Because as soon as he said the words, she believed them. Believed that he would do everything in his power to make them true. "It might take a day or two," he continued, "but we will find her and bring her to safety. I give you my word."

Unable to keep her gaze away, she looked up then and was surprised to see something that looked remarkably like tenderness in his gaze. But just as quickly as she glimpsed it, the emotion was gone, replaced with friendly, distant concern.

"Why would you agree to it?" she asked, unable to keep her curiosity at bay any longer. "You do not know Maggie. And we don't really know each other beyond a slight acquaintance thanks to the marriages of our mutual friends. That is no reason for you to risk your name and reputation, and indeed, your own friendship with George Grayson."

"You must have a very poor opinion of what it means to be a gentleman if you think one would simply go on about his business after learning that a lady had been taken away against her will," Trent said wryly. "Not to mention saw another lady of closer acquaintance brought low from a blow from those same captors."

"But you might have simply summoned the runners and washed your hands of the thing," Ophelia persisted. "But you did not."

He sighed. "You are persistent, I will give you that."

They were both silent. And she thought for a moment that he would not continue at all.

But finally, he turned back to her. "My reasons are multifold. But the most pressing now is that while I haven't known him for long, George Grayson did not strike me as the sort of man who would sign away his wife's freedom and then go about his business as if nothing had happened. And I dislike being wrong.

"And then," he continued, thrusting a hand through his short, dark hair, "there is this."

And to her surprise, he looked her boldly in the eye before raising his hand to cup her cheek, and kissing her softly, sweetly on the mouth. When she opened her mouth in a gasp, he took it a bit deeper and she felt her world tilt as he lightly sucked her lower lip. Then, almost as quickly as it had begun, he pulled away.

A hand pressed against her bosom in a ridiculous pantomime of every surprised young lady ever, Ophelia knew her eyes were wide and her cheeks were flushed as she stared at him.

For his part, Trent looked both smug and rather boyish.

"Oh," she said, blinking up at him.

"Yes," he said wryly. "Oh."

"I supposed that's a . . ." she stammered, searching for just the right word, "a reason."

"Indeed," Trent said before he turned his attention back to the horses. "So, be assured that I have my *reasons* for assisting you in the search for your friend. And for the time being, let's leave it at that."

Reaching up a hand to clasp her hat firmly upon her head, Ophelia nodded. "I think that is a very good idea, your grace."

And as they turned a corner onto a busy street, she added, gravely, "For the time being."

Seven

As soon as he dropped Ophelia off, Trent went in search of Freddy and Mainwaring at Brooks's. Though neither was acquainted with George Grayson, they might be able to point him in the direction of someone who could advise him about the legality of the order that had come from Dr. Hayes.

He turned his thoughts firmly away from the ill-advised kiss he'd so clumsily pressed on Ophelia. He was hardly the world's most debonair of men. Far from it. And he could only imagine the delighted guffaws that would consume Freddy and Mainwaring if they ever got wind of it. But in the face of Ophelia's persistent questions about his motives, he'd been unable to resist giving her a clue as to why he'd agreed to go along with her search for her friend.

It wasn't that he didn't care about the reputation of the Lords of Anarchy. Of course he did. But the truth of the matter was, he'd not have cared nearly as much if Ophelia hadn't stumbled into his house looking as white as a sheet and needing his help. And though he'd finally noticed her as a damsel in distress, she'd not remained one for long. Instead she'd transformed into a strong-willed lady of grim determination. And the truth of it was, he was drawn to both.

The kiss had been both a warning for her that his motives weren't quite as pure as she'd supposed them to be, and to himself. Getting involved with an unmarried young lady could be dangerous for his freedom. But the damnable thing about it was that it had only whetted his appetite for more.

He'd been caught in his own trap, dash it.

Knowing that his friends would rib him mercilessly if he let on what had happened between himself and Ophelia, he schooled his features and shoved the encounter firmly into a corner of his mind to be examined at some later time. Preferably when he was alone and could go over every last detail.

Stepping into Brooks's, he found his friends in their usual corner, looking far too self-satisfied for Trent's comfort. Ever since his best friends had married they'd smelled suspiciously of April and May and were often seen to smile for no apparent reason. Which had until today made him slightly ill. Now, he reluctantly understood why they might have undergone such a change.

Not that he was thinking about . . . anything remotely related to romance or love or the like.

"Hard at work, I see," he said, pulling out the third chair at their table and propping his booted foot on his knee. "I find it difficult to believe you escaped the apron strings long enough to make it to St. James's Street."

But if he expected an argument, he was sadly mistaken.

"Jealous, old thing?" asked Freddy, stretching languidly, like a cat enjoying a bit of late afternoon sunshine. "You sound quite cross."

"Clearly he's lonely," Mainwaring said with a shrug. "Been as angry as a bear with a thorn in his paw for weeks. I suspect he's been too long without a mistress. I know that my own mood has improved greatly thanks to regular bouts of . . ." Then, perhaps realizing it was indiscreet to speak about his wife thus, he coughed. "You know what I mean."

"Marriage," Freddy said gravely. "I know indeed. It's quite a satisfactory state."

"You should try it," Mainwaring said to Trent with a nod in his direction.

"You both sound like recent inductees into a cult," Trent said with a roll of his eyes. "And I have no wish to join you in your lodgings inside the parson's mousetrap, thank you very much."

"Your loss," Freddy said with an elegant shrug. "One day you'll see."

"And we'll welcome you with open arms," Mainwaring nodded, flicking a bit of fluff from his sleeve. "Despite your nastiness this day."

"Speaking of nastiness," said Freddy with a frown, "how are things with the new and improved Lords of Anarchy? Any attempts on the part of the old regime to wrest back power?"

"Well you should ask," Trent said, grateful for the turn of subject. Quickly he explained to them what had happened that morning. But when he came to the bit about Ophelia's arrival at his door sporting a bruised face, Freddy stopped him.

"Who hit her?" Clearly he felt some sort of protectiveness for the chit since she was Leonora's particular friend, but Trent was rather annoyed that the other man seemed to think him unequal to the task himself.

"I was getting to that," Trent said curtly. In as few words as possible he told them what Ophelia had said about Maggie Grayson's abduction.

"Can they just do that?" Mainwaring asked. "Just go about armed with a piece of paper and cart someone off to the nearest asylum? With nothing but the say-so of a near relative? I find that quite terrifying."

"And well you might," Trent said with a frown. "I'm not sure of the legality of the thing. I feel sure this Dr. Hayes will tell us it is all aboveboard, but I wish to know from someone who isn't the same man who signed the writ. It would be in his best interest to make us think that he was perfectly within his rights to send his men out to take her away. I daresay he makes quite a nice living from the family members of people who would like nothing better than to have their troublesome relatives taken away."

"Good God, I could likely pay my household expenses for a year solely on what he earns from the aristocracy alone," Freddy said with a grimace. "Perhaps even two."

"But surely a medical man would have an obligation to ensure that the accusations were true before he signed his name to such a writ," Mainwaring argued. "I mean, if it were that easy then we'd see a whole spate of drunken uncles and temperamental aunts being taken up by the good doctor's men on a daily basis."

"Who's to say there isn't?" Trent asked seriously. "It's not as if the nobility are open about such matters. It's an embarrassment to have a family member taken to the madhouse. Much easier to explain away their absence by claiming they've gone to Scotland. And no one would be the wiser. I can even imagine a grateful head of the family sending the doctor a gift of a few hundred pounds in gratitude."

Freddy whistled. "When you put it that way it does sound rather ominous. I'm glad my family never heard of this chap. It would be just like one of my brothers to have me carted off as a joke."

"Your family is odd," Mainwaring said with a shake of his head. Turning back to Trent, he asked, "So, do you believe that this Maggie Grayson is indeed mad or that her husband lied to have her taken up?"

"I know Ophelia, that is, Miss Dauntry," Trent corrected himself, "believes that Mrs. Grayson is no more mad than you or I, but not knowing the woman myself, I cannot judge that. What I do know is that George Grayson was reputed to be a good officer, and I find it hard to believe that the man I spoke with at length this morning did such a thing."

"But if not him, then who?" Freddy asked. "And where has Grayson gone? Surely his disappearance is suspicious if nothing else is."

"Oh, it's suspicious as hell," Trent said, clenching his jaw. "If for no other reason than to see if my own instincts have degraded to such a degree than I can no longer tell the difference between sincerity and barefaced lies. And he's a member of the Lords of Anarchy, so there's also that."

"Because you're the president, you mean?" Mainwaring asked with a raised brow. "I'm not sure the past presidents would have been so conscientious."

"Need I remind you that one of them is in exile and the other is dead? I do not believe either are examples I wish to follow," Trent said wryly. "I swore to turn this club into something that its members can be proud of. And that means investigating the matter when one of the members appears to have acted in bad faith."

"Well, when you put it that way," Mainwaring said with a dismissive wave of his hand.

"Just don't get yourself into trouble," Freddy said, taking a deep drink of claret.

"And if you do," Mainwaring said, raising his own glass, "feel free to call on us for help. We've got a bit of experience in this sort of thing."

"I think I've got it handled," Trent said, biting back a grin. "I did manage to go to war for a decade without your assistance. Surely I can handle a physician with delusions of grandeur and a certain demanding young lady."

At least he hoped so. Otherwise he was in for quite a difficult few days.

"Was that the Duke of Trent's curricle?" asked Ophelia's mother from the doorway to her sitting room.

Ophelia had hoped to sneak into her own bed-chamber without notice. Especially after that shock-ing kiss. Unfortunately her mother's windows faced the front of the house and therefore gave her an unobstructed view of the street below.

With a sigh of resignation, she obeyed her mother's unspoken demand and followed her into the cozy parlor where Mrs. Dauntry spent most of her free afternoons.

After requesting her maid to bring them some tea, Mrs. Dauntry gestured for Ophelia to take a seat on the chintz sofa across from her, then waited with an expectant look on her still attractive face.

"Well, my dear," Mrs. Dauntry said, brows raised. "I'm waiting."

Though most mothers of the *ton* with unwed daughters would see the Duke of Trent as a matri-monial prize of epic proportions, Mrs. Dauntry had her heart set on one of her daughters marrying the son of her dearest friend, the dowager Lady Goring. And since Ophelia's sister Mariah had been fortunate enough to receive a proposal from the Marquess of Kinston earlier in the year, it was up to Ophelia to accept the addresses of Lord Goring.

"It was merely a ride in his curricle, Mama,"

Ophelia said patiently, crossing her fingers behind her back at the fib. She didn't bother to explain for the umpteenth time that the idea of marrying the amiable but utterly dull Lord Goring made her want to flee to the Continent and join a convent. Not to mention that Trent's kiss had told her in no uncertain terms that what she felt for him was not mere friendship. But she said anyway, "We are friends. That is all."

She had no intention of talking through her confused feelings about Trent in light of the kiss they'd shared. But she did know that it hadn't made her any more eager to spend time in the company of Lord Goring. If anything it had solidified her aversion to him.

Whenever a potential rival for Goring came on the scene, Ophelia was forced to listen again to all the myriad reasons why her mother thought Goring would be such a wonderful husband and why the supposed rival would not. She was not in the mood to hear all of Lord Goring's supposed virtues praised to the heavens. Not when she'd spent the afternoon investigating the disappearance of a dear friend whose loving husband might have had her locked away. And definitely not when she'd been thoroughly kissed by another man.

One of those reasons alone might have put her off Goring temporarily, but both together meant that there was no conceivable way that she could contemplate accepting the man's advances.

"I fail to see how you can call the Duke of Trent your friend, Ophelia," said Mrs. Dauntry sharply, making her feel guilty despite herself. "Not when you are all but promised to Lord Goring. It isn't appropriate for a betrothed lady to have male friends."

Sighing, Ophelia wished she could point out that there was no betrothal between herself and Lord Goring, but in Mrs. Dauntry's mind it was all agreed to but for the technicality of the actual betrothal. It was Trent who was the usurper in Mrs. Dauntry's mind, not Goring. And nothing Ophelia said would change her mind.

"We happened to be visiting a mutual acquaintance and the duke offered to give me a ride home," Ophelia said aloud, wishing she could simply leave the room and retreat to her own. "There is nothing to concern yourself over."

She felt a trifle guilty about the half-truth, but she knew that Mrs. Dauntry would not be any happier with the news that she'd been with Maggie earlier in the day than she had been about Trent. As someone who took her social standing quite seriously, Mrs. Dauntry saw her daughter's friendship with Maggie Grayson as a threat. Not only did Maggie write for a newspaper, she also encouraged Ophelia to do so. Which in turn endangered Ophelia's nonexistent understanding with Lord Goring.

"There is everything to concern myself over," Mrs. Dauntry reminded her with a frown, "especially when you parade around town with a man who is not your—"

The arrival of the tea tray stopped Mrs. Dauntry

in mid-reply, which Ophelia could tell from the set of her lips put her nose out of joint. But once she'd poured for both of them and her maid was safely out of the room, she continued as if she'd not been interrupted.

"You may not be officially betrothed, but it's been accepted by both of our families since you and Lord Goring were children. So it is highly untoward for you to be seen in the Duke of Trent's carriage." Mrs. Dauntry frowned suddenly and Ophelia knew she'd just noticed the bump on her forehead.

"Where did you get that injury?" she asked, setting her teacup down and hurrying to her daughter's side. "I sincerely hope that the Duke of Trent is not responsible for it or I fear your father will have words with him. And that's nothing to what Lord Goring's response will be."

She hovered over Ophelia and leaned closer to better observe the spot, touching it gingerly before Ophelia pushed her away. "Mama! Stop. You needn't treat me like a child. It is merely a bump on the head."

"Pray excuse me for being concerned about your well-being, Ophelia," said Mrs. Dauntry, though she did step back. But she rang the bell again. And when her maid returned, asked for some bandages and liniment.

"It's already been cleaned once today," Ophelia said, relaxing a bit. It was, she was forced to admit, good to know her mother still cared about her well-being. But it was hardly the ordeal she was making it out to be. "Truly, I'm fine. It doesn't even hurt anymore."

"But what happened?" her mother asked again, resuming her seat and pouring herself another cup of tea.

Ophelia bit her lip, debating whether telling her mother the truth would make her more or less upset. Finally, realizing that she'd likely hear the truth through gossip, she explained what had occurred with Maggie earlier in the day. Though she omitted the trip to the Hayes Clinic because she knew that would be more inexcusable in her mother's eyes than riding in an open curricle with the Duke of Trent for all the world to see.

"How ghastly," Mrs. Dauntry said, clasping a hand to her bosom. "I hope you see now why I disapprove of your friendship with Mrs. Grayson. Her husband might be the son of Sir Michael Grayson, but only someone of bad *ton* would get herself taken to the madhouse."

"I am not upset at the damage it might have done to my reputation, Mama," Ophelia said, fighting the urge to roll her eyes. "Maggie might have been killed in the scuffle. And I would not wish my worst enemy to be taken against her will to a madhouse. Much less a dear friend. Where is your compassion?"

"Oh, pooh," Mrs. Dauntry said with a frown. "I have plenty of compassion for the lady. But as my daughter of course you are my first priority. I cannot sit idly by while your reputation is put into danger by a dispute between husband and wife. Truly, I fear what Lord Goring's response will be."

And, Ophelia reflected with an inward sigh, this was why she wished to avoid her mother altogether when she arrived home. It wasn't that Mrs. Dauntry was callous, she simply had a single-minded dedication to seeing the realization of the match she and her dearest friend had hatched between them when Ophelia was born. And her daughter's reluctance thus far to abide by her mother's wishes was making her press even harder.

"Mama," Ophelia said aloud, "I barely even know Lord Goring." And what she did know of him was that he was quite dull and seemed to have as little interest in Ophelia as she had in him. Since seeing her two dearest friends wed men who adored them, and they in turn adored, she'd come to feel even more strongly that a match like the one her mother proposed for her would bring nothing but unhappiness.

"Oh, that won't matter," Mrs. Dauntry said with a wave of her hand. "I barely knew your father before we were wed and look how well we rub along together."

Ophelia forbore from pointing out that her parents spent most of their time apart from one another and barely exchanged three words at a time.

Even so, Mrs. Dauntry must have decided to try a different tack in the present conversation.

"The Duke of Trent is quite handsome," she said

thoughtfully. "Though not, I fear, as handsome as some gentlemen."

It was all too clear to whom she was referring when she said "some gentlemen."

"For all that his title is so illustrious, Trent is rather rough around the edges. A bit . . . harsh. Don't you agree? I much prefer a more refined countenance on a gentleman."

Since it didn't matter what Ophelia said, she simply made a noise that could be construed as either agreement or protest depending on how the recipient interpreted it. As she'd hoped, her mother accepted the noise for a hearty agreement.

"Now that your sister is settled," Mrs. Dauntry continued, pressing on despite Ophelia's lack of encouragement, "I think it's time for you and Lord Goring to come to some kind of formal agreement. Especially before any gossip about your involvement in this business with Mrs. Grayson comes out. And it would be lovely to announce your betrothal as soon as your sister's wedding celebrations are concluded. Perhaps as soon as they embark upon their wedding journey."

Ophelia supposed she should be thankful that her mother hadn't encouraged her to press for an announcement at the wedding breakfast itself. She and Mariah were hardly best friends, but Ophelia had no wish to ruin her sister's wedding day.

"Oh, do not be so stubborn, my dear," Mrs. Dauntry chided when she rightly interpreted Ophelia's silence for what it was: disapproval.

"You may never get a better offer. And Lord Goring is willing to marry you despite your determination to ruin your reputation by writing for that dreadful publication."

"That dreadful publication, as you call it," Ophelia said stiffly, "is something I am quite proud to be associated with. Indeed, I enjoy writing my articles for the *Ladies' Gazette*, and I do not plan to stop anytime soon. Whether Lord Goring approves of it or not."

Mrs. Dauntry's lips pursed. "Any occupation is shameful for a gentleman's daughter. As I have told you more than once."

"And I have told you that there is no shame in accepting pay for my work," Ophelia said sharply. "You are fond enough of Leonora and she made quite a good living by her pen before she was married."

"Before she was married, yes," Mrs. Dauntry said, still displeased. "But there is a world of difference between her birth and your own. Both your fathers might be gentlemen, but you know as well as I do that the Dauntrys have been in England since before the Conquest. And the Cravens? Why, they can only trace themselves back to the Reformation at best. There is simply no comparison. And I will point out that Leonora has not written nearly so much since she married into the Lisle family. She knows what is expected of the wife of a duke's son even if you do not."

"Mama, you will not convince me to give up my

writing," Ophelia said firmly. "Especially when Father has seen fit to allow it."

"He is far too lenient with you," her mother said with a shake of her head. "He of all people should know what is expected of this family. But when has he ever shown any care for our reputations? He's too concerned with finding the next card game to pay any attention to us."

Since to Ophelia's knowledge, her father limited his play to the card rooms at various *ton* entertainments, he was hardly making the Dauntry name a byword in society. It was just her mother's frustration with his refusal to bow to her on this one matter that made her speak so. Not for the first time, she wondered what on earth had brought her parents together in the first place. It certainly hadn't been mutual respect and affection.

Mistaking Ophelia's silence for censure, Mrs. Dauntry sighed. "I do not expect you to marry Lord Goring tomorrow, my dear. Just give the man a chance to woo you properly. I feel sure he will do so with the least bit of encouragement from you. Eleanor has assured me that he is quite fond of you."

Wonderful, Ophelia thought. Marriage to a man who was "quite fond" of her according to his overbearing mother was just the sort of dream marriage she'd longed for as a little girl.

Unbidden, a memory of Trent's soft lips on hers flooded her with feeling. If just a kiss could move her thus, what would it be like if there were more between them? A slight shiver ran through her at the thought.

She knew now more than ever that she would never be able to settle for the sort of passionless match her mother was determined to force her into.

"You have been patient, Mama," she said aloud now. "But I cannot make myself feel affection for someone when I don't. Even if he is the son of your dearest friend in the world. Why can I not choose my own husband as Mariah has done?"

"What makes you think your sister chose Kinston?" Mrs. Dauntry asked, frowning. "I am the one who first introduced her to him."

"But she had to hold him in some degree of regard in order to agree to the match," Ophelia argued, wondering if she'd read the situation all wrong. Perhaps Mariah hadn't been as defiant as Ophelia had thought.

"Oh, she likes him well enough," Mrs. Dauntry said dismissively. "But it's hardly a love match. Unlike you, your sister knows how to show filial obedience. When Kinston asked for her hand she was more than eager to accept him. Both for her own sake and the family's."

"Then let me make it clear now that I will not allow myself to be pushed into a similar situation by you or anyone," Ophelia said firmly. "I know you mean well, but I will not sacrifice my own happiness just to fulfill some dream you and the dowager Lady Goring have concocted between you."

For a moment Mrs. Dauntry stared at her daughter, as if trying to understand how such a creature could possibly be her very own. Then, when Ophelia didn't back down, the older lady huffed out a laugh. "All right. You've made your point. I will consider allowing you more time to get to know Lord Goring. I'm sure once you are better acquainted with the man you'll be more eager for the match."

As concessions went, it was a poor one, but Ophelia was not so foolish as to look the gift of more time to escape the proposed match in the mouth.

"Thank you, Mama," she said sincerely. "I will do my best to get to know him." What she didn't say was that she doubted a dozen years on a deserted isle with the man would endear him to her. Even so, she knew further open defiance of her mother's wishes would only encourage her to be more determined about the matter.

They were silent for a moment as they both became lost in their thoughts. Then, looking up from her contemplation of her empty teacup, Mrs. Dauntry said, "I know you think me mad when it comes to this, but I do have good reason for my determination to see the two of you wed. I promise you."

"I do not think you mad, Mama." *Only stubborn.*

"So, no more flaunting your relationship with the Duke of Trent where Lord Goring might hear of it?"

Really, she was like a dog with a bone, Ophelia cursed inwardly.

"Not without good reason," she said aloud, giving herself an out so that she could spend more time with Trent without gaining a guilty conscience.

After all, they would likely need to go on one or two more outings before they were able to get Maggie out of that awful place.

Was it too terribly shameful that she was looking forward to it for reasons that had nothing to do with rescuing her friend?

Eight

After supper at Brooks's with Freddy and Mainwaring, Trent left the two married men and returned home to dress for the card party at Viscount Wrotham's lodgings where he knew the majority of the Lords of Anarchy would be that evening.

Because many of the newer members of the club were either familiar with one another or indeed were already friends, from their time together in the military, such gatherings as tonight's party at Wrotham's had become commonplace. Trent saw the frequency with which the men assembled outside sanctioned club meetings as a good thing. Something that would ensure the club's strength even after his own tenure as president ended.

Still, as he handed the reins of his curricle to a waiting groom outside the apartments where Wrotham had lodgings, the sight of men spilling out of the entryway to the building did not reassure him that the club wasn't up to its old, rowdy tricks.

"Trent!" shouted Lord Edward Findlay from

where he leaned against the balustrade smoking a cheroot. "Just the man we wanted to see!" He turned to the man next to him, Mr. Adam Vessy, and clapped him rather hard on the shoulder. "Didn't we just say that, Vessy?"

"S'truth," Vessy said, screwing up his face to squint past the cloud of smoke shrouding both men's heads. "Just this very moment, Duke."

Trent fought back a cough as he stepped closer to the smokers. "While I am, of course, grateful to be missed," he drawled, "I'm afraid I didn't come to blow a cloud. I was wondering if either of you has seen George Grayson this evening."

Lord Edward's eyes widened at the mention of Grayson. "No," he said, his mouth forming an O as he did so. "I heard there was a bit of trouble this morning with his lady wife."

Vessy nodded, and added in a stage whisper, "Had her sent to the . . . the . . ."

"Bedlam," Lord Edward finished for his friend with a sage nod. "Or someplace like it. Not sure precisely the lady's destination. Only that Grayson sent her there, poor sod."

If these two were to be the future of the club, Trent reflected with an inward sigh, then the club didn't have much of a future.

Aloud, he said, "I had heard about that, yes. But neither of you has seen Grayson this evening? Or even earlier in the day?"

"Just at your fencing do this morning, Duke," Vessy said with a shake of his head. "Fellow's probably at home with a bottle. S'where I'd be."

Lord Edward nodded his agreement, and Trent took his leave of the two men and pushed into the entrance of the building, making his way through the throng upstairs to Wrotham's rooms.

Once there, he was greeted by the sight of multiple card tables set up throughout the large sitting room. Several of the players called out their hellos, as did the ladies of the evening who were seated on several of their laps.

Scanning the room, Trent finally saw his quarry at one of the far tables, his teeth clamped around a cigar and a drink in his hand.

"Trent!" cried Viscount Wrotham as the club's president approached his side. "I didn't think you'd be coming tonight after this morning's debacle."

"Bad business, that," said the man to Wrotham's left as he discarded. "Not the thing to shame the family publicly like that. Much better to have waited until she got home."

Trent didn't bother to suggest that it might have been even better for Grayson not to have his wife sent to an asylum at all. He wasn't here to argue the merits or lack thereof of the way Grayson had handled things. He wanted only to know where the man was now.

"Haven't seen him," Wrotham said, glancing down at his cards for a moment before he discarded. "Which is a bit strange, now that I think of it. Grayson and I spend most Tuesday afternoons at Tatt's. A bit horse-mad is our Grayson. But he disappeared this morning before the gathering at your house was finished and I haven't seen him since."

Trent leaned a shoulder against the wall behind the card table, deciding to wait for Wrotham's game to end before he tried to speak further to him.

Finally, with a victory cry from the winner, who was not Wrotham, the game was over and, having seen Trent waiting patiently throughout the game, Wrotham indicated with a jerk of his head toward the French doors.

Stepping outside onto the small balcony, Trent took a deep breath of the foggy London air. It was hardly as clear as it would be in the country, but given the amount of smoke, alcohol fumes, and body odor inside the apartment, the balcony was relatively fresh.

"What's the problem, Duke?" Wrotham asked as soon as he'd shut the door behind them. Trent was unsurprised to note that despite his having imbibed several drinks while he watched, the viscount didn't sound the least bit drunk. "I know you're looking for Grayson, but it's not like you to get involved in a domestic dispute."

Trent was hardly going to confess that most of his reason for coming here tonight had been related not to Grayson's problems, but instead to the pleading in a certain young lady's eyes as she sat next to him in the curricle earlier in the day.

Aloud, he said, "I've just managed to reestablish the club after two corrupt leaders have run the Lords of Anarchy into the ground. It concerns me that a club member might have recklessly endangered our reputation once more by lying to have his wife locked in a madhouse. If I can undo what damage this morning's fracas caused, then I will do it."

Wrotham's eyes narrowed as if he were trying to determine whether Trent was being truthful. "I'm not sure why it would damage the club's reputation for Grayson to lie about such a thing. It's not as if he were acting on behalf of the club."

"But you forget, Wrotham," Trent said sharply, "that Grayson's wife was a correspondent for the *Ladies' Gazette*. Much as we might think Grayson's actions shouldn't be a reflection on the club, it is all too possible that the publication will use this opportunity to paint an altogether different picture of the club's role in Mrs. Grayson's incarceration."

Swearing, Wrotham shook his head. "Damn Grayson for a fool. Any other man would keep his wife's removal to the madhouse out of the public eye. But not George."

"So you knew what he was planning?" Trent asked, turning to face the other man.

But the viscount shook his head. "No. Not in so many words. I knew he was having difficulty with his wife, but not that he was planning something like this. If I had you can be sure I'd have talked him into either not doing it at all, or at the very least keeping it under wraps."

He stared out across the darkened back garden of his apartment building. "I've been proud to be a member of this club again. Thanks in large part to your leadership. I won't lie and say I didn't enjoy myself during some of the things that used to pass for entertainment in this group. But a man can only attend so many orgies before they begin to pall."

Trent couldn't help himself. He laughed. "I am sorry to hear you've become so jaded, old man. When even an orgy begins to pall, you know it's time for a change."

"You may well laugh, your grace," said Wrotham with a shudder, "but there were some things at that last one that I can't unsee. I could go the rest of my life without seeing Vessy's naked arse again and it wouldn't be too soon."

"So noted, Wrotham," Trent said, grateful for the moment of levity. "No more orgies."

"I do not know where Grayson might have gone," Wrotham continued, turning serious again. "If I did you can be sure I'd tell you. But to be honest, I'm rather surprised he's gone to ground. If he were convinced he'd done the right thing by having his wife taken away, then what reason would he have to hide? And if he wasn't the one who gave the order, then his disappearance is even more suspicious."

Which is exactly what Trent had been thinking.

He might do worse than to have Wrotham's assistance in this matter. He filed away the notion for future reference.

Thanking his host, he made his way back out of the crowded party and took himself home. Vowing to start fresh the next morning.

* * *

After a night spent tossing and turning as she worried about Maggie, Ophelia set out after breakfast the next morning for the offices of the *Ladies' Gazette* in Fleet Street. Though she'd found some of her friend's notes about the home for unwed mothers in her rooms yesterday, there was a slight chance that Maggie had left more at her desk in the newspaper offices. And Ophelia wasn't quite sure which notes Maggie had referenced yesterday in the haberdasher's.

She alighted from the Dauntry carriage outside the newspaper offices with its front windows crowded with colorful prints and lampoons related to political scandals of the day. Mr. Carrington produced the broadsides and prints to supplement the money earned from advertisements in the *Gazette,* which was hardly what the larger papers could bring in. And as she knew at times the editor paid his writers from the proceeds from the smaller print jobs, Ophelia didn't begrudge their place of prominence.

Pausing a moment to gird her loins before her editor's inevitable questions about Maggie, she had her hand on the door, when it opened suddenly to reveal the man himself.

"Are you going to come in or stay out here all day loitering, Miss Dauntry?" he asked with a raised brow and a grin.

Before she could reply, though, his eyes narrowed as he noticed the bruise the cosmetics hadn't quite managed to hide fully.

Cursing under his breath, he took her by the arm and steered her into the newspaper offices and urged her into a chair near her desk.

"What the hell happened?" he demanded, his mouth tight as he stepped back to survey her. "And does it have anything to do with Mrs. Grayson? I was expecting her this morning but she hasn't come. Which isn't like her."

In his way, Edwin was protective of his lady reporters as he called them. Not many men would take it upon themselves to provide the sort of stories enjoyed by the ladies of London's middle and upper classes. But he was both a shrewd businessman, who could see a market potential when it presented itself, and a bit of a radical, who wanted to change the system from the inside. And he saw London's ladies as the perfect conduit for that change.

Maggie had already worked for the *Gazette* for months before she convinced Ophelia to join her, and the relationship between her friend and the editor had at first made Ophelia uncomfortable. For it was obvious to her that not only was Edwin grateful for Maggie's innovative approach to the news, but he was also head over ears in love with her.

That Maggie was a married lady seemed not to bother him one bit.

Whether they'd acted on that attraction or not, Ophelia had no idea. And she didn't actually want to know. She was terrible at keeping secrets, and besides that, she didn't want to sit in judgment of her friend. Someone had once told her that a marriage was only truly understood from inside it. And she had no wish to know anything more about Maggie's marriage to George than she could see from the outside.

Still, she should have known that telling Edwin about Maggie's predicament would be difficult.

Quickly she told him everything that had happened in the haberdashery from the moment the two thugs had arrived until they left with her friend in chains.

As she told her story, all the color drained out of Edwin's face. "Dear God!" he said, leaning back against the desk behind him, as if afraid his legs would no longer hold him up. "Why would that bastard do something like that? Does he know what goes on in those places? We have to get her out of there."

For the moment, Ophelia chose not to tell him about her visit to the Hayes Clinic with Trent, and the fact that Maggie wasn't there. It would only worry Edwin further. And the fewer people who knew that Maggie was truly missing, the better.

"We won't know his reasons until we can actually speak to George Grayson," she said aloud. "And when I tried to ask him he was nowhere to be found."

"Well, we'll just have to keep looking for him." Edwin thrust a hand through his untidy hair. "Miss Dauntry, you know as well as I do how awful some of those places are. My God. Of all the ways he could think to punish her, this is the worst."

Ophelia didn't ask why George should punish his wife, because she suspected that if that was the direction Edwin's mind had run to, then he knew all too well for what. Considering the unhappiness of her friend's marriage, she had little doubt that the punishment was related to some infraction real or imagined involving Edwin.

Still, that didn't explain why Maggie had suspected her notes on the unwed mothers' home would hold some clue to freeing her. It was clear that she needed to speak to Dr. Hayes himself to see if he could shed some light on both Maggie's whereabouts and George's motive in having her taken up in the first place.

Now, however, she needed to calm down Mr. Carrington before he tore across London searching for George Grayson to teach him some sort of lesson.

"A friend and I are going to see Dr. Hayes later today," she said aloud as she watched her publisher stalk from one end of the room to the other. She wasn't sure if Trent had a visit to Dr. Hayes on the agenda for today, but if he didn't wish to accompany her, then Ophelia would visit the man herself. "But in the meantime, just as she was being led away, Maggie asked me to look for her notes. Could she have found something while working on the story about the unwed mothers' home? Something that would put her in danger? Or would . . ."

At the mention of Maggie's story, which he'd only rejected yesterday, Mr. Carrington looked stricken. "I told her—told you both—that I didn't want stories like that. If this is what got her taken into that place then I'll never forgive myself. I shouldn't have encouraged the two of you to flex your journalistic muscles." He thrust a hand through his hair. "Damn it!"

Ophelia watched as he turned his back to her, to regain his composure, she supposed.

Feeling a pang of sympathy for him, she touched him briefly on the shoulder. "Do not blame yourself, Mr. Carrington. I doubt there is anything you could have done to dissuade her from pursuing the story. We can be quite stubborn, you know."

He gave a rueful, if pained, laugh and turned back to her. "I daresay you're right. Though I will have your word that you will not pursue stories like that in the future. It is far too dangerous for ladies to go to the sort of places necessary to get these stories. And I know neither of you is willing to cut corners."

"You have my word," Ophelia agreed. "Now, let's search for Maggie's notes. I'm hoping we can find something that will give a clue as to who, if not her husband, wished to get her out of the way."

Standing, she strode over to where four desks were pushed together into a table of sorts.

Maggie and Ophelia had the desks on the far side, while two other reporters had the two on the other side. Ophelia was grateful that they were out today so that she and Mr. Carrington could search without interruption.

Unlike Ophelia's desk, which was messy with

scraps of paper, pots of ink, and past issues of the *Gazette*, Maggie's was neat as a pin. Stepping up beside her, Mr. Carrington began to open drawers and rifle through them. Ophelia, meanwhile, pulled out sheafs of paper from the cubbies of the hutch atop the desk's surface.

It wasn't long before Mr. Carrington, squatting before the bottom drawer of the desk, gave a cry of triumph and held up a notebook bound in kid leather. Ophelia recognized it immediately as the journal Maggie often used to take notes for stories or longer pieces like the one she wrote about the unwed mothers' home.

"This is the one," he said, standing up and stroking a hand over the cover—as if trying to find some trace of Maggie on its surface.

"May I?" Ophelia asked gently, aware that he was more vulnerable at the moment than she'd ever seen him. With a sharp nod, he placed the notebook in her hand and stepped back, as if disavowing his response to both Maggie and the notebook.

Taking a seat at her own desk, Ophelia pulled the small oil lamp she and Maggie shared over to her own side of the desk surface. With an annoyed sound, Mr. Carrington brushed her hands away and set about lighting it himself.

Once the light was bright enough to read the pages, Ophelia began to scan Maggie's notes, looking for anything that might tell them who Maggie might have upset during the course of her investigation.

The first was what looked to be an interview

with the superintendent of a girls' orphanage in Whitechapel where Maggie had been investigating some new method of teaching girls discipline. While the method sounded rather grim from Maggie's description, there was nothing about it that might possibly place Maggie's own freedom in danger. Indeed, the man she spoke to—a Daniel Swinton—seemed sincere if a bit harsh. From her interviews with the girls at the school, however, they seemed happy enough. And though they found the cold-water-bath punishments uncomfortable, and the food less than appealing, none of them would admit to having been mistreated at the school.

Continuing to thumb through the book, Ophelia finally came to a notation that made her gut clench.

"Hayes Clinic," the note read. "Possible location for the discarded girls?"

"What's this about?" Ophelia asked Mr. Carrington, holding up the page so that he could read it. "I haven't read her article, only spoken with Maggie about it. But you have."

He took it from her, scowling at the words. "Discarded girls? There was no mention of anything like that in her story. And I'm not sure what she means by 'discarded.' From what Swinton said in her article no one is turned away from his home. And it's the same for the orphanage that's mentioned."

Taking the book back from him, Ophelia flipped through the next few pages and found a list of names and addresses. A quick glance revealed that

Mr. Carrington, having grown impatient, had moved on to flip through a stack of broadsides on the other side of the desk.

Some sixth sense told her to keep the list of names to herself, so she closed the book with a thump and clasped it to her bosom. Mr. Carrington's response to the news about Maggie had been emotional, and she didn't wish to reveal anything to him that might provoke him to do something rash.

"I'll just take this with me," she said, hoping to appear normal. "It likely won't come to anything, but I'll see if the orphanage has any information about missing girls."

"But how is this going to help us get Maggie out of the asylum?" he demanded with a scowl. "Even if someone from the orphanage is involved, until we know who we won't be able to find her."

And Ophelia was suddenly quite glad she hadn't revealed to Mr. Carrington that Maggie wasn't at the Hayes Clinic. If he learned that Maggie was missing altogether, in his current mood he just might take it into his head to confront Dr. Hayes himself. And that might make the doctor angry enough not to speak to them at all.

Just then the bell on the front door chimed to indicate someone had entered the offices.

Looking up, Ophelia saw the Duke of Trent striding toward them.

"We're closed right now, my lord," said Mr. Carrington with a dismissive smile. "I'm sure if you'll come back tomorrow—"

"I'm here to see Miss Dauntry," Trent interrupted with a raised hand. "And it's your grace, so you needn't try to fob me off like a creditor with an outstanding bill."

Surprise and annoyance flashed across Edwin's face, then he turned to look at Ophelia, who felt a blush rise in her cheeks.

"What a pleasant surprise, your grace," she said with a dampening glance at Trent. "I do apologize, Mr. Carrington. I hadn't realized that his grace was meeting me here. He has kindly agreed to help me get Maggie set free."

Now Mr. Carrington frowned. "Your grace, it's a pleasure," he said, bowing. "I do not believe we've met."

"Just so, Carrington," said Trent with a nod. "I apologize for turning up unexpectedly. Miss Dauntry's mother was kind enough to give me her whereabouts when I paid a call there this morning. And I must admit I was curious to see the offices of the *Ladies' Gazette*."

Ophelia would have spoken up, but Mr. Carrington did so first.

"Are you familiar with Mrs. Grayson, your grace?" he asked, his eyes narrowed. "I must admit your name has never come up in our conversation."

Turning to look at her editor, Ophelia was surprised to see what looked like jealousy on his face.

But if Trent was put off by it, he didn't reveal as much. "I don't see why she would mention me, Carrington. I am better acquainted with her husband, George. Though as Miss Dauntry has said, I have agreed to assist her in trying to free her friend. I dislike the notion of her friend being held against her will."

Mr. Carrington looked as if he'd respond, but Ophelia suddenly had the feeling that she needed to get these two away from one another. She disliked the ire in her editor's face when he looked at Trent. And Trent himself wasn't looking particularly well disposed toward Carrington either.

"Don't we need to leave if we're to make it to Dr. Hayes's offices on time, your grace?" she asked pointedly, stepping forward to stand beside Trent.

As if he'd come there with no other object in mind, Trent nodded smoothly and offered her his arm. "Yes, indeed, Miss Dauntry. And I have heard that Dr. Hayes has a dislike of tardiness above all things."

"I will keep you informed, Mr. Carrington," Ophelia assured her editor. "And thank you for your help. I know Maggie would appreciate it."

"Think nothing of it, Miss Dauntry," he said.

And as she turned just before Trent closed the door behind them, Ophelia noted that rather than looking either despondent or jealous, Mr. Carrington instead looked thoughtful.

Nine

*O*nce they were outside, out of earshot of Carrington, Trent said in a low voice, "Why didn't you wait for me?"

He couldn't quite put into words why finding that Ophelia had already left when he arrived at the Dauntry town house had been so unnerving, but it had been. For some reason he'd expected her to practice more caution in the wake of what had happened to her friend. Though any fault was his own since he'd not expressly told her not to go anywhere alone, he supposed.

He'd not make that mistake again. Ophelia's safety was too important.

"Why should I have done?" she asked, frowning up at him as she stopped beside the curricle, her blue eyes narrowed. "Surely I'm in no danger. And I've come to the offices of the *Gazette* hundreds of times without incident. Why should I stop now?"

Without answering, Trent placed his hands on her waist and lifted her into the curricle. It was something he'd done before without remarking on it. But something was different about it today. He found himself leaning in a little, to catch the elusive floral scent of her. And his eyes lingered for the barest moment on her mouth as he deposited her in the seat. The realization of where his thoughts had gone in that moment—to thoughts of tangled sheets and flushed skin—was so jarring that he pulled his hands away with rather more speed than necessary and drew a puzzled frown from his passenger.

"Are you quite well?" she asked, brows drawn.

Not bothering to answer, he tossed a few coins to the boy who'd held his horses, and launched himself into the seat beside her.

"I was merely concerned for your safety," he said, relaxing a little now that he had something to do with his hands.

When it had occurred to him the night before that the editor of the *Ladies' Gazette* might use this circumstance as an opportunity to further blacken the name of the Lords of Anarchy, Trent hadn't for a moment considered that the fellow might also pose a threat of a different kind. To Ophelia.

But as soon as he'd seen the other man's head against hers as they leafed through what he assumed to be Maggie's papers, Trent had been struck with a pang of what could only be jealousy. Which was absurd, of course. He and Ophelia were friends.

He was merely misinterpreting fear for her safety as something more commonplace. That was all.

"We don't know the full story of why your friend was taken away," Trent said aloud, regaining his composure. "And though George is named on the writ, there's nothing to say someone else didn't go to Dr. Hayes claiming to be George."

Her sharp intake of breath told him she hadn't considered that option. Nonetheless, it was clear she still didn't quite trust him. "I suppose it is possible that Mr. Carrington might have done so, but how do I know you aren't simply attempting to remove suspicion from your friend? It would be another black eye for the club if it were learned one of your number had wrongfully had his wife locked away."

"You don't," he said with a glance in her direction. "But you can hardly fault me for wishing to find the club blameless. Reforming its public image is my main goal as the new president. I will not, however, alter the facts we find to suit that notion. No matter how damning those facts might be."

She was silent, apparently thinking that over.

"Another reason I was disconcerted to find you gone was because I'd hoped you would accompany me to see Dr. Hayes."

At the mention of the not-so-good doctor, Ophelia turned. "You didn't go without me, I hope?"

"Of course not," he said simply. "I'm the one who persuaded you not to go to him yesterday. It wouldn't be cricket for me to go without you."

That must have satisfied her, because she nodded. "I thought you said we needed some strategy before we approached him."

"I did," he said, placing an arm across her body as the horses slowed to accommodate a fruit seller's cart. For the barest moment their eyes met, and he was startled to see a flare of heat in them. A cry from the street broke the spell, however, and he returned his attention to the road.

"Strategy," he said, shaking his head a little to clear it. "I think ultimately we will be best served to consult a solicitor. But for now I believe a strong offensive front will get the information we need."

"And what will that entail?" she asked, frowning. "I doubt I'll be much use in a physical confrontation."

"I don't think that will be necessary," he said wryly. "I was thinking in terms of strong words rather than confronting him with pistols or a sword."

"That's a relief," she said with a grin. "So what will we say?"

"A man like Hayes is used to being in control," he said as they pulled onto Harley Street. "He literally has the power of life or death over his patients. I imagine that means it takes a fair bit of strength in an opponent to cow him."

"That seems reasonable," she agreed. "So you will confront him with your military presence?"

"Much more intimidating than that," he said with a flash of teeth.

She gave a puzzled frown, and he continued, "I will confront him as the Duke of Trent."

In the past months, Ophelia had spent a great deal of time with Trent. Not on a one-on-one basis, but they'd both been visitors at the Lisle and Mainwaring homes many times. And thus she'd come to know him not so much as a duke, but as a friend to Freddy and Mainwaring. Someone to make up the numbers so that she wouldn't be left out of outings with Leonora and Hermione and their husbands. A decent conversationalist, and at times quite amusing.

But one thing she'd come to take for granted was Trent's rank.

As a member of the *beau monde*, or rather, from the outer fringe of the upper reaches of society, she was quite aware of the gulf that stretched between herself, a gentleman's daughter, and Trent, a duke. But because they both ran tame in the same houses, and counted the same couples as friends, it had been easy for Ophelia to forget about that difference in their stations.

He was just Trent.

Something happened to him between the curricle and the doorway leading into Dr. Hayes's offices, however. Somewhere in between he'd become . . . ducal.

"Please inform your master that the Duke of Trent is here," he said languidly to the dapper little man who responded to their knock. Wordlessly he extended his card to the butler, who had stood up straighter as soon as Trent announced himself.

"Of course, your grace," the butler said with a low bow. "Please come in and make yourself comfortable. I will tell Dr. Hayes at once that you are here."

At Ophelia's sideways glance, Trent raised one dark brow, and pulled a quizzing glass from some hidden pocket in his waistcoat. "Is there aught amiss, Miss Dauntry?" he drawled.

Was that a wink? It was difficult to tell. But Ophelia shook her head and allowed him to take her arm. She wondered when she'd get used to this formal version of Trent. She was almost looking forward to Dr. Hayes's response. She had a feeling that he would be much more forthcoming with Trent than he would be with plain Miss Ophelia Dauntry.

"If you will both just wait here," the butler said, ushering them into a finely appointed sitting room. "I'm sure Dr. Hayes will be here momentarily. May I offer you some refreshment?"

The thick Aubusson carpets, luxurious wallpapers, and finely turned furniture spoke to the prosperity of Dr. Hayes's practice. So did the portrait of what she assumed was the doctor hanging over the mantelpiece. Ophelia wondered how many men had slipped Hayes a few quid to have their inconvenient wives disappear for a bit.

"Nothing for me," Trent said dismissively. And the butler didn't bother to ask Ophelia if she wished for anything. Between the two of them, she might not have even been there.

"Very good, your grace," said the butler, as he reversed from the room.

"If this is the Duke of Trent," Ophelia said in a low voice, "then I'm rather afraid to see what he will do next."

Remaining in character, Trent shook his head slightly, indicating that she shouldn't let on that he was pretending.

If that was the case, then she would probably do best to keep silent, she reflected.

Wandering over to a shelf of what she knew to be expensive bits of art glass and pottery, Ophelia's back was to the door when Dr. Hayes entered the room. So she missed the moment when he took in Trent in all his glory.

Still, there was no mistaking the mercenary glint that flashed in his eyes as she turned to get a look at him. Her second thought was that the portrait hadn't been of him after all. Not unless he'd lost several inches in height in the last several years.

"Your grace," he said, bowing deeply before Trent, who looked down from his superior height with patent boredom. "What an honor to welcome you here in my humble offices. I wish you had known to call upon me at my home. I do not expect clients of your rank to visit me here in the rudeness of Harley Street."

Oh dear. Ophelia's eyes widened at the doctor's obsequiousness. It was toadying of the first order, but she supposed that when one relied upon the condescension of the nobility for one's bread and butter, it was all of a piece.

For a man who wielded such power from his position, he was remarkably unremarkable, she reflected as Trent examined him with his quizzing glass.

"I wish you had warned me," Trent said with a

nod of agreement. Though how Dr. Hayes might have known to warn him, when Trent didn't know he was even coming here until this morning, she didn't know. "But now that we are here . . ." He let the words dangle in the air, as if he were too fatigued to even complete the thought.

"You have my abject apologies, your grace," Hayes said sorrowfully. "But now that you are here, perhaps I can assist you?"

He was about a head shorter than Trent, and had hair of a color somewhere between brown and blond. His features were regular, but nothing stood out. It was almost as if he were making himself fade in deference to his noble visitor.

"My lady friend here," Trent said with a wave in her direction, "you know how ladies are, I trust?" He asked the question as if it made all the sense in the world. As if there were an agreed-upon thing that ladies were, and he expected Hayes to know it.

If Hayes were confused by the aside, he didn't show it. "Of course, of course. Your friend . . . Oh dear, I'm afraid I do not know your name, madam."

He said it as if the fault were his own rather than Trent's for failing to introduce her from the first.

Trent raised his quizzing glass once again and peered at the doctor. "Miss Dauntry," he said with boredom. "Miss Ophelia Dauntry."

"Miss Dauntry," the doctor said with a nod. "Please have a seat and make yourself comfortable, Miss Dauntry. I'll ring for some refreshments."

Trent sighed. "We already told the other fellow

that there was no need of that. I really must insist you speed this along, Doctor." He shook his head mournfully. "I've an important appointment in an hour or so and I must get Miss Dauntry back to her mother before I do so."

He whispered, as if Ophelia were several rooms away instead of a few feet. "Gentleman's business." He laid a finger alongside his nose, as if she were blind as well.

"Quite so," Hayes whispered. Aloud to Ophelia he said, "How may I assist you, Miss Dauntry? Is it your nerves?"

She was startled from her amusement at Trent's charade by annoyance at the doctor's question. "Certainly not. My nerves are as sound as horses."

"My apologies, Miss Dauntry," he said hastily. "It's just that I see a number of ladies complaining of such things. Please tell me what it is you wish to consult me about. Perhaps you have a relative who is suffering from a temperament that requires them to be removed to somewhere more suited to their needs? I can assure you that it can be done quickly and painlessly. Without much fuss."

But that only made her angrier. Of course his pockets were brimming with gold, she thought sourly. If he approached every visitor to his offices with the suggestion to lock away their relatives, then he likely was making a fortune.

"Is that what you told Mr. George Grayson when he came to you about his wife?"

At the mention of George, the doctor's eyes narrowed. "I've not had the pleasure. Is Mr. Grayson a relative, then? Or perhaps it's Mrs. Grayson to whom you are kin?"

"I find it difficult to understand how you might not be able to place either of the Graysons, Doctor," she said, anger at his pretense coursing through her, "when I read your name just yesterday on a writ declaring Maggie Grayson insane, and ordering her to be taken to the Hayes Clinic."

At Ophelia's words, the doctor's eyes narrowed. Gone was the fatuous smile he'd given Trent, and by association, her. In its place was a shrewd examination of both his visitors. "What is this about? I thought the duke was here to seek my assistance."

"And so I am, Dr. Hayes," Trent said, stepping forward to lend Ophelia his support. He was every inch the nobleman, and it had nothing to do with his quizzing glass. "I wish you to answer Miss Dauntry's questions about the bodily removal of Mrs. Margaret Grayson from a public establishment, which, according to the paper presented by the thugs who took her was sanctioned by you and her husband, George Grayson."

"You deceived me," Dr. Hayes said accusingly to Trent.

"I believed the ends justified the means," the duke said with a slight shrug. "And that doesn't negate our reason for coming here. Did you even see Mrs. Grayson in person before you diagnosed her?"

But Dr. Hayes was not interested in answering questions. "I'm sure you'll both excuse me. I made time to see you specially but I'm afraid that I have much work to get to this morning."

Ophelia almost shouted with frustration, but she needn't have worried. Trent stopped the physician's progress to the door with a few words.

"Not. Yet. Sir."

As if a string had pulled him up short, Dr. Hayes stopped in his tracks.

"I would like an answer to my question," Trent said in a deceptively casual tone. "And I believe Miss Dauntry is still waiting as well. What possible motive could you have had for declaring Mrs. Grayson mad sight unseen?"

"I would imagine," Ophelia said softly, "it was a financial incentive."

Hayes turned and glared at her. "If you were a man, Miss Dauntry, I could call you out for that."

"That would require you to be a man of honor, Dr. Hayes," she retorted coldly. "And we know by now that you have none. No man who would take money in exchange for a woman's freedom could."

"For your information, Miss Dauntry," the doctor said through clenched teeth, "I make sure the streets are safe for ladies like you by making declarations of insanity against those whose relatives have deemed them unbalanced. There is nothing dishonorable about it. If at times I have them taken up before I have a chance to see them personally, then it is always with good cause. And if I have made a mistake, which I beg to inform you that I never have, then that person would be set free as soon as it was discovered."

It was what she'd expected, of course. Ophelia shouldn't be at all surprised. Even so, hearing him declare it so baldly, admitting that it took no more than the suggestion from a relation that the person in question was unbalanced, was terrifying. For who could be safe when there was such a practice? It would take only the word of a disapproving parent, or a jealous sibling, to see to it that their offending relation was removed from society indefinitely.

"And what was it that George Grayson told you about his wife's condition that deemed her worthy of committal?" Trent asked. "Or was it just his coin that spoke for him?"

The flush that rose in the doctor's face told the tale more eloquently than words could have done.

"I had a long talk with Mr. Grayson," Dr. Hayes said defensively. "He was quite worried about his wife's condition. Quite worried."

"When was it that you spoke to him?"

Ophelia had by now stepped aside to let Trent do the questioning, since he seemed to be making better headway than she had.

"Yesterday morning," Dr. Hayes said. "Around nine. I remember because it was rather early in the day for a gentleman. I generally do not see members of the upper classes until later in the day."

At the doctor's admission, Ophelia saw Trent scowl. "What did Mr. Grayson look like?"

"I thought you were acquainted with this couple,"

Dr. Hayes said darkly. "If you've come here under false pretenses . . ."

"Just answer the question, Doctor," Trent said in a tone that would brook no demurral. "What did this man who called himself George Grayson look like?"

"He was around your height," Dr. Hayes said, dropping all show of defiance. "With light brown hair. And he had an eye patch. I assumed it was from a war injury. He did tell me he'd fought against the French at Waterloo."

"An eye patch?" Ophelia asked, surprised despite herself. It certainly wasn't George he was speaking of. Not only did George not have an eye patch, but he was also quite fair-haired. Far too fair-haired to be called a brunet. She exchanged a look with Trent who looked just as shocked as she was. "Doctor, I don't know who you spoke with but it wasn't George Grayson."

But Dr. Hayes was not convinced.

"Now see here," he said sharply, "I have only your word that the man I spoke to is not the actual George Grayson. I take my authority as a physician seriously and would never declare someone mad on a stranger's word." Once more he tugged the bellpull.

Before Trent or Ophelia could retort, two large men entered the room. But not the men who had taken Maggie.

How many of these giants did Dr. Hayes have in his employ? she wondered with irritation.

"See these two out, please," said Dr. Hayes haughtily. "I have said all I care to say on the subject of your friend. And I have grown quite tired of your insults."

When the guards made to put their hands on Trent, however, he held them off with a look. Then he turned and took Ophelia by the arm. "Thank you for your time, Dr. Hayes. I feel sure we'll be seeing one another again."

Ophelia was quite sure he had the right of it.

Ten

So this is what those bullies did to you?" Hermione, Countess of Mainwaring, asked, inspecting the bruise on Ophelia's forehead. "It's monstrous that anyone can simply be placed in manacles and led away without a by-your-leave. You must do something about this in the House of Lords, Jasper."

"It's certainly worth looking into," Ophelia said, grateful to be back among friends after the tense meeting with Dr. Hayes.

As soon as they'd left the physician's office, Trent had suggested they pay a call at the town house Lord Frederick Lisle and his wife, Leonora, shared with her aging father. Ophelia had agreed with alacrity. She badly needed to talk about what she'd found at the newspaper office that morning. Fortunately Hermione and Jasper were also paying a visit to the Lisles, which meant she could discuss Maggie's disappearance with all of them.

"My dear," said Leonora, whose pregnancy was

disguised by a generously cut gown, as she ushered Ophelia to a comfortable settee. "You must be exhausted. When I got Trent's note I was desperate to see you myself just to ensure that you are still in one piece."

"I thought we'd put all this derring-do and grappling with ruffians in the past when Trent took over the Lords of Anarchy," Hermione said with a speaking look at the duke. "To think that those horrid men actually struck out at you. It's getting impossible for respectable ladies to go about in public without being interfered with in some way."

"I can assure you, Lady Mainwaring," said Trent from where he stood to one side with Freddy and Jasper, "that this time the Lords of Anarchy are most certainly without blame in the matter. Though Mrs. Grayson, the friend whom Miss Dauntry was attempting to prevent from being taken, is married to one of the new members."

"That has yet to be proved," Ophelia said sharply. "While we can find no connection just yet, I am not ready to absolve the driving club so easily. It is entirely possible that whoever it was that approached Dr. Hayes pretending to be George Grayson was a club member."

She felt Trent's annoyed gaze, but refused to meet his eyes. When they were alone together it was quite easy to believe that he and the club weren't involved. But she didn't wish to allow their new amity to cloud her judgment on the matter. So until she was convinced otherwise, the club would remain on her suspect list.

Ignoring the six feet of exasperated male in her peripheral vision, she related what had happened the day of Maggie's abduction and all she and Trent had learned since then. "At this point, I'm not sure who we should be focusing on. It is certainly damning that George Grayson has gone missing, but I found something in Maggie's notebook that might give someone else a motive."

"You didn't share this with me," Trent said crossly. "I thought we were working on this together, Miss Dauntry."

"Oh, I think with all the time you've been spending together you can dispense with formalities, Trent," Freddy said, clapping his friend on the shoulder as he crossed to sit on the arm of Leonora's chair. "Unless you object to that, Ophelia?"

Ophelia knew better than to believe that Freddy's suggestion was innocent. Her friend's husband had an impish sense of humor and didn't mind poking fun at his friends when he thought they needed it. Still, it was rather silly to continue addressing Trent as "your grace" or to expect him to call her "Miss Dauntry" when they were among friends. "I have no objection," she relented. "What say you, your—Trent?"

When she looked over at him, he caught and held her gaze for a moment and Ophelia felt curiously breathless. It would be all too easy to allow herself to imagine that such intensity meant far more than it did. But she had seen enough ladies make fools of themselves over the handsome duke to know that he wasn't easily susceptible to flirtation.

Still, it was hard to resist that pull between them when he looked at her the way he did now, as if they were the only two people in the room. "I'm agreeable to it, Ophelia."

The way he said the words, it was difficult to know if he meant using their Christian names, or something far more dangerous.

Mainwaring clearing his throat let her know that she'd perhaps been staring a bit too long. "What were we talking about?"

"Maggie's notebook," Leonora said with a broad smile. "I believe Trent was complaining that you hadn't shared finding it with him?"

Not daring to look at him again, Ophelia sank onto the overstuffed chair beside the fire. "Yes, it was the notebook Maggie used when she was investigating the story about homes for unwed mothers."

"That sounds rather dark for a ladies' newspaper," Freddy said with a frown. When Leonora, who wrote quite serious essays for several journals and newspapers, pinched him in the arm, he yelped, and amended, "Not that ladies' newspapers cannot be serious. I just thought you and your friend wrote lighter fare for the *Ladies' Gazette*. Nothing that would require you to visit the parts of London that might pose a danger to you."

"That is actually quite true," Ophelia said. "But both Maggie and I have been trying to convince our editor, Mr. Carrington, to publish more stories about the sort of things ladies care about. Like what happens when a girl bears a child out of wedlock."

"What was the topic of your serious story?" Trent asked, an edge in his voice that told her he did not like her investigation into such dark topics any more than Mr. Carrington had.

"I hadn't started mine yet," she admitted, feeling somehow disloyal because she'd let Maggie put herself in danger while she stood safely out of the way. "We had agreed that she would write hers first to show Mr. Carrington that it could be done in a way that would appeal to the *Gazette*'s existing readers. Then, when he saw that, I would write the next one."

"So what did her notes say, Ophelia?" Hermione asked, curious.

"They weren't explicit, but it did mention the Hayes Clinic in conjunction with one particular home for unwed mothers run by a Mr. Daniel Swinton, and the words 'discarded girls,'" Ophelia said. "And I do not believe that was a coincidence."

"You might have mentioned this before we met with Dr. Hayes," Trent said, his arms crossed over his broad chest.

"I could hardly make an accusation based on a few scribbled notes," she retorted. "And you saw how Dr. Hayes reacted to our questioning. Can you imagine what his response would have been if I'd asked about his clinic in reference to children born out of wedlock?"

"We might have seen if he had any response to

the name Swinton," Trent countered. "If you don't confide in me, Ophelia, I don't see how we will ever find out what happened to Mrs. Grayson."

She felt a flush rise in her cheeks. He was right, of course. But she was not one who refused to admit when she was wrong. "You're right," she said with a sigh. "I'm just so used to keeping the details of Maggie's investigation a secret that I didn't tell you."

"Well, I'm here now," he said calmly. "And I need to know everything you know if we're to find your friend."

She nodded. "That is everything, I promise."

Feeling all eyes in the room on her, she quickly got back to the subject at hand. "So, have any of you heard of the Hayes Clinic? Or an orphanage run by a Daniel Swinton?"

"In fact," Mainwaring said with a frown, "I have heard of this Daniel Swinton fellow." He glanced at Freddy and Trent. "You know Lord Knox. Older chap, will talk your ear off if you give him half a chance? Lurks in the reading room at Brooks's in search of innocent victims to sacrifice on the altar of his long-winded sermons?"

Freddy groaned. "He is relentless. I vow, he caught me a few weeks ago and I thought I'd have to fake a fainting spell to get him to let me leave."

"What did he have to say about Swinton?" Trent pressed, leaning his shoulders back against the mantel.

"Well, he trapped me in much the same way as he had Freddy," Mainwaring said with a grimace.

"And his topic of conversation was Daniel Swinton and how he's successfully reforming the children in his orphanage using some sort of miraculous technique that is able to turn even the most recalcitrant of youths into law-abiding citizens."

"What is it?" Ophelia asked. "There was something in Maggie's notes about 'the method' in relation to Swinton, but she didn't give any details of it."

"From what I remember," Mainwaring said, wrinkling his brow, "I think it had something to do with immersion in cold water followed by strenuous labor."

"Sounds delightful," Leonora said acidly. "Just the thing to make a young prostitute being pimped out by her own mother change her evil ways."

"I say," Mainwaring objected with a stern look at their hostess. "That's a bit dark."

"Don't be priggish, darling," Hermione said to her husband. "Ophelia and I are quite aware of the horrors that occur every day in the poorer parts of the city."

"And unfortunately, Leonora is right," Ophelia said with a sigh. "It's very likely that this method is being used on young prostitutes, given that the topic of Maggie's story was unwed mothers. For what it's worth, she seemed to conclude that there was nothing criminal about the practice."

"Just heartless," Trent said grimly. "I wonder how this Swinton would like to be the one enduring the cold baths and hard labor."

"Like most men of that ilk," Freddy said dryly,

"I can only guess that he would scream bloody murder and claim to have been abused dreadfully."

"Bullies are much the same wherever you go." Mainwaring nodded. "Cowards, every last one of them."

It was difficult for Ophelia to imagine herself trapped in such a place. She only hoped that wherever Maggie was, it wasn't Daniel Swinton's orphanage.

"Speaking of cowards and unwed mothers," Leonora said, her eyes troubled. "I have recalled just where I had heard of the Hayes Clinic."

Ophelia didn't miss the comforting arm Freddy slipped around his wife's shoulders. "I don't like the sound of this," he said, not taking his eyes from her face.

"It's nothing to do with me personally," Leonora assured him, patting his hand. "But you both remember my cousin Daisy, don't you, Hermione and Ophelia?"

At their nods, she continued. "I'm quite sure she was confined at the Hayes Clinic."

Ophelia's eyes widened. "Daisy? Wasn't she the one who went on an extended tour of Italy just a couple of years ago?"

Nodding, Leonora continued, "She was. But what wasn't for public consumption at the time was the fact that she first spent several months in the care of Dr. Hayes."

The room was silent as a tomb while they waited for Leonora to speak.

"Daisy was the sweetest little girl imaginable," Leonora said with a smile. "I recall her as a sunny-natured child, who loved her dolls and was always ready with a laugh. But something changed when she began to mature. And, not to put too fine a point on it, she became somewhat difficult to manage around the age of sixteen. She was lovely—I mean, so beautiful that it was remarked upon by everyone who met her. And she attracted the notice of men. Many of whom were not eligible in the least."

A knot formed in Ophelia's stomach. She had a bad feeling about where this story was headed.

"This wasn't a problem when she was in her right mind," Leonora continued. "But when she was seventeen she suffered a brain fever that left her with a diminished capacity to make sound decisions. All the ineligible young men whom she'd rejected before the fever she suddenly allowed to pay her court. And . . . other things. And I am quite certain if she'd been a boy no one would have remarked upon it."

"You are likely correct," Freddy said with a frown. "There is a frightful double standard when it comes to such things."

"The worst of it was that every time she became involved with one of these men, no matter what his motives," Leonora said sadly, "Daisy fancied herself desperately in love. She wanted to marry each and every one of them, but my aunt and uncle refused to give their consent. It was their only means of controlling her. And because she had a handsome dowry that they were convinced the men wanted access to."

"But what of her reputation?" Hermione asked, her brow furrowed. "Surely they would wish her to marry as quickly as possible to save it."

"They didn't trust any of the men to do right by her once they'd gained her fortune," Leonora explained.

"So what happened?" Ophelia asked, dreading the answer.

"Aunt Sibyl placed her under the care of Dr. Hayes, who recommended immediate confinement in his clinic," Leonora continued, "and for a little while at least, it worked. Out of the reach of the fortune hunters, she was able to gain some sense of perspective. Or at least that's what my aunt said. It's hard to know whether it was being out of reach or a change of heart that made the difference in Daisy's behavior."

"But," Trent said, his voice grim.

"She wept frequently," Leonora said sadly. "And her beautiful hair began to fall out. She complained to her mother that the medications they were giving her made her ill. Until finally Aunt Sibyl convinced Uncle Harold that they should remove her from the clinic altogether and take her away to the Continent for treatment."

"So they took her to Italy," Ophelia said.

"They did," Leonora confirmed. "And slowly but surely she began to regain her health. And before long she even met a young man there on holiday, who fell in love with her. Who had a fortune of his own, so my aunt and uncle trusted him. And soon after they married."

"So Dr. Hayes's treatment made her ill," Trent said. "As indictments go that's not particularly damning."

"There is one thing I failed to mention, however," Leonora said, her mouth tight with anger. "When my cousin and her new husband returned from the Continent, they brought someone with them."

"Who?" Mainwaring asked, eyes narrowed.

But Ophelia already knew. "A child," she said softly. "A child that her new husband claimed was his own."

"Precisely," Leonora said. "But the timing was all wrong—at least I knew that from my aunt's letters. No one else is aware of it as far as I know."

"So, you think she was with someone at the Hayes Clinic?" Trent asked. "Or is it worse than that? You think she was raped?"

"I cannot know," Leonora said with a shake of her head. "The thing is that Daisy was very persuadable. It's why her parents were so concerned about her. She fell in love at the drop of a hat. And I can quite easily imagine her allowing one of those young fortune hunters to make love to her. But she was at the clinic for months without any sign of pregnancy. I know because I visited her there. It had to have happened after she went into the clinic and before she left for Italy. Remember, she complained that the medication was making her ill. It's equally possible she was suffering from morning sickness."

"Is it possible that someone at the Hayes Clinic is preying on vulnerable patients?" Ophelia asked thoughtfully, her mind teeming with images that made her skin crawl. "And then, what, when the victims become pregnant sending them to Daniel Swinton's home for unwed mothers?"

"It's a possibility, certainly," Trent agreed. "And a logical reason for Maggie to have both the Hayes Clinic and Swinton in her notes."

"I should like to speak to Daisy," Ophelia said to Leonora. "Do you think she would feel comfortable answering some questions? I don't wish to upset her. And I know she's been through a great deal."

"She'll be at the Kinston ball tonight," Leonora replied. "She doesn't like to talk about her time in the Hayes Clinic, but I suspect she will wish to help you as much as she's able. I'll see you two are introduced tonight."

"I promise to be gentle with her," Ophelia said gratefully. "And discreet. I have no wish to intrude upon her newfound happiness."

"Don't tell me you mean to attend a ball after the drama of the past couple of days," Trent said with a frown. "You suffered quite a serious blow to the head yesterday."

Ophelia frowned at his high-handed tone. Just because they were working together did not mean he had the right to make decisions for her.

"And now I am feeling much better," she said coolly. "Besides which, my sister is betrothed to the Marquess of Kinston so my mother is expecting me to attend whether I feel up to it or not. And I most certainly do feel up to it."

He looked as if he would like to say more, but perhaps seeing the mulish set of her jaw, he kept silent.

"I can promise to look after her." Leonora exchanged a sly look with her husband, who winked. "Unless, of course, you mean to attend too, Trent."

"He must attend," Freddy said guilelessly. "For I mean to keep you busy dancing, my dear. You will have no time to watch over Ophelia."

"I'm sitting right here, you know," Ophelia said, rolling her eyes. "And I have no need of a keeper. At least not the last time I checked."

Trent muttered something under his breath, but when she scowled at him, he shrugged as if to say, "Who, me?"

Annoyed with all of them, she stood. "I believe I'll walk home. It is a fair enough afternoon and my house is only a few streets away."

"Of course I'll take you," Trent said, looking offended. "As I said, you've had an eventful couple of days. And as I am going in that direction anyway it will be no inconvenience."

It would serve him right if she refused, Ophelia thought stubbornly. But it was true that she was tired. And if she were going to attend a ball that evening she'd do better to conserve her energy. "Very well," she said.

"We'll see you there tonight," Hermione said as she and Leonora ushered their friend into the hallway and toward the front entrance.

* * *

Trent made to follow Ophelia, but was stayed by Freddy's hand on his arm.

"What's going on here?" his friend asked with a speaking look in the direction of the departing ladies. "I was unaware that you and Ophelia were more than speaking acquaintances."

"Certainly not close enough to ride about town together in your curricle for two days in a row," Mainwaring added, his eyes bright with mischief.

"Don't be daft," Trent said with a frown. "We are only working together to find her friend because George Grayson is a member of the Lords of Anarchy. Nothing more than that."

"But it would be easy enough for you to look for Maggie Grayson on your own, surely?" Freddy asked, pinning him with his blue gaze. "Especially considering that you don't know what's in store when you find her. Shouldn't you leave Ophelia to her own devices for safety's sake if nothing else?"

At the suggestion he was endangering Ophelia in some way, Trent stiffened. "Now see here, Lisle," he said with a voice that sounded threatening even to his own ears. "I am doing my utmost to see that she remains safe. If I were to leave her to her own devices as you so helpfully suggest, then she would be God knows where poking her nose into the devil knows what. That lady is as stubborn as a mule and the only reason she is still safe is because I've ensured that she doesn't take the sort of risks she'd doubtless undertake if she were allowed to go about unchecked."

There was an eerie silence in the hallway for a moment as Trent realized his mistake.

Damn. Double damn.

"That was some speech, old fellow," Mainwaring said, diffidently picking a bit of lint from his sleeve. "I believe you've made our point."

"You are both asses," Trent said, turning his back on his oldest friends and stalking down the stairs toward the entry hall.

"You don't suppose I was too hard on him?" he heard Freddy say from above. "I sometimes can go a bit too far."

"Not a bit of it," Mainwaring replied. "How else were we to learn the truth of things? It's not as if he'll tell us he's head over ears on his own."

Grateful that Ophelia and her married friends were already outside, Trent collected his hat and coat and stomped out the door.

Eleven

"Remember, you promised to dance at least two sets with Lord Goring," Mrs. Dauntry reminded Ophelia as they rode, along with Mr. Dauntry and Mariah, to the Kinston ball that evening. Though in many households it would be unusual for the elder daughter to remain unmatched while the younger was betrothed, in this case, Mrs. Dauntry had tolerated the situation because she considered Ophelia and Lord Goring all but betrothed already.

Mr. Dauntry, however, had other ideas. "Why are you encouraging her to dance with that milksop?" he demanded of his wife. Though they'd doubtless discussed the matter any number of times, Ophelia suspected he pretended to forget about her mother's plans for Lord Goring out of sheer dislike for the man and a wish to needle his wife. "She's got more spirit in her little finger than that fellow has in his entire body."

"You know very well, Mr. Dauntry," her mother said stiffly, "that Ophelia has been promised to

Lord Goring for some time now. It's just a matter of his asking the question. And I will not have you speak of him in that way. He is the son of my dearest friend, as you well know."

"How is that being promised?" he demanded, his dark brows contrasting with his white hair. "Sounds to me like something you and Lady Goring cooked up between you two without consulting Ophelia or her supposed suitor."

Though she knew it was wrong to take pleasure in her mother's discomfort, Ophelia could not help but appreciate her father's championship. Especially since she was no more eager to marry Lord Goring than her father was to call the man son-in-law.

"It would be better for Ophelia to simply accept the match with good grace," Mariah interjected with the insufferably smug air she'd adopted since she'd accepted Kinston's proposal. "It's not as if she has any other prospects. And this way, she will avoid being the butt of jokes as the unmarried elder sister."

"There's no possibility of a match if the fellow doesn't ask me," Mr. Dauntry reminded Mariah archly. "And even if he did I wouldn't give my consent. Bad enough we're allowing a bacon brain like Kinston into the family. I don't think we can stand to add someone like Goring."

Fortunately for Mr. Dauntry's continued health, his wife and Mariah were diverted from their ire at his statement by the halt of the carriage before the Kinstons' town house.

Ophelia allowed her mother and sister to disembark first, and was rewarded with a grin from her father as he handed her down. "Find yourself some other man with a bit of sense tonight, my girl," he said, chucking her under the cheek. "I should hate to see your spirit broken by a match with that milksop. Son or no son of your mama's dearest friend, he's not good enough for you."

Though he was, at times, gruff and distant, Ophelia loved her father for these times when he stood up for her. Her mother loved her, she knew, but it always seemed as if she'd love her more if she'd only do this or that. Her papa loved her as she was.

"I shall try, Papa," she replied as he handed her down. "Though it will make Mama quite cross."

"You let me handle your mama," he said with a wink. "I should hate to be saddled with two addle-pated sons-in-law. One will be bad enough."

The line of guests snaking its way up to the receiving line was longer than Ophelia had anticipated, but the parties before and behind theirs were merry enough, and when they finally reached where Lord Kinston and his mother were waiting, she was in a better mood than she had been on the drive over.

"I am delighted to welcome you to Weatherford House, Mr. and Mrs. Dauntry, Miss Mariah, and Miss Dauntry," said the marquess as they reached where he stood in the glittering candlelight of his entry hall. "I do hope you will enjoy yourselves."

He really was a pleasant man, Ophelia thought with relief for her sister. She might be a nuisance at times, but Ophelia loved her and was pleased to know she'd have an amiable husband at the very least.

Once she'd made it through the receiving line, Ophelia excused herself to her parents and Mariah—but not without an admonishment from her mother to save dances for Lord Goring—and stepped a little bit away, scanning the ballroom for her friends. Finally she spied Leonora and Freddie on the opposite side of the room in conversation with one of Freddy's multiple brothers.

Before she could step away, however, a familiar voice sent a frisson of awareness through her.

"Miss Dauntry," said the Duke of Trent, his eyes intense as he stepped before her and bowed over her hand. "You're looking well. I trust you are recovered from your accident yesterday."

Though she'd known him for almost a year, Ophelia was struck with a sudden breathlessness on hearing his voice. What a difference one little kiss could make.

Even so, she might be forgiven for her response if one were to actually take a good look at the Duke of Trent this evening. If he'd been impressive in his shirtsleeves with a sheen of sweat, Trent in evening finery was truly a sight to behold. Following the fashion set by Brummel years ago, he wore a perfectly tailored black coat over a silver-threaded waistcoat of deep blue that matched his eyes. The blue was also echoed by a sapphire pin winking amid the folds of his simply knotted cravat.

"Your grace," she said as she curtsied deeply, well aware of the blush creeping into her cheeks. "Thank you, I am quite well. I hope you are enjoying your evening."

Feeling his eyes upon her, Ophelia was quite glad she'd chosen to wear her new deep green gown. Once upon a time she'd allowed her mother to choose the design of her gowns, and the result had been a disaster. As a taller-than-average lady, Ophelia ran the risk of looking rather like an overly festooned Christmas mantel when her gowns were covered in ribbons and tucks and decorations. But after one too many balls spent watching everyone else dance from the isolation of the chaperones' seats, she had put her foot down. She would choose her own gowns and the result was nothing short of miraculous. Whereas before she'd drawn attention for all the wrong reasons, now she was, if not a diamond of the first water, at least pretty and presentable in her simple evening silk with its puffed sleeves and deep neckline.

"I am now," he said with an appreciative scan of her figure and a wide grin that made his usually austere countenance almost boyish. Then, offering her his arm, he added, "I believe I see Lord Frederick and Mrs. Lisle over near the refreshment table. Shall I escort you there?"

Taking his arm, Ophelia was pleased that he'd singled her out. Because it would mean avoiding Lord Goring, she told herself firmly. And as they walked, she saw more than one young lady glance at her in envy as they passed through the throng of guests along the perimeter of the dance floor.

"I hope you will save a waltz for me," Trent said as they neared their friends. "And perhaps the supper dance?"

Her heart skipped a little at the invitation. At any other evening entertainment his request for saved dances would have been unremarkable. But in the context of their time spent together yesterday and today, coupled with the kiss, it was evident that the Duke of Trent was feeling a level of interest in her that went beyond mere friendship.

But her excitement was dampened when he continued. "We can use the time to discuss all we've learned today about the Hayes Clinic. And perhaps talk about what we should do next."

Ah. How foolish of her to think he might be asking her for personal reasons. Of course it was because he wished to discuss Dr. Hayes. He was after all trying to clear the name of the Lords of Anarchy. And prove his friend had had no hand in Maggie's disappearance. He likely kissed any number of ladies over the course of a week. He was a highly sought-after duke, after all.

"Of course," she said, careful not to let her disappointment show. "We have much to discuss."

They had reached Freddy and Leonora by then, and she was grateful for the distraction.

"You should always wear that shade of green," Leonora said with a bright smile as she gave Ophelia a hard hug. "It goes so nicely with your black hair. Just lovely."

"I have to agree," Freddy said, kissing her on the cheek. "If I didn't know better I'd never have guessed you're the same lady who fought against a pair of brutes yesterday."

"That's me," Ophelia said with a dry grin, "the ladies' counterpart to Gentleman Jackson."

"Just the same," Trent said with a frown, "it would be much better if you tried not to do so in the future, Miss Dauntry. You were lucky yesterday, but that might not be the case next time."

"Tut-tut, Trent," Freddy scolded his friend. "I sincerely doubt Miss Dauntry goes out of her way to court danger. I've always found her to be a sensible lady."

"I said nothing about her sense or lack thereof," Trent said defensively, "only that it is not always going to end as well as it did yesterday."

"I believe you have made your point, your grace," said Ophelia, disappointed in his lack of faith in her.

Changing the subject, she turned to Leonora and asked, "Have you seen your cousin Daisy?"

Blinking as she looked from Ophelia to Trent then back again, Leonora said, "Yes, as a matter of fact, I have. She is dancing the current set with Lord Kimball." Gesturing to a red-haired lady who was dancing the steps of the Sir Roger de Coverley with a handsome young man on the other side of the dance floor.

"She's quite lovely, isn't she?" Ophelia asked in a low voice as she watched the other lady dance.

"Indeed," said Leonora gravely. "I suspect that might have been as much a source of her trouble as anything else. I somehow think being that beautiful is a double-edged sword in that way. You are both assumed to be better than you are, and infinitely worse than you are."

"True enough," Ophelia agreed. Though she herself hadn't dealt with such an affliction, she did suppose the attention such beauty would bring with it could make life difficult.

"As soon as this set is over I will take you over to her," Leonora said with a nod.

But before Ophelia could respond, the sound of her mother's voice intruded. Turning, she saw Mrs. Dauntry approaching with Lord Goring by her side.

It was really too bad for Goring that she happened to be standing with two of the most handsome men in the room when he approached. Whereas Freddy bore the sleek and fine-boned good looks of all the Lisle family, and Trent was darkly handsome with a military bearing, Goring seemed callow by comparison. Thin, almost bony, with unremarkable features and light brown hair, he was sadly overshadowed by the other two men.

Still, Mrs. Dauntry pulled him along into the circle of Ophelia and her friends.

"Here she is, Lord Goring," Mrs. Dauntry trilled, in a tone that made Ophelia cringe in embarrassment. Even with the noise of the ballroom she was sure everyone was able to hear her. "My dear daughter, did you forget that we were to meet Lord Goring and his dear mama when we arrived? I'm sure I reminded you on the drive here. Did I not?"

There was no mistaking the steel in her mother's eyes, and Ophelia wished fleetingly that she had managed to find that convent.

"Of course not, Mama," she said with politeness, but no real enthusiasm. "I simply thought to seek out my friends when I arrived. As one does."

"Miss Dauntry," said Lord Goring, with no sign that he'd heard what she said. "It is a delight to see you again. And I vow you are lovelier each time we meet."

It was obvious that Goring's compliment was as empty as his vacant smile, but that didn't stop Mrs. Dauntry from beaming at him as if he'd paid her daughter the highest possible compliment. "Oh, Lord Goring, you will turn her head with such flattery, I vow. Won't he, Ophelia?"

Ophelia smiled painfully, neither agreeing nor disagreeing. With a polite curtsy, she said, "Thank you, my lord. How nice to see you again."

They were the same words she'd say to any distant acquaintance upon meeting them again, but Goring took them as his due.

"Your devotion to your friends is admirable," Lord Goring said, bowing over her hand. "But you mustn't forget who your true friends are, my dear."

Before she could respond to *that* odd statement, Trent stepped up beside her. "I'm not sure you give

Miss Dauntry enough credit, Goring. I am quite sure she can tell paste from a diamond."

A flash of annoyance crossed Goring's face before he replaced it with a fatuous smile. "Of course she can, your grace. Dear Miss Dauntry has excellent taste."

Though she was hardly Lord Goring's staunchest defender, Ophelia found herself annoyed that Trent had decided to engage the other man on her behalf. If he didn't want her for himself then he would do well to leave her alone.

Before she could raise an objection, however, Mrs. Dauntry spoke up. "Ophelia, Lord Goring wished to ask you to dance, I believe. Did you not, my lord?"

Could she not even allow the man to ask her to dance on his own? Ophelia wondered in exasperation.

But Goring didn't seem to mind the assistance. "Indeed I did, Mrs. Dauntry," he said. "I hope you will save me a waltz and the supper dance, Miss Dauntry."

"Unfortunately," Trent said before Ophelia could respond, "Miss Dauntry has already promised the supper dance to me."

Much as she'd have liked to disagree, it was the truth. She didn't care for the way Trent had spoken on her behalf. She had her mother for that, thank you very much. And again, he was behaving like a dog in the manger, growling to protect the bone he didn't even want.

"I'm afraid that's true, Lord Goring," she said

with feigned sadness to the viscount. "But I can save you a waltz." She made sure to make it clear to Trent that she was not grateful in the least for his championship of her.

Even so, Lord Goring was suspicious. Surely she hadn't been that dismissive of him, she thought with a pang of guilt. "That will be quite acceptable, Miss Dauntry," the viscount said after a nervous glance between Ophelia and Trent. "And perhaps you will take a turn with me on the terrace later?"

Much as she'd dislike the time with Goring, she agreed with a gracious nod. "That would be delightful, my lord," she said, smiling. "I shall look forward to it."

She felt Trent's gaze on her as she extended her hand to Lord Goring.

But now that his mission had been accomplished, Goring seemed to lose interest in her entirely, and bowed his good-bye.

"I am quite pleased to see you have decided to follow my advice," Mrs. Dauntry said in a low voice, beaming at Ophelia once her favorite had left them. Then, not waiting for a reply, she turned and left them as well.

"I had hoped she'd have given up her plan to marry you off to Goring," Leonora said, stepping up beside her. "He really is quite smarmy, isn't he?"

"An excellent description, my dear," Freddy said from beside her. "He positively oozed with it."

"He's not so very bad," Ophelia objected, still

wanting to keep up the pretense that she was interested in Goring while Trent was looking on.

"Surely she won't force you to marry him," Trent said, frowning. "That would be a disaster."

"I'm not sure why it should interest you, your grace," Ophelia said coolly. "My mother wishes our families to be joined through a marriage between myself and Lord Goring. It is a private family matter."

She held her head high though she felt Leonora and Freddie's startled gazes on her as well as Trent's baffled one.

"My apologies, Miss Dauntry," he said stiffly. "I had thought that since you'd confided in me about the matter . . . well, I was wrong, clearly. I beg your pardon." Then, excusing himself, he left them.

"Well, I have no compunction about counseling you against the match," Leonora said, breaking into Ophelia's thoughts as she stared after Trent, giving her a quick hug. "No one should have to wake up to that cloying smile every day."

A shudder ran through Ophelia at the very idea, and she felt bad for having been so cold to Trent. He was only trying to be her friend.

It wasn't his fault his kiss had meant nothing.

Having done his duty by dancing with several wallflowers, and stinging a bit over Ophelia's setdown, Trent made his way to one of the refreshment tables for a glass of what was sure to be tepid punch, but was stopped by a hand on his arm.

Turning, he saw it was Freddy who indicated with a jerk of his chin that they should step away from the crowd.

Once they were standing in an empty pocket at the side of the ballroom, Freddy spoke up.

"What the devil was that about?" he demanded. "You greeted Goring as if you suspected him of having killed your favorite spaniel. And then Ophelia reacted as if he were the greatest thing since mint-flavored tooth powder. Which is not her usual reaction to that bounder."

Turning to put his back against the wall, Trent shrugged. It wasn't as if he could tell him about the kiss he and Ophelia had shared yesterday. Nor was he ready to admit that he'd been jealous as hell at the sight of Goring's proprietary air.

"Don't know what you're talking about," he said finally, deciding denial was his best course of action, and hoping Freddy would drop the matter so that they could speak of something else.

"You might be able to fob others off like that," his oldest friend said with a scowl, "but it won't work with me. I've never seen you appear more unfriendly on meeting someone for the first time. And I sincerely doubt it has anything to do with the man's countenance. And that does nothing to explain Ophelia's reaction to him. Every other time she's encountered him she's all but openly cut him."

"Something about him rubbed me the wrong way," Trent admitted with a shrug, not daring to meet Freddy's gaze. "You said yourself the man is smarmy. No need to become distraught about it.

As for Ophelia's reaction, I'm sure I don't know why she does anything."

As soon as the words left his mouth he realized his mistake.

"Interesting you should say such a thing," Freddy said, brows drawn, "when only this afternoon the two of you were finishing each other's sentences and seemed fast friends. What might have happened to set the cat among the pigeons? I wonder."

"What's interesting?" asked the Earl of Mainwaring as he stepped into their little corner, a glass of champagne in his hand. "Leonora said something queer happened earlier but she wouldn't explain what."

"Our Trent has developed a *tendre* for Miss Ophelia Dauntry," said Freddy with a wink. "You missed seeing him slay his rival for her hand with a mere glance. It was something to behold. Truly."

"Oh, is that all?" Mainwaring asked, obviously disappointed. "I'd guessed that already. Not the slaying bit but definitely the *tendre* bit."

"I'd like to know how you can be so sure of it when I myself am unaware of any such thing," Trent said in a low grumble.

"Well, as to that," his friend said with a shrug, "it's not uncommon for the man to be the last to know. You agree, don't you, Freddy?"

Freddy nodded. "He's right. Creeps up on a fellow, love does. Like a thief in the night."

"While I greatly appreciate your poetic imagery," Trent said, crossing his arms over his coat of black superfine, "you are both talking bollocks.

And couldn't be more wrong if you had suggested I was pining after Lady Sefton or Sally Jersey.

"Not to mention," he added with a scowl, "that Ophelia is clearly not in the least bit interested in me, given the way she told me in not so many words to bugger off after I complained about Goring."

"Oh," Freddy said with a shake of his head. "That was just because you'd done something to offend her. Probably said something dismissive. Or, knowing how ladies react to things, you mightn't even have known you were doing it. They are rather inscrutable sometimes, ladies."

"And, deny all you want," Mainwaring said with a grin, "but you haven't seen your face when you think she's not looking."

"Or when she enters a room unexpectedly," Freddy added, nodding.

"And vice versa," Mainwaring added with a wink at Freddy.

"Might we speak about something else?" Trent demanded, though he didn't take his gaze off where Ophelia and Goring continued to dance. "Perhaps you could tell me if you've learned anything more about Dr. Hayes?"

Doubtless realizing that they would get no more of a reaction out of Trent, the other men shrugged.

"I asked my mother if she'd heard anything untoward about Hayes," Mainwaring said thoughtfully. "She had quite an interesting tale to tell. It seems that several years ago the good doctor was accused of wrongfully having a young heiress locked away."

His full attention on the other man, Trent pressed him for more. "Go on."

"Well, it seems Miss Langley's mother was afraid that the chit would have her head turned by a fortune hunter," Mainwaring explained. "And since she, the mother, had no control over the inheritance Miss Langley was to receive, she decided her only recourse would be to have the girl locked away so the mother could be named trustee. Which she did."

Freddy whistled. "How did the good doctor fit into this?"

"Hayes declared that Miss Langley was insane without ever having met the girl, and just as he did with Mrs. Grayson, he sent his thugs to abduct her and take her to his clinic," Mainwaring said. "The only trouble was that the girl was of age, wasn't insane, and unbeknownst to her dear mama, had already secretly married the alleged fortune hunter."

"What happened?" Trent demanded. He had a feeling that this story might be just what he and Ophelia needed to find Mrs. Grayson.

"The husband, a Mr. Volpe, protested the physician's orders in court and was able to have the new Mrs. Volpe removed from the clinic, and the court rebuked Dr. Hayes for attempting to take away the chit's freedom without ever having examined her."

"That is definitely promising," Trent said with a grin. "And if Hayes was willing to do the same thing in the case of Mrs. Grayson, perhaps he was willing to lie about Mrs. Grayson's actual condition in this case as well."

"And this time he wasn't quite as scrupulous about checking the identity of the person requesting the declaration," Freddy added. "But what's his incentive?"

"I'd be very surprised if he weren't demanding quite an exorbitant fee," Trent said. "These families are in difficult positions, with a daughter or son embarrassing all of them in public. They're willing to pay just about any sum that Dr. Hayes demands of them just so that he'll lock them away, making the public displays stop. Why would he question their assurances of madness? He not only gets the initial fee for the declaration, but then they pay him monthly for room and board in his clinic."

"But wouldn't the affair with Miss Langley, or Mrs. Volpe rather," Freddy asked, his brow furrowed, "have damaged Hayes's reputation?"

"Not when it's his word against that of a fortune hunter and a purported madwoman," Mainwaring said with a grim smile. "There was some mention of it in the papers, but they were more interested in the tale of poor duped Mrs. Volpe. And it didn't help that Volpe spent all of her fortune in short order. It made it look like Hayes was right in the first place."

"Nice work, Mainwaring," said Trent with a clap on his friend's shoulder. "O . . . I mean Miss Ophelia is going to be quite pleased at the news. If she is still speaking to me."

Before Freddy or the earl could continue their good-natured ribbing of their friend, the set ended and Ophelia herself approached.

"Gentlemen," she said gravely. "I hate to steal your friend away, but I believe you asked me for the supper dance, Trent."

"I did," he said, ignoring the way his friends were ogling their every move. Offering Ophelia his arm, he led her onto the floor.

As the opening notes of a waltz sounded, Ophelia took Trent's proffered hand and gazed at some point just over his left shoulder.

He'd danced the waltz countless times since it became fashionable in London, and before that in the ballrooms of Europe during the campaign against Napoleon. But as he placed his other hand at her waist, he found himself for the first time realizing just how intimate a thing it was.

"Miss Dauntry," he said as they began to whirl across the ballroom floor. "Ophelia. Have I done something to offend you?"

And rather than answer him truthfully, to his disappointment, she smiled brightly. "Of course not, your grace," she said. "Why would you think so?"

Twelve

*O*phelia was quite sure Trent had seen right through her attempt to behave as if nothing were wrong. It was perhaps an overreaction on her part to have taken offense at his admission that he looked forward to their dances solely as a means for discussing Dr. Hayes.

But when she glanced up, Trent was frowning. "You seemed a bit annoyed, I suppose," he said. "But if you say all is well, then I will take you at your word."

It was difficult to hold on to her pique when he looked so confused about it, Ophelia thought as they twirled around the ballroom. "I was just," she admitted, "a bit disappointed when you seemed more eager to talk about our investigation than actually dance with me. But it's silly. I see that now. My focus should be on finding Maggie. I apologize for being so silly."

If anything, his frown deepened. "I would have thought it went without saying that I wished to

dance with you," he said. Was it her imagination
or did he pull her just the slightest bit closer?

"It did?" She lowered her lashes, the intensity of
his gaze making her heart beat a little faster.

"In fact," he continued, in a voice only she could
hear, "if anything, it was the investigation that I
used as an excuse to dance with you. Not the other
way round."

She dared a glance up and he raised one dark
brow.

"Oh."

"Yes, oh."

They danced in silence for a few beats before she
spoke up again. "Now that that's settled, we really
should discuss the investigation."

He looked as if he'd like to argue, but nodded.
"Mainwaring might have gotten us some information that could be useful."

"What is it? Has he learned something about
Maggie?"

Quickly he told her the story of Mrs. Volpe, née
Langley, who had been wrongfully imprisoned by
Dr. Hayes.

As he related the tale, Ophelia became more and
more disgusted and, at the same time, excited. "This
is just the sort of thing I was hoping we'd learn," she
said, her eyes wide. "If we can confront Dr. Hayes
with his wrongdoing in this case, perhaps we can
leverage that to force him to tell us where Maggie
is now."

But Trent didn't seem as optimistic.

"Since the man has escaped thus far without

suffering any consequences for his behavior," he said, "I don't think he will be particularly afraid if we threaten him with exposure now. And without George we won't be able to prove that the writ was produced without Hayes having set eyes on Maggie."

Recognizing the truth of his words, Ophelia felt herself deflate a little. "That makes sense," she said with a frown. "I had so hoped this would be the break we were looking for."

"And it might still be," Trent said soothingly. "We now know of two other people who have been in the care of Dr. Hayes. And as such they might have heard, while they were in his clinic, about the location of another, more secret place where recalcitrant patients were kept. Patients like Maggie."

Though she knew he was right, Ophelia couldn't stop the wave of frustration that she'd felt on realizing that this wasn't the clue they'd needed to find her friend. Even so, it was better than nothing, and she was glad to know that they were a bit closer.

As they spun across the floor, Ophelia glanced up at Trent and found his blue eyes were watching her intently. "May I ask you something?" he said, his hand warm at her hip.

Not sure she liked the intensity in his gaze, she nodded.

"Is your mother always so unwilling to take your wishes into account when it comes to suitors?" he asked, a frown line between his brows.

Ophelia wasn't sure what she'd expected him to

ask but it wasn't that. "I . . . that is to say . . . Mama is very . . . determined," she finally managed to say.

"In what way?" Trent asked, clearly intent on her words.

She sighed. Wondering what the best way would be to explain her mother's reasons for wanting to see both her girls settled down happily with a man of good fortune.

"Now that my sister is betrothed to Kinston," Ophelia said carefully, "she has turned her attention to me. And that means she will do her utmost to ensure that Lord Goring, who is the son of her dearest friend, comes up to scratch."

"And yet, you clearly have no liking for the man," he said, his mouth tight.

"Well," she admitted carefully, "I am three and twenty and as yet unmarried, so she is afraid time is running out. Though I'm not even altogether sure that I wish to marry."

"But doesn't every lady wish to marry?" he asked, looking genuinely puzzled. "I should think you would not wish to live with your family forever."

"Well, the two do not necessarily relate to one another," she said wryly. "As it happens I would like to have a household of my own. But I'm not sure I would like to take on the infringement of freedoms that marriage would entail, however."

"It had never occurred to me until recently that a lady might not view marriage as a boon," he admitted. "Not until Freddy brought Mainwaring and myself into your circle, that is. I have learned a great deal about the plight of women since I met you and Leonora and Hermione."

"Only consider the number of men who never achieve such an understanding," Ophelia said. "I believe we'll make an enlightened male out of you yet, your grace."

Rather than take offense, Trent laughed. Ophelia wasn't sure she'd ever seen him look so carefree in his amusement. She was quite pleased with herself.

Since it was the supper dance, when the dance ended they sought out Freddy and Leonora, Mainwaring and Hermione, and found a table.

As soon as Trent and the other two men were gone to fetch plates for them, Leonora and Hermione began peppering Ophelia with questions.

"You looked to be in serious conversation during that waltz," Leonora said, her eyes wide. "What were you talking about? Surely not your investigation the whole time because I'm quite sure I saw Trent laugh more than once."

"And I saw him smile," Hermione added with a grin. "Do you know how rare it is to see him drop that somber countenance and actually enjoy himself?"

Though Ophelia had noticed the same things, she wasn't quite ready to discuss them with her friends. No matter how much she might love them.

"You're both incorrigible," she said with a shake of her head. "We were merely talking. As you do during a waltz. It's not as if we are both mutes who suddenly found our voices, after all. And a great deal of it was about my missing friend."

"She's holding something back from us, Nora," Hermione said with mock shock. "I cannot believe our dear Ophelia is refusing to share every last detail of her interaction with a handsome man. Is that not some sort of breach of the code of friendship?"

"At the very least." Leonora nodded. "I think we'll have to bring you up on sanctions, Miss Dauntry. It is regrettable, but you leave us no choice."

"About what?" Freddy asked as he took the empty seat beside his wife and presented her with a plate piled high with delicacies. "I got you extra crab cakes, my dear," he said. "Just as the babe requested."

"You're the dearest man," Leonora said, patting him on the hand as she picked up a fork. "The child is quite grateful."

Fortunately, Mainwaring and Trent also arrived then and presented Hermione and Ophelia with plates of their own.

The group was silent for a few moments as everyone began to eat.

Then, unfortunately, Freddy remembered what he'd overheard before he arrived with the food. "So what were you chastising poor Ophelia about?"

Ophelia exchanged a look with Leonora and Hermione.

"Nothing you gentlemen should concern yourselves with," Leonora assured him. "We ladies must keep some secrets, my dear. You know that."

"Sounds suspicious to me," Mainwaring said with a wink at his wife. "I believe you ladies just tell us that when you're discussing us."

"We are a fascinating topic of conversation, Mainwaring," said Freddy. "Do you not agree, Trent?"

But the duke shrugged. "Never having conversed about myself, I wouldn't know."

Determined to get the conversation back into safer waters, Ophelia spoke up. "I'm sorry Mama's interruption meant we missed the opportunity to speak with your cousin, Leonora. Do you suppose Daisy might be willing to chat once supper is finished?"

Leonora shook her head. "I'm afraid she's already left. She doesn't like staying at these things for very long. I think something about the crowd overwhelms her. But I feel sure we'll be able to set up something tomorrow or the next day. I'll invite you both to tea."

"I'd be grateful for it," Ophelia said, glad that her friends were so determined to help her any way they could to find her friend. "Tonight will be Maggie's second night in the care of whoever has taken her."

"We'll find her, Ophelia," Trent said quietly. "We'll unravel Dr. Hayes's lies and find her. Have no fear on that score."

But that was just it. "I do believe we'll find her," she admitted as, to her mortification, tears threatened. "But in what state? I can't help but recall what Leonora said her cousin endured at Dr. Hayes's hands. If that was in the main clinic where visitors were allowed, then what sort of horrors must Maggie be subjected to in the secret one?"

Unable to hold back her emotions any longer, she quickly excused herself and hurried from the crowded supper room.

"Oh dear," Leonora said, looking in the direction where Ophelia had fled. "This must have been a hard couple of days for her."

"Poor girl," Freddy said, patting his wife's hand.

"I'll go check on her," Hermione said, placing her napkin beside her plate.

But Trent was already on his feet, and ignoring his friends' curious stares, he threaded his way through the tables in search of where Ophelia had gone.

Even as he headed into the hallway leading to the public rooms of the Kinston town house, his conscience was demanding answers to his motive in searching for Ophelia when she'd certainly wanted only privacy in which to unleash her emotions.

Leonora had been right, it had been a hard couple of days for Ophelia, and he'd been insensitive not to pay closer attention to just how difficult they'd been. Not only had she endured an attack upon her own person, but she'd watched helplessly as two strange men absconded with her dear friend. And no one seemed to know where to look for her. Then on top of all that, her own mother was trying to force her into a loveless marriage with a man she clearly had little respect, let alone affection, for.

After walking in on an embracing couple in one small firelit chamber, and apologizing before beating a quick retreat, he finally discovered Ophelia alone in a room a few doors down. It must be some sort of music room, he reflected on seeing a pianoforte and a harp positioned on either side of the lit fireplace.

Ophelia herself was seated on the bench before the pianoforte, her shoulders bent as she dabbed at her eyes with a handkerchief.

"There you are," he said, wanting to alert her to his presence before he approached her.

From this angle, he could see the elegant curve of her slender neck, tendrils of her glossy dark hair kissing the porcelain of her skin.

At the sound of his voice, she stiffened, but did not turn around. "One moment, please," she said in a teary voice. "I'll only be a moment."

But he couldn't just leave her there to suffer on her own. She was so strong. So composed most of the time. But there were occasions when it was necessary to unleash the emotions one kept at bay. And if she needed a shoulder to lean on, could he not be the one to provide it?

Cautiously, he stepped closer and wordlessly took the seat beside her.

When she looked up, her eyes were bright with the sheen of tears. "You needn't have come after me," she said in a low voice. "I only needed some time alone."

"But you don't have to be alone," he said, giving in to temptation and reaching out to stroke a tear from her cheek. "Your friends are all there to listen when you need to talk about your worries."

She leaned into his hand, almost unconsciously, like a cat accepting a caress.

"And what of you?" she asked, boldly meeting his gaze. "Are you my friend?"

He felt something spark between them. The same pull that had made him kiss her yesterday—could it only have been the day before? It felt as if they'd been creeping toward this moment for months, years, decades, centuries.

"I'm afraid not," he said carefully, noting the flare of disappointment, before adding, "At least, not only your friend, I hope."

Her brows drew together. "What else?"

But he could no longer rely on words to explain things.

Stroking his thumb over her lower lip, he leaned in and kissed her.

Thirteen

*O*phelia had read a great deal about kisses. In the Minerva Press novels she read, they were copious, but annoyingly vague about what happened beyond the actual touching of lips. There had been that quick one yesterday in Trent's curricle, but it had hardly lasted more than a moment. This, she knew, was a proper kiss.

And when Trent bent his head to hers, she realized that the vague descriptions in novels might owe to the fact that so many thoughts and feelings occurred when one was being kissed that it was impossible to catalogue them.

She closed her eyes and was reminded again of how surprisingly soft his lips were, and was assailed by so many sensations she could never name them all. The only thing she knew for certain was that he smelled like sandalwood and man and when he shifted closer to wrap her in his arms, she would rather have died than pull away.

And when he nipped lightly on her lower lip, she

opened her mouth and welcomed his tongue against hers, eager for more of this intimacy she'd imagined but never experienced. A fleeting worry that she might not be doing it right disappeared in the maelstrom of sensation. His mouth was gentle but firm, and when he made a small moan she realized that untutored as she might be, he was just as swept up in the moment as she was.

Every part of her was aching to be closer. And it was more, much more than just their lips that touched.

Her breasts, pressed against his hard chest, ached to be touched. And as she slid her hands up and around his neck, she felt his own hands trace up her sides and pull her closer.

Then she gasped as his hand covered her breast, and his kiss grew more demanding, more urgent. And she met him stroke for stroke, kiss for kiss. Heady with the need to have him touch her, the need to touch him, everywhere. Arched her neck so that he could kiss his way down her throat to that spot on her collarbone where she suddenly knew his mouth belonged.

So caught up were they in the moment, neither of them heard the door of the music room open.

But there was no ignoring the angry gasp of Mrs. Dauntry a moment later.

"Ophelia!" she hissed. "What on earth is this?"

At her mother's words, Ophelia felt a jolt of alarm run through her and she immediately pushed away from Trent.

Trent gave a low curse and stood just behind

her. He did not, however, let go of her completely. Rather he slipped his hand over her shoulder and gave it a squeeze.

Only then did Ophelia notice that Lord Goring was also there, standing just behind her mother. Was the man actually raising his quizzing glass to see them better? Well, she thought, on the verge of hysteria, let him look. This might finally prove to Lord Goring that she had no interest in marrying him.

"I might have expected such a thing of some other men, your grace," Ophelia's mother snapped, moving closer to the pianoforte, "but I thought you were at least a gentleman."

Watching helplessly as Mrs. Dauntry moved away from him, Lord Goring lowered his eyeglass and began to back away. "I'll just leave the three of you to—"

But Mrs. Dauntry turned, grabbed him by the arm, and pulled him back into the room. Then shut the door behind him.

"You stay here, Lord Goring," she said with an implacability that Ophelia knew all too well. "Do you not wish to fight for your bride?"

Goring blanched. "We are not . . . that is to say, Mrs. Dauntry, Miss Dauntry and I haven't yet . . ." He ran a finger beneath his suddenly too-tight cravat. "There is no . . ."

"Mrs. Dauntry," Trent cut in sharply, "you do both Ophelia and me a disservice."

Ophelia was pleased to see her mother gape at being spoken to in such a way.

"And," he added with a scowl directed toward the other interloper, "Goring is correct to want to leave. He has no place here. Any agreement you might have had with him about Miss Dauntry's hand is void."

"Unless what I just saw was the conclusion of a marriage proposal," Mrs. Dauntry said with a cynical laugh, "then I think not."

To her shame, Ophelia heard the disbelief in her mother's tone. She clearly didn't believe that a man like Trent would bother offering marriage to Ophelia.

She opened her mouth to explain to her mother that it didn't take a proposal from another man to prove she would never marry Goring, but before she could speak, Trent said, "That is precisely what you saw, ma'am. And I will not tolerate such disrespect of Ophelia either while I am here to offer her protection or when you are alone with her."

What the—

Ophelia gaped at Trent, unable to decide whether he was serious, or had some other reason for telling her mother an outright lie.

But rather than grinning and declaring that he'd only been bamming her, instead he simply stared back at her.

"Is this true, Ophelia?" Mrs. Dauntry asked, looking as shocked as Ophelia felt. "Why would you accept a proposal from another man when you are clearly promised to Lord Goring?"

But Goring, seeing who held the power in the

room, perhaps, was already slipping out of the room. Behind Mrs. Dauntry's back, of course. He was not such a fool after all.

Mrs. Dauntry looked as if she'd like to go after him, but was arrested when Ophelia responded. "It is true, Mama," she said, deciding to trust that Trent had some sort of plan. Even so, however, she left herself a means for escape. "I had not yet given him an answer, however."

When she turned to Trent, he gave her a slight look of exasperation but did not object.

Her mother, however, was not going to be so easily cowed.

"It is customary for a gentleman to approach a young lady's father with an offer of marriage, is it not?" Mrs. Dauntry asked. "I feel sure Mr. Dauntry would have informed me if he'd received such a visit from you."

"And for that I apologize, ma'am," Trent said with an inclination of his head. "I was carried away in the moment and forgot all propriety. But rest assured I will approach Ophelia's father at the first opportunity."

As Ophelia watched, her mother's nostrils flared with annoyance. "You both seem to have things all figured out, don't you?"

Since any response to that would mean angering her further, both Ophelia and Trent held their tongues.

"I had hoped, Ophelia," Mrs. Dauntry said with a shake of her head, "that you would allow yourself to be guided by me in your choice of a husband, but clearly you are as headstrong as you are disobedient."

"Mama, I have tried to tell you again and again that I do not wish to marry Lord Goring," Ophelia protested, grateful that Trent was here to offer her some support. "But you refused to listen. I know you and his mother had dreamed of joining our families, but I'm afraid that's a dream that will not come to fruition."

"Clearly," Mrs. Dauntry said with a frown.

Trent cleared his throat then, and said, "There is just the matter of gaining Miss Dauntry's consent to my proposal."

"Is that not beside the point, at this juncture?"

And Ophelia suddenly realized that her escape route was not quite so convenient as she'd hoped.

"Even so," Trent said smoothly, "I should like a moment with Ophelia before you take her home."

Mrs. Dauntry looked as if she'd like to object, but perhaps realizing that this whole matter was now out of her hands, she shrugged. "Ophelia, I will go find your father and inform him that we are leaving." To Trent she added, "You have five minutes, your grace."

When her mother was gone, Ophelia turned to Trent with a speaking look.

"You needed rescuing," Trent said with an elegant shrug. "And it's not as if you wished to marry Goring."

Then, perhaps doubting himself for a moment, he asked, "Did you?"

"Of course not," she said, poking him in the chest with a finger. "I hadn't thought to marry anyone in the near future."

"Well, sometimes," he said with an innocent air, "things change."

She shook her head in exasperation. "What made you say that? What could possibly have made you do it?"

Trent stepped closer, and despite what she hoped was her annoyed face, he slipped his arms around her. "I thought," he said, before kissing her on the nose, "that since you were kissing me quite thoroughly before we were so rudely interrupted, you might not be averse to marrying me."

It was very difficult to remain angry when someone kissed you on the nose, Ophelia realized with a sigh.

"You were not entirely wrong," she said, keeping her gaze firmly on his chest.

"Good," he said. Then, pulling away, he gave her a little push in the direction of the door. "Go find your mother and I'll wait for a few minutes so no one sees us leaving together."

"We're already being rushed into a betrothal," she argued, though she did as he said. "What more is there to lose?"

"Just go, Ophelia," he said with exasperation of his own.

"Only betrothed for a few minutes and you think you can order me around," she groused.

Then with a backward glance at him, she shut the door firmly behind her.

* * *

After a sleepless night, in which he went back over the events of the Kinston ball again and again in his mind, Trent rose early and dressed with more care than he was accustomed to.

"I don't know when I've seen you go through this many cravats, yer grace," grumbled his valet, Bamford, after Trent had crumpled the fourth neck cloth in as many minutes and tossed it aside. "One would think you was in the petticoat line."

At the valet's tart words, Trent supposed he might as well tell the man about the upcoming change in their circumstances. "If you must know, I'm paying a call on Miss Ophelia Dauntry's father this morning to ask for her hand. So you're not far off."

"Huh," the grizzled ex-soldier grunted. "I knowed it was coming up one of these days. Might have guessed it when she showed up at the door in a faint. In the family way is she?"

"Damn you, Bamford, she is not," he growled as he finally managed to tie a decent Corinthian knot. "I'll not have you speaking of your future mistress in that way either. Show some respect, man, or I'll toss you out on your arse."

Having been with Trent for long enough to know when there was steel behind his words, the valet threw up his hands in apology. "Easy, yer grace. I was just putting two and two together to make seven. You can't blame a man for making assumptions when yesterday morning you weren't thinking marriage but today you are."

"Well, next time perhaps don't make such a miscalculation," Trent said grudgingly. "I shall count on you to ensure that the rest of the house treats her with the respect she deserves. Especially since our marriage will likely happen quickly. Can I count on you?"

They exchanged a look in the pier glass and Trent saw surprise in the other man's eyes. Surely his servants had expected him to marry at some point.

But Bamford nodded and said, "O'course, yer grace. I'll see to it, don't you worry."

Trent glanced down at his waistcoat again. It was a peacock blue with silver-threaded embroidery throughout. Against the black of his coat and the pristine white of his shirt and neck cloth, it was eye-catching. He wondered if he was perhaps overdoing it a bit.

As if he'd spoken aloud, Bamford shook his head. "It ain't every day a man gets betrothed, yer grace. Miss Dauntry will like a bit of dash, see if she don't."

Feeling rather like a prize fool, Trent nodded his thanks.

"I'll be out for most of the day, Bamford. Tell cook to hold supper."

"Of course, yer grace," the valet replied.

As Trent turned to leave, he heard the man clear his throat behind him.

"What is it?" he asked, his hand on the knob.

When he glanced round at the man he looked more serious than he'd seen him since their days on

the Continent. "I just wanted to offer my congratulations, yer grace. I'm pleased for ye."

Trent found himself surprisingly touched by the
other man's words. They'd been through a lot, the
two of them.

"My thanks, Bamford," he said with a grin. "I
don't think either of us thought this day would
come when we were in Belgium, did we?"

"Psh," the ex-soldier responded with an answering grin. "I knowed if anybody could face
the frogs and live to tell the tale it would be you.
Why do you think I stuck by ye for such a long
stretch?"

"Why indeed?"

When Trent lifted the brass knocker of the Dauntry town house some time later, it was with an
oddly uplifting sense of optimism.

While it was true he was preparing to put his
bachelor days behind him, Ophelia was a beautiful, intelligent woman. And he wanted her rather
badly. He might not yet feel the sort of overwhelm-
ing passion that Freddy and Mainwaring felt for
their wives, but he was confident that he and
Ophelia could be happy together.

If, that is, her mother didn't put up another
obstacle before he managed to make a formal proposal. She'd appeared to accept defeat in her plan
to marry Ophelia to Goring last night, but that
could have been a temporary appeasement.

He might no longer be an active soldier, but that
was no reason to abandon his head for strategy.

And Mrs. Dauntry was as wily as any general he'd ever encountered.

But when he was ushered into Mr. Dauntry's study, he was relieved to see the man was alone. From what Ophelia had said about him, Trent suspected Mr. Dauntry was the more reasonable of her parents.

"Why do you want to marry my daughter, your grace?" the older man asked after greeting Trent and gesturing for him to have a seat, then taking one for himself behind his enormous desk. "What is it about her that makes you single her out for your attentions? You are quite the catch, I would imagine. And while I am quite proud of my daughter, I do not delude myself into thinking that she is the most eligible young lady in London."

Resisting the urge to straighten his cravat, Trent said, "I believe, sir, begging your pardon, that you quite mistake my requirements in a wife if you think I care one whit about a potential bride's standing in the *ton*. I am far more concerned with her ability to carry on an intelligent conversation."

"And yet," Mr. Dauntry said wryly, "it was not conversation that my wife found you engaged in last evening."

Trent felt a suspicious heat in his cheeks. "That is correct, sir. But let me assure you that I do not take what happened last night lightly. I know what honor demands, and I am more than willing to do my duty. But let me assure you it is no hardship. I want to marry Ophelia, and had been seriously contemplating asking for her hand before last night."

As he spoke, Trent saw something in the older man's expression relax a bit.

"I do not mind telling you, your grace," Mr. Dauntry said with a nod, "that I was prepared to toss you out on your ear if you'd come to me with a proposal wrapped in the usual pompous nonsense. I know parents are not supposed to have favorites, but Ophelia is mine. And she is a bright girl. I would not have thought she'd look twice at a man who couldn't keep up with her intellectually. But stranger things have happened. And if you'd been the typical young nobleman with more hair than wit, I'd have rejected you. But now I am much more sanguine about you."

Trent wondered idly how it was that Mr. Dauntry had allowed Mrs. Dauntry's attempts to force Lord Goring on her for so long if Ophelia was indeed his favorite daughter. But he wasn't prepared to look this particular gift horse in the mouth, so he bit his tongue and thanked the man instead.

As if he had heard Trent's thoughts aloud, Mr. Dauntry then said, "It has been my wife's dearest wish for many years for one of her daughters to marry the son of her dearest friend. Lord Goring, to be precise. She is not best pleased at the way events have unfolded between you and my daughter. But as far as I'm concerned, you have my blessing. While Goring does not. I just thought you should know lest my wife attempt to make one last effort at bringing her plan to fruition."

"I am well aware of Goring's desire to marry Ophelia, sir," Trent said. "And I can assure you that my suit is strong enough to withstand anything your wife might attempt in order to prevent me from marrying Ophelia."

Mr. Dauntry nodded with approval. "Very good, your grace. Then it's settled. All it needs is for you to speak to my daughter."

He stood and extended his hand to Trent. "She's in the drawing room. Third door on the left."

Taking his leave of Ophelia's father, Trent left the study and went in search of Ophelia.

Fourteen

Ophelia sat over her needlepoint—about which she was indifferent at best—in the drawing room of Dauntry House the next morning, feeling rather like a prisoner waiting for the executioner.

It wasn't that she found Trent to be repugnant in any way. Of course not. She'd kissed him quite willingly the evening before. And though she had no experience to compare it to, she was convinced he was very good at it, kissing.

There was no denying the attraction between them. Though only last week she would not have credited it.

She'd always found him handsome, of course. That was obvious to anyone with eyes. But the time they'd spent together these past two days had revealed him to be kind, fair, and if his pursuit of Maggie was any indication, determined.

And he was determined, now, it seemed, to marry her.

Her mother's reminder at breakfast, however,

that she had no choice in the matter had stoked Ophelia's defiant streak. Given a choice between Trent and Goring, she would choose Trent of course. And she liked Trent well enough when it came down to it. It had nothing to do with the man, and everything to do with the circumstance. Willing participant though she had been.

Looking down at the rose she was embroidering, she realized she'd just stitched using the wrong color entirely. Perhaps close work was not the best choice of an occupation this morning, she thought ruefully as she removed the stitch.

She was threading her needle with the correct shade when a brisk knock on the drawing room door made her jump and poke herself with the needle.

"Come in," she called, ignoring the stinging of her thumb.

As she stood and shook out her favorite deep blue morning gown, which made her feel both attractive and confident, she turned to the doorway.

And froze.

Instead of the Duke of Trent, Lord Goring crossed the room, his hands extended as if to reach for hers.

"My dear Miss Dauntry," he said, his face a mask of desolation. "I couldn't sleep a wink last night for thinking of your awful predicament."

Taking her hands before she could offer them, he squeezed. Hard.

"I . . . that is to say, thank you, my lord," she said, trying and failing to extricate herself from his surprisingly strong grip. "But I don't think such concern is warranted. And I wouldn't call it a predicament."

"My dear," he said, shaking his head at her, "you are far too innocent to realize the repercussions of what happened last night. But I can assure you that reputations have been decimated for far, far less. It is truly a dreadful situation. One that can be resolved if only you will say yes to my proposal."

Was this not the same man who all but ran from the room last night as soon as things got the least bit contentious?

"I assure you, there is no need for you to intervene, Lord Goring," she said with more charity for his offer than she felt. "I have an understanding with the Duke of Trent, and I am expecting him this morning."

But if she'd been hoping for Goring to take the hint and leave, she was sorely mistaken.

"Let there be no mention of that brute's name in my presence, Miss Dauntry," Goring cried dramatically, actually clasping his hands to his breast. "I fear I am unable to answer for the consequences if you do. I find it quite unthinkable that you can consider marrying him after what he did to you."

Stopping herself just short of rolling her eyes, Ophelia said, "Not that it's any of your affair, sir, but I am quite happy to marry the duke." *Instead of you*, she added mentally.

"After he left you soiled, like a handkerchief discarded in the gutter?" Goring said with a shudder.

"No, it's not to be borne. Fortunately for you, your mother has convinced me, against my natural instinct to shy away from ugliness, to offer you my hand in marriage."

"I'm not sure what my mother told you, Lord Goring," Ophelia said, moving away as Goring moved closer, "but I have no need of your sacrifice. In fact, I'd be quite happy for you to leave me now. Please go."

But for such a thin man, Goring was surprisingly strong, and when he pulled Ophelia to him, his grip was unbreakable. "Your missishness does you proud, my dear," he said as he attempted to kiss her.

At that moment a brisk knock sounded on the drawing room door. Instead of leaping away, Goring only held harder.

"Help me," Ophelia cried, without knowing who interrupted, but desperate for escape. "Please."

"You have exactly one minute to let go of her, Goring," Trent said. "Before I ask you to name your seconds."

Perhaps Goring wasn't the fool Ophelia thought him, because he dropped his hands at once.

That didn't stop him from arguing, however. "It is laughable to me that you should be the one to threaten a duel, your grace, when it is I who am protecting Miss Dauntry's honor."

Ophelia saw one of Trent's brows rise at Goring's hyperbole, even as he moved to stand beside her, slipping an arm around her waist as she stood rubbing her upper arms where Goring had gripped her.

"Goring," Trent said in a deceptively languid drawl, "I don't know what sort of arrangement you've made with Mrs. Dauntry, but you may be assured that I have an agreement with Mr. Dauntry that negates yours. So, get out. Now."

"I'm afraid I cannot do that, your grace," Goring persisted. "Honor demands that I remain here. If only to prevent you from further damaging Miss Dauntry's reputation. In fact, I could not forgive myself if I were to flee now."

"There is no danger of Miss Dauntry's reputation suffering a blemish," Trent said coldly, "if you will only keep your mouth shut."

"You forget that I was not the only one to witness your indiscretion, your grace," Goring said with a nasty smile. "Mrs. Dauntry was also a witness. And she has assured me that my suit has been accepted. If Ophelia is reluctant, it is only because she fears angering you."

"Do not put words in my mouth, sir," Ophelia said, growing impatient with the man's persistence. "What has my mother promised you that you refuse to be dismissed? Money? A house? What?"

As Goring's face turned scarlet, she realized she had the right of it. It shouldn't have come as a surprise given how quick he'd been to make his escape previously. Even so, the knowledge did nothing to endear her mother to her.

"I . . . I can assure you, Miss Dauntry," Goring

said, his Adam's apple bobbing furiously, "that any agreement I have with your mother is strictly a business arrangement that does not concern you."

By this time, Trent, it seemed, had had enough. Carefully he removed his arm from around Ophelia's waist, and walking easily up to the other man, he unceremoniously grabbed him by the cravat and all but carried him over to the door, opened it, and pushed the other man through it.

This done, Trent closed the door and locked it.

"I apologize for using such language in front of you, my dear Miss Dauntry," he said with a shake of his head. "But, what an ass."

Unable to stop herself, Ophelia giggled. "He is, isn't he?"

"However," Trent said, his face turning serious, "I did not come here to discuss Lord Goring." He began to prowl toward her, and Ophelia felt a small shiver run through her. "I came, as you likely suspected, to speak to your father, Miss Dauntry. And, thankfully, he has given his consent."

Before she could respond to that, he continued, taking both her hands in his, the touch achingly gentle. "I know we spoke of it last night, but today I wish to make you a formal offer. Miss Dauntry, will you do me the honor of becoming my wife? I realize we have only truly known one another for a couple of days, but I believe during that time we have proved to be compatible. And there is no question that there is friendship between us."

If she'd been hoping for a romantic proposal that would sweep her off her feet, Ophelia thought wryly, then she was doomed to disappointment. It was likely not something that the practical, rational ex-soldier turned duke had in him. But there was much to appreciate in his words, not least of which was his claim of friendship between them, which she knew was not something most couples in the *ton* could attest to.

Still, some imp of mischief prompted her to step even closer to him, and lifting her face to look up into his eyes, she whispered, "Do not forget, your grace, that we also have this." And trembling with nerves at her own boldness, she brought her lips up to kiss his.

She would have pulled away, but Trent was no fool, and slipped his hand up to cup the back of her head and hold her in place even as he waited for her to continue the kiss. Recalling last night's embrace, she pulled back a little, then lightly scraping her teeth over his lower lip, she was rewarded when he opened for her. Fusing her open mouth over his, she tentatively stroked her tongue into his mouth and was soon losing herself in sensation as he kissed her back, met her stroke for stroke.

When he slid his hand up to close over her left breast, she moaned, and it must have awakened something in Trent, because he drew back with a groan, and put a little distance between them.

Both of them were breathing hard as he thrust a hand through his hair. "Zounds," he said with a breathless laugh, "I think you proved your point there."

"Then why did you stop?" she asked. "I wasn't

very good at it, was I?" She'd known just how un-tutored she was at such things, but she'd hoped her eagerness would make up for it.

Something like tenderness shone in his eyes as he moved over to her once more. He stroked his thumb over her cheek. "You couldn't have been better," he said with a sweet smile that made her stomach do a little flip. "But we are under your father's roof. And it would be disrespectful for us to do anything more than kiss here. Not to mention the fact that we aren't wed yet." His eyes darkened as they held hers. "When I take you, it will be in the privacy of our own bedchamber. Where I can take my time, and there will be no chance of someone disturbing us."

"Oh," she whispered.

"Yes," he whispered back, leaning in to kiss her once on the lips before drawing away. "Oh."

Just then, a rattling at the door startled them both.

"Ophelia!" Mrs. Dauntry shouted from the other side of the door. "Ophelia, open this door this instant."

"Let me handle her," Trent said with a staying hand on her arm, as she'd begun to move toward the door.

"But she's my mother," Ophelia said in a low voice. "My responsibility."

"I'm the one she's truly angry with, however," Trent said simply. "Let me do this for you. I may not be able to slay actual dragons, but the least I can do is handle your mother."

Perhaps she'd been wrong about him, Ophelia thought as he turned to walk over and unlock the door. That was perhaps the most romantic thing anyone had ever done for her.

After Trent had, as he'd said he would, handled Mrs. Dauntry, he left to petition the archbishop for a special license. Leaving Ophelia with an urgent need to escape the house and her mother's ire, though Trent assured her she had nothing to worry about.

She'd had many more years of experience with her mother than he had, however, so she decided to be safe rather than sorry.

Donning her bonnet and pelisse, she called for the carriage to be brought round and set off to call upon Leonora.

"My dear," her friend said when Ophelia entered her pretty sitting room. "I wasn't expecting you this morning, was I? I fear this child has wreaked havoc on my memory. I don't know what's happening from one minute to the next some days."

The two shared a quick hug and Ophelia took a seat on the chair beside the settee where Leonora sat with a book beside her.

"Not at all," Ophelia said, smiling at her friend's complaint. She knew as well as anyone how pleased Leonora and Freddy had been when she discovered she was with child. Though it was not common knowledge, they'd had reason to believe that she might not be able to conceive. The fact that she had, and not very long after they were wed, was something that had made both the couple and their closest friends incredibly happy. "We had no plans. I simply had some news to share and, to be honest, thought it would be better if I didn't interact with Mama too much today."

"Oh dear." Leonora grimaced at Ophelia's words. "I had hoped things were getting better between the two of you. Is she still pressing you to wed the dreadful Lord Goring?"

"Not exactly," Ophelia said sheepishly. "There's more."

Quickly she told Leonora about the events of last evening and this morning. Punctuating the tale with gasps and groans where appropriate, her friend actually clapped her hands when Ophelia's tale was complete. "I suspected something when we learned you'd left early with the headache," she said, bemused, "but I had little notion it was because you'd been caught kissing Trent! Was it wonderful? Of course it was, one has only to look at you to know it was. I am so happy for you! I had hoped there was something building between you, but I never suspected it had gone this far."

Ophelia was a little bemused as Leonora pulled her into a hug. "I am so thoroughly pleased about this. You have no idea. Wait until I tell Freddy! And Hermione! We must send her a note and ask her to come round at once. We have to make plans for your wedding. You shall have five hundred at the wedding breakfast, at the very least."

"Slow down, Nora," Ophelia said with a laugh,

feeling rather like a sailor caught in his first hurricane. "We can certainly ask Hermione to join us, but you must remember the circumstances. Something quiet and soon will be more appropriate. Trent has gone to ask the archbishop for a special license as we speak."

"Oh." Nora sank back down onto the settee. "Well, you cannot blame me for being pleased. It's such a surprise. And yet, so wonderful. I didn't even realize the two of you knew one another that well before you embarked on the search for Mrs. Grayson. Though of course you've spent enough time together since Freddy and I wed."

"You're not far off the mark," Ophelia admitted, feeling a blush rise in her cheeks at the thought of how well she'd come to know him. "I believe I've spoken to Trent more in the past two days than I have in the last several months. But it doesn't always take years to determine whether a man is decent. And we both know that he is honorable and can be amusing when the mood strikes him."

"And he must be quite the romantic to have wooed and won you in such short order," Leonora said with a laugh. "Freddy said once that it is easier to get a bill passed in the Lords than it is to make Trent do something he is disinclined to do. So you know that he must indeed want you very badly to go to the effort of stealing you from beneath that awful Lord Goring's nose."

At that assessment, Ophelia felt slightly uncomfortable. "I'm not sure I'd say he was eager for the match," she said ruefully. "I doubt he'd have asked if Mama and Lord Goring hadn't walked in on us."

But Leonora shook her head. "You may set your mind at ease on that score, my dear," she said with a sweet smile. "For I have no doubt that Trent had already made up his mind to have you before he kissed you. You musn't forget that he spent a decade or more in the military. He doesn't move a muscle before he's thought the thing through most thoroughly. Rest assured that he does nothing by accident."

That gave Ophelia pause. "That makes it sound as if Trent intentionally compromised me." Something about that notion dimmed her enthusiasm for the betrothal. She'd been so busy avoiding her mother's attempts to trap her into marriage to Lord Goring, it hadn't occurred to her that she might have gone from the frying pan into the fire.

But Leonora would have none of it. "Of course not!" she said with a shake of her head. "I only meant that he would not have kissed you if his intentions weren't honorable. That's all. Please do not think that I am saying he maneuvered things so that you'd be forced to marry. Indeed, I have no knowledge of what was in Trent's mind. I have enough trouble trying to figure out what Freddy is thinking. And half the time with him I'm only guessing, and incorrectly at that."

Ophelia was quick to reassure her. "I don't think that, I assure you. For one thing, he'd have had to arrange Maggie's kidnapping in order to orchestrate the circumstances that would throw us together for two days. And even he couldn't have predicted I'd go to him first on the day Maggie was taken."

"Speaking of Maggie," Leonora said, sobering. "Is there any news? I had hoped by now you'd have learned something."

And like the sun going behind a cloud, Ophelia's world dimmed. "No," she said to her friend. To her shame, in the drama surrounding her betrothal she'd forgotten about Maggie for hours at a time today. Which made her feel like the worst friend in the world. "In all honesty, I don't quite know where to look next. We still should speak to your cousin Daisy, but that will need to be postponed until after the wedding. For I sincerely doubt Mama will be put off long enough for me to speak to her. Even if I'm to wed Trent and not her preferred candidate."

"Since you don't know that Daisy will be able to tell you anything new," Leonora said sensibly, "then I think it best that you don't put too much hope into it. Otherwise the disappointment might be too much for you to handle."

"There's no fear of that," Ophelia admitted with a sigh. "I've begun to expect disappointment rather than success in this matter. There are simply too many possibilities for where she might have been taken. For all I know she's been put on a ship bound for America and I'll never see her again."

"Oh, my dear," Leonora gave her an impulsive hug. "Do not think that. You will find her. I know it. Have no fear of that."

"If only there were something I could do right

now to look for her," Ophelia said with a shake of her head. "I should like very much to visit the orphanage run by Daniel Swinton, to follow up on what I found in Maggie's journal. But there's little chance of that before the wedding."

Frowning, Leonora tapped a finger on her lower lip. "Perhaps there is a way to do so this afternoon."

"How?" Ophelia asked, frowning. "I can hardly go into Whitechapel by myself to make inquiries of the man."

"But why not?" Leonora asked. "Is it not the sort of thing you would do to research something for the *Ladies' Gazette*?"

"But that's the sort of story Maggie writes," Ophelia countered. "I write strictly about light, fashionable things."

Leonora, however, had already gone to the bell-pull, and rung. "Then it's high time you remedied that, isn't it?" she asked with a wink. "And we can call and pick up Hermione on the way."

Leave it to Leonora, Ophelia thought with a rueful grin, to simply set things in motion whether Ophelia was ready or not.

"I do love you," she said to her friend once they were in the carriage, two burly outriders accompanying them. "I'd never have done this on my own."

"Think nothing of it," Leonora said with a wave of her hand. "I also wish to know what happened to your friend Maggie. I don't know about you, but I cannot sit idly by while Dr. Hayes simply declares someone to be mad, sight unseen, and has them locked away indefinitely. It's the most frightening thing I've ever heard of. And you must remember I was acquainted with both past presidents of the Lords of Anarchy, so I know whereof I speak."

And with that assurance, they were on their way.

Fifteen

It turned out that securing a special license was not as difficult as Trent had thought it would be, thanks to Freddy's brother, who was conveniently in town and, as a clergyman himself, known to the archbishop. It was only a matter of a couple of hours before Trent had the license in hand and was on his way back to Brooks's to have a celebratory drink with his friends, which turned out to be a much shorter celebration than either Freddy or Mainwaring had intended.

"Why are we leaving so soon?" Freddy asked as Trent hustled both men out into St. James's Street and into his waiting carriage. "I barely had time to make a toast before you were calling for the carriage."

"Not to mention that we had only managed a few sips of brandy," Mainwaring groused. "Really, Trent, if this is what you'll be like as a married man, I must recommend against it."

Trent peered out the window as the vehicle began

to move, and once he was sure they were under way, he turned to his friends. "My apologies, gentlemen," he said with a not very regretful expression. "But I wished for you to accompany me to Whitechapel. And I was unsure you would do so if I didn't make it impossible for you to refuse."

"What the devil is wrong with you, man?" Freddy asked, rolling his eyes. "You're about to get married and you wish to make a trip into the most notorious part of town? I realize it is customary for a man to have some sort of last hurrah before he weds, but I never took you for the sort who'd favor the type of wares offered in Whitechapel."

"Rest easy, Freddy," Trent said, leaning back against the squabs. "Your assessment of my character is correct. I am not the sort who'd favor Whitechapel wares as you so poetically call them."

"Then why the devil are we going there?" Freddy looked more puzzled than angry now.

Before Trent could answer, however, Mainwaring spoke up. "I think I've got it, Freddy. And it's something in the way of a bridal gift he's after."

But poor Freddy looked more confused than ever. "Are you telling me that Ophelia has some sort of fascination with Whitechapel—"

Trent cut him off before he could complete the thought. "No, Freddy. No one is going to be sampling any of the base pleasures Whitechapel has to offer. At least no one in our immediate circle. Mainwaring does have the right of it, though. We are here because I wish to do something for

Ophelia as her bridal gift. I want to find her friend Maggie."

Freddy let out a sigh of relief. "Thank the Lord. I was quite overset at the idea I'd have to explain to her before you were even wed that you'd died at the hands of an angry pimp or the like. Clearly I am not made for a life of vice."

"Is this the same man who spent years gambling his way through Paris?" Mainwaring asked Trent idly. "For I cannot imagine that Freddy tolerating this Freddy for more than a few minutes before shooting one or both of them."

"I'm a married man now, Mainwaring," Freddy said without rancor. "With a child on the way. You cannot expect me to get up to my old tricks when such a momentous occasion is only a few months away."

"I too am married, old chap," Mainwaring said, training his quizzing glass upon Freddy. "And you do not see me cowering like a scared debutante at the mere mention of Whitechapel."

"Stop bickering, you two," Trent snapped before Freddy could argue. "Or I'll put you both out of the carriage. And I have a feeling neither of you would wish to walk back to Mayfair from this distance."

"That was quite masterful, Trent," said Freddy admiringly.

"I think you'll make a splendid father when the time comes," Mainwaring said, turning the quizzing glass from Freddy to Trent. "Quite masterful. But sensitive too."

"Yes," Freddy agreed. "Like the sort of father

one wouldn't be afraid to tell about a little tipple into his brandy."

"Or a kiss behind the rosebushes," Mainwaring added.

"Or losing the cricket match for the whole team," Freddy agreed.

"You are both quite mad," Trent said, shaking his head at them. "You know this, do you not?"

Freddy shrugged. "Leonora has said it once or twice. But I can generally make her change her mind with a bit of persuasion." He winked.

"So, tell us what it is we're doing in Whitechapel for Ophelia," Mainwaring said once their verbal sparring had died down. "I'm guessing we're paying a visit to an orphanage run by one Daniel Swinton?"

Trent nodded. The idea had occurred to him while he was waiting to see the archibishop—or rather, the archbishop's clerk. The fact that he and Ophelia were going to have to wed just now necessarily meant that their search for Maggie would need to be postponed. And though he knew Ophelia had consented to the marriage, he also knew that she would regret it if Maggie had to spend any more nights wherever she was being kept than she absolutely had to. So, it had occurred to him that he could visit this Daniel Swinton and question the fellow about the connection between his orphanage and the Hayes Clinic. And if he and Freddy and Mainwaring happened to find the missing woman as a result, he knew that having her friend safe would be the best wedding gift he could possibly give Ophelia.

Aloud he said, "Well done, Mainwaring. It's obvious you weren't just a pretty face at the Home Office."

The other man rolled his eyes. "Don't make me regret agreeing to accompany you, man."

"So, what is it we suspect this Swinton fellow of?" Freddy asked, frowning. "And what's his connection with Maggie Grayson?"

Quickly, Trent filled both men in on what Maggie's journal had said about the orphanage Swinton ran—about the the disciplinary methods used on the girls, and Maggie's note about the possibility that some "discarded girls" might have been sent to the Hayes Clinic.

"What does that mean exactly?" Mainwaring asked, frowning. "I don't like the sound of 'discarded girls' a bit."

"Nor do I," Trent admitted. "Which is why I want to question Swinton. There's no suggestion that he's done anything wrong in Maggie's journal. But even so, the connection with Hayes means that we have to check it out."

The carriage slowed then, and soon the three men were being welcomed into the front room of the Whitechapel Orphanage.

"If you'll wait just a minute, my lords," said the mobcapped young lady who'd ushered them in. "Mr. Swinton will see you as soon as he's finished with the little ones and the ladies. I'll have cook bring you some tea and biscuits."

When she'd closed the door behind her, the three men wandered around the simply furnished room, looking for anything that might give them a clue about the nature of the institution. Or the man who ran it.

"He's got a taste for the classics," Freddy said as he scanned the tall shelves of books on either side of the fireplace. "Latin, Greek, the usual things you'd expect to find in a schoolmaster's rooms."

"I wonder if he teaches the young girls with them," Mainwaring said with interest. "That would be quite progressive of him. Though rather unusual."

"More likely they're his own books and the girls aren't allowed in this room very often," Trent said, examining a quartet of paintings over a side table. "Or perhaps only a few of the older girls are allowed to use them. They'd not last long if they circulated among the entire school."

"I think Maggie was right about there being a connection between Swinton and Hayes," Freddy said from where he was examining a plaque on the far wall. "Come look at this."

Trent and Mainwaring hurried over to look. Pointing to the words etched on the brass plates, Freddy stepped back so the other men could see it better.

" 'Most Improved—Miss Jane Dawson— Presented on Behalf of Dr. Hayes of the Hayes Clinic,' " Trent read aloud. "So Hayes is some sort of benefactor, it would seem."

"Looks that way," Mainwaring said. "Perhaps that's what she meant by 'discarded girls'? That they were discarded, then he helped them improve?"

"Sounds like a rather optimistic way of interpreting things, to me," Trent said grimly.

"It needn't be so terrible," Freddy said with a shrug. "It's possible that Maggie's removal had nothing to do with this place."

Before either Trent or Mainwaring could reply, voices sounded in the hallway—male and female—and all three men hurried to look casual, spreading themselves across the room from one another.

"It was such an honor to welcome you, ladies" said a warm male voice from the other side of the door. "Now, if you'll just wait in here, I'll have one of the girls go tell your driver that you're ready to depart."

When he opened the door, however, the man looked surprised to see that it was already occupied. "Oh, well," he said, smiling nervously. "This must be our day for unexpected guests. If you gentlemen will wait here for a few minutes, I'll be right back."

"Oh, we do not need to be taken somewhere else," Trent heard a familiar voice say from behind the man he assumed to be Swinton.

"Indeed," said another familiar voice, "we are most willing to share your anteroom. We don't wish to discommode you."

Stepping forward, Trent saw the man's eyes widen with alarm. But he ignored that and focused on getting a glimpse of the ladies behind their host, as he sensed Freddy and Mainwaring stepping up on either side of him.

"Miss Dauntry," he said dryly, "and Mrs. Lisle, and that's Lady Mainwaring as well, isn't it? What a surprise to see you three here."

* * *

"I'm afraid I have little more to tell you, Miss Dauntry," said Daniel Swinton as he accompanied Ophelia, Leonora, and Hermione on their tour of the orphanage. "Your friend was quite inquisitive, of course, but I was pleased to answer her questions."

Far from behaving suspiciously, he'd welcomed the three ladies into the orphanage with open arms. A tall, pleasant-looking man in his early forties, Ophelia would have guessed, Swinton was about as different from what she'd expected as could be. While it was true he did appear to stress discipline with the children, he also seemed to hold them in genuine affection. And they seemed to return it.

Ophelia had informed him only that Maggie was missing. She hadn't gone into detail about what might have happened to her, both for Maggie's privacy, but also because she wished to know how much Swinton himself knew about what had happened.

They were currently in the library where the girls as young as five and as old as fourteen either read quietly or were taught to read by one of several teachers. It was all much more civilized than Ophelia would have credited. She'd heard many terrible tales about what went on in such places, but it did appear that her impressions of Maggie's notes had been correct. There had been nothing untoward about Swinton or the school.

"Have you heard of a Dr. Hayes, Mr. Swinton?"

she asked, as Leonora and Hermione spoke to two of the smaller girls who had been bold enough to approach them. "He runs a sort of hospital for those with unbalanced minds called the Hayes Clinic."

Swinton turned sharply, staring at her. "Why would you ask me about Dr. Hayes?"

Careful not to show her excitement that she'd seemed to touch a nerve, Ophelia said, "I came across something in Maggie's notes that seemed to make a connection between the Hayes Clinic and your orphanage. Something about 'discarded girls.' Do you know what that means?"

He pinched the bridge of his nose, then sighed. "Dr. Hayes is no longer associated with my school, Miss Dauntry. There was a time when I sent girls who suffered from maladies too serious for me to cure for treatment at the Hayes Clinic. But when I learned about the unorthodox practices used by Dr. Hayes and his staff, I stopped sending them. Now I have an arrangement with a Dr. Barnes who comes here to treat the girls. It is much more agreeable for all of us."

"And the discarded girls?" Ophelia pressed. She sensed that there was much more to the story than Swinton was letting on, but she could hardly force the man to tell her.

"That," he said, his mouth white with anger, "was what Hayes called my students who were sent into his care. As if they were scraps of old clothing tossed into the ragbag. I fear my cousin has little respect for my girls as children of God. Indeed, I wonder if he has respect for anyone but himself."

Ophelia bit back a gasp. "Dr. Hayes is your cousin?" she asked in surprise.

"Not that it's something I am proud of, Miss Dauntry," said the headmaster. "I'm afraid my cousin and I had very different upbringings. My parents were missionaries and taught me to love my neighbor, and to care for those who could not care for themselves. My cousin, though, was taught to do whatever he could to get ahead. He is not a bad man, Miss Dauntry, but I must admit that there are times when I cannot understand that we share the same blood."

Leonora and Hermione returned to them just then and soon they were on their way back to the small room where they'd been taken upon their arrival.

They had just reached the door to the waiting area when Ophelia heard Leonora gasp.

It was difficult to say which group was more surprised to see the other: the ladies, who had been so immersed in their discussion with Mr. Swinton they'd forgotten their visit was supposed to be a secret, or the gentlemen, who had not expected to find the ladies were already there.

"How lovely that you came to collect us," Leonora said upon seeing her husband, scowling though he might be. "I must admit I was rather put out that you were unable to join us this morning, gentlemen. I'm so pleased your errands were completed in time."

Ophelia watched as a cascade of emotions ranging from annoyance to exasperation flashed over Freddy's countenance. Finally he shrugged and said, "I'm not sure those are the precise words I'd have chosen, my dear, but nevertheless we are here now. And it's high time we got you home."

"I hope your visit was fruitful," Trent said after they'd all said their good-byes to Mr. Swinton, and the Mainwarings and Lisles left in one coach while Ophelia and Trent took the other. "Though I admit a certain degree of frustration that you chose to go there without any sort of protection."

He had taken the seat beside her rather than the one opposite, and Ophelia was reminded once again of just how much larger than she he was. The inside of the vehicle seemed rather close suddenly and she was all too aware of the press of his thigh against hers.

"We took footmen," she said, sounding rather breathless to her own ears. "We were perfectly safe. Mr. Swinton was all that was polite. Truly."

Turning, she saw that he was watching her with an expression somewhere between frustration and affection. "I am delighted that Mr. Swinton turned out to be so unexceptional, but what if he had not been? You went there asking the same sort of questions that Maggie did. And she is now missing." He picked up her hand and threaded their fingers together. "I do not want anything to happen to you. And I certainly do not want to be the one to tell your parents that you've been injured or worse. Have a care. For yourself as well as for me."

"Of course I am careful," she said, staring down at their joined hands. "That is why I took Leonora and Hermione. He could hardly dispose of three of us at one time."

Trent gave an exasperated sigh. "If you think that then you are far more naïve than I at first thought."

Annoyed, she tried to prise her hand away from his. "I am not naïve. I am sensible. And as you can see nothing untoward happened. So I'm not quite sure why we are arguing over this."

Letting her take her hand back, he shook his head. "We are quarreling because I was damn near terrified to find you'd gone to what might have been a hellhole without so much as a note to inform me," he said sharply. "Because if something had happened to you I'd have never forgiven myself. Because I don't know what I'd do if I had no idea where you'd gone!"

By this time he'd gripped her by the shoulders and was staring down into her shocked face. "Do you have a response for that?" he demanded, all the frustration and fear and affection he felt for her combined into that one question.

"I . . ." she stuttered, never having faced this sort of interrogation."I am sorry I worried you, Trent. Truly."

But his confession had unleashed something in him and he responded by pulling her against his chest and kissing her. Hard.

This was not the gentle seduction of the night they'd become betrothed, but a claiming. Every press of his lips, every stroke of his tongue, every firm caress told her in more than words that she belonged to him. In body and mind and soul. And far from feeling her usual frustration at being hemmed in, she instead felt a return sense of claiming. If she was his, then he was also hers. And she told him so with every returned caress.

When his hand slid up her side and over her breast, her own hand slid around his neck to pull him closer. When he lightly pulled at her lower lip with his teeth, she did the same with his upper one. She matched him move for move and felt no shame in it, only triumph.

When finally they each pulled away, breathless and aching with unspent passion, he gave her a crooked frown. "You cannot even let me give you a proper set-down without taking over." But it was clear from the way his eyes shone that he bore no grudge over it.

"Why should I?" she asked archly. "When there is a time that I agree with your assessment I will acquiesce. Until then, I will continue to give as good as I get."

He looked as if he'd like to object, but then surprised her and laughed. "I suppose I have no one to blame but myself," he groused. "I suspect there is a general out there who is laughing his head off at how the mighty have fallen."

But Ophelia would have none of it. Clasping his hand in hers now, she only said, "Would you like to hear what I learned from my visit with Swinton?"

Gesturing for her to go ahead, Trent listened carefully as Ophelia outlined what the orphanage headmaster had said about Maggie's visit to them, as well as his admission that Dr. Hayes was his cousin. When she was finished, Trent whistled.

"That's quite impressive," he said with a nod. "It never occurred to me that he and Hayes might be relations. There certainly seems to be no love lost between them."

"No," Ophelia agreed, "and what's more, he said that 'discarded girls' was Hayes's way of describing girls sent to him from the orphanage. Swinton was quite angry over it still. So I don't think he'd kidnap the person who threatened to expose the man's lack of compassion for his cousin's charges."

"Good point," he conceded. "If anyone had something to hide as result of Maggie's article it was Hayes, who was trying to keep his hospital afloat. If it got out that he was mistreating orphans as well as wealthy young women like Leonora's cousin, then his reputation would suffer a serious blow."

"And the worse his reputation, the fewer paying patients he can get," Ophelia agreed. "It all comes back to the article Maggie wrote. If Hayes could stop her from getting it published then he could potentially keep his business from losing money."

Just then the carriage began to slow and Ophelia frowned. It didn't seem as if they'd been driving for long enough to have returned to Mayfair.

"Where are we?" she asked, frowning.

"I don't know," Trent said, his brows lowered. Opening one of the compartments beside the carriage seat, he removed two pistols. Handing one to Ophelia, who wasn't quite sure what to do with it, he took the other for himself. "Now, if for whatever reason, something happens to me, do not hesitate to shoot."

"What?" she demanded, eyes wide, holding the pistol in one hand gingerly. "I don't understand."

"One of the only reasons we'd be stopped at this point in our journey is because of footpads. I simply do not wish you to be unarmed should the need arise."

Just then, the carriage door was wrenched open and a handsome man around Trent's age glanced inside, before his eyes fell on Trent. "There you are, your grace. I was beginning to fear we'd have to wait all day."

"What the devil are you doing, man?" Trent demanded. "I might have killed you."

"So you might," said the other man with an elegant shrug. "But you didn't so that's no matter now." Turning to Ophelia he offered her a slow grin. "You must be the lovely Miss Dauntry. If you don't mind I shall steal your betrothed for a few minutes. It won't take long, I promise."

With a wink at Trent he shut the door, leaving Ophelia to stare after him. "Who was that?" she demanded of her betrothed.

"That," he said with a shake of his head, "is one of my lieutenants in the Lords of Anarchy,

Viscount Wrotham," Trent growled. "Let me go see what he wants. I'll be right back."

And without another word, he stepped out of the carriage and shut the door behind him.

Sixteen

"Why the devil would you stop my carriage like a footpad, Wrotham?" Trent demanded with a scowl. "That's a good way to get yourself shot."

If he'd thought Wrotham would be cowed, however, he was doomed to disappointment.

"It's hardly the Great North Road, your grace," the other man said dryly, "and it's the middle of the day. And we're on the edge of Mayfair. Truly, I think you're overreacting a bit."

"Just tell me what the devil you're up to," Trent pressed. "I should like to get Miss Dauntry home."

"It's about Miss Dauntry," Wrotham said grimly, "or rather that newspaper of hers, that I needed to speak to you." He pulled a rolled-up broadside from his inside pocket. "Take a look at this."

Wordlessly, Trent took the page and unrolled it, seeing that it was the sort of one-page announcement that was circulated all over the city to advertise coming shows or carnivals or the like. Only this one had a crude drawing of a curricle with the words "Lords of Anarchy" posted above it, and a short paragraph beneath telling exaggerated details of the club's exploits. Nothing libelous, or bad enough to incur any kind of government crackdown, but enough to make Trent feel ill at the sight.

"Carrington," he spat out as soon as he handed it back to Wrotham. "If he thinks to shame the club with this nonsense then he is sorely mistaken. Everyone who actually knows the club, or its new roster of members, knows that we are reformed now. And dredging up past history will do no good at all."

"So, you intend to simply ignore it?" Wrotham asked with a skeptical look. "But what of our reputation?"

"Our reputation will suffer whether we confront Carrington or not," Trent assured him. "And in case you haven't heard the news, I've got a wedding to attend tomorrow. And I have no intention of letting this fellow ruin it."

"So you don't even want a couple of the lads and me to go speak to him?" Wrotham asked, deflated.

"No," Trent told him with a shake of his head. "I'll handle it. Have no fear."

After saying his good-byes to the other man, Trent climbed back into the carriage, only to be peppered with questions. Who was it? What did they want? Was it something good or something bad? Did he need to go take care of something?

Finally, he picked up her hand and kissed the

back of it. "Nothing for you to worry about," he assured her. "Now, let us get back to your father's house at once. I'll tell you about this business later."

As he stood at the altar of St. George's Hanover Square some three days later, Trent tried to recall when he'd last felt this nervous.

Even before a battle he'd been able to arrive at a sense of calm, pushing any worries about his safety or the safety of his men into a far corner of his mind where they wouldn't affect his ability to fight.

But today was different.

Today was about forever.

"You'll wear a hole in the marble if you keep pacing like that," Freddy said from his place next to the spot where Trent should be stationary. "I have a feeling you would not like to hear the cost of replacing it."

Sighing, Trent fiddled with his cravat and came to a stop beside his friend. "I'd be a damn sight more easy about it if I didn't know her mother was so opposed to the match. Who's to say that Goring hasn't managed to convince Mrs. Dauntry to allow him to spirit Ophelia away to Scotland? She seems perfectly capable of it."

"She might," Freddy said, clapping him on the shoulder, "but I sincerely doubt Ophelia's father would allow such a thing. Mrs. Dauntry might be foolish enough to wish for Goring as a son-in-law, but Dauntry has a great deal more sense than his wife. Besides that, the announcement is in the papers this morning, so there will be a great deal of explanation involved should she attempt to change the plan at this late date."

Clenching his teeth, Trent knew that Freddy was right in his assessment of Ophelia's parents. And added to that, Ophelia would not allow herself to be forced into marriage with Goring no matter how much her mother might wish for it. She was a determined young lady when she had the bit between her teeth and she would fight like hell if her mother so much as mentioned Goring again.

"You're likely correct," he admitted aloud. "I just wish I knew what was taking so cursed long."

Freddy raised his brows in skepticism. "Can you think of nothing that might delay a lady on her wedding day? The day when she cares the most about how she looks? Even one such as Ophelia, whom I will admit is far more sensible than most of her sex, will take a bit of extra care in her toilette on this day."

Unbidden, a mental picture of Ophelia clad in a revealing wrapper, seated at a dressing table, came to Trent. Though he hadn't seen her in such a state of undress, his mind had no difficulty filling in the gaps and he found himself rocked back on his heels by the knowledge that all the curves his imagination was currently sketching for him would soon be his to touch.

Before he could get too carried away, however, there was a noise at the rear of the church, and as he watched, Ophelia's mother hurried up the aisle. She didn't meet his eye, and he held his breath—

waiting for her to approach and reveal that Ophelia wasn't coming—but she stopped long before the altar, moving to stand next to her other daughter, who stood beside her own betrothed, the Marquess of Kinston.

At a speaking look from the archbishop, Mrs. Dauntry nodded, and to Trent's great relief, the rear door of the church opened, and Ophelia, on her father's arm, walked slowly up the aisle toward them.

He was surprised to see her eyes were bright with tears, but since she was smiling, he supposed they were happy ones. He'd never understand the distinctions between the various types of weeping.

Even so, he was relieved when the archbishop began the ceremony.

And soon, Mr. Dauntry was kissing Ophelia's cheek and placing her hand on Trent's arm. When he felt it tremble a little, he couldn't help placing his other hand over it, offering what comfort he could and realizing only a moment later that it had calmed him as well.

When it came time to say their vows, it was Trent whose voice cracked as he slid the family ring over her knuckle, saying, "With this ring, I thee wed, with my body, I thee worship."

Ophelia's voice rang out clear and strong as she said her own, but there was a moment where he thought he saw a brief longing in her eyes. But whatever it was, she quickly masked it again and soon they were pronounced man and wife. And being congratulated by the few friends and family they'd invited to witness the ceremony.

"I am so pleased for you both," Hermione said as she pulled him into a hug. "I couldn't have arranged things better myself. It's as if the heavens were making all of my greatest wishes come true before me."

"If we are to be blessed with a sudden onslaught of miracles enacted on your behalf, my dear," Mainwaring said from behind her, "then I believe we should warn the authorities. For I fear some of your 'greatest wishes,' as you call them, are quite bloodthirsty."

Hermione scowled at her husband. "I am only bloodthirsty in those instances in which it is called for, my lord, and well you know it."

From her place at Trent's side, Ophelia laughed. "He is right, you know, Hermione. You can be most vengeful when prompted."

Lady Mainwaring scowled. "If that's the case," she said, her gaze going from Trent to Ophelia and back again, "then what sort of punishment do you two expect from me? For I cannot quite believe denials of any sort of romance between the two of you before the Kinston ball."

"I will simply not hear any more talk of vengeance and punishment on such a lovely occasion," Leonora said, stepping up beside her friend. "It is a wedding, Hermione."

"Oh, pish," Hermione retorted with a most uncountesslike roll of her eyes. "The happiness of these two wouldn't be dampened by the most dire of proclamations."

"Be that as it may," Trent said firmly, "I will whisk my bride away now."

"Spoilsport," Hermione said with a grin. "Go on, the two of you. We will see you at Trent House."

Not waiting to hear if his new wife was ready to leave, Trent slipped his arm through hers and hurried her out of the church and into his waiting carriage.

"I cannot believe it's actually over," Ophelia said once they were safely inside the carriage. "I must admit, I did wonder for a brief moment this morning if it were all some elaborate fantasy I'd dreamt up."

"It is quite real, I assure you," he said, lifting her from where she sat primly across the carriage from him, and depositing her most indecorously upon his own lap.

"Trent!" she squealed. "This is quite improper."

"I am attempting to kiss my wife," he said, sliding his arm around her back and pulling her close. Then he lowered his head and hovered his lips over hers for the barest moment before taking her mouth. "Which," he added between kisses, "is allowed."

Knocked off balance when the carriage began to move, Ophelia grasped his coat with one hand and slid the other around the back of his neck. His kiss was every bit as intoxicating as she'd remembered it, and when he opened his mouth over hers, she was ready for him and gave back as good as she got.

She thought of her married friends and wondered if they'd felt the same kind of contentment upon their wedding day.

Unfortunately that led her to wonder about Maggie. Where was she? What was she doing today? Was she even still alive? Ophelia hoped that she was, and that wherever she might be she was warm and dry and knew that Ophelia and Trent and their friends were all working to find her. The very notion that her friend might possibly think that she'd been abandoned was almost too much to bear. The sooner she found Maggie the better.

"A penny for them," Trent said, stroking a finger along her cheek. "What's bothering you? This should be a happy day."

Blushing, Ophelia recalled where she was. "I am sorry, your grace. Please forgive me. I was woolgathering. It's just something I do sometimes."

"That's not much of an answer, my dear," he said with a frown. "And though I do believe you were thinking, I don't believe it was idle at all. You were thinking of Maggie, weren't you?"

How, after truly knowing her for only a few days, could he possibly be able to read her thoughts? she wondered.

"I was," she admitted with a sigh. "I had hoped we would find her before we married. But it seems as if every clue we find leads to a dead end. At this point I don't think we'll ever know what happened to her. Or George for that matter."

"I hate to hear you sound so despondent, my dear," Trent said, kissing the top of her head. "I wish I had some news that would make it all seem better. But alas, I do not. My fears perfectly mirror your own."

"I am sorry to be so morose on our wedding day," she said, feeling guilty for her sadness.

"Don't say that," he assured her. "Your loyalty and compassion are two of the things I admire most about you. I can imagine any number of foolish *ton* ladies who would breeze through their wedding festivities without sparing a thought for a lost friend. You on the other hand have been perfectly celebratory. You only let your guard down after we were here alone. Which is just as it should be."

"You make me sound like some sort of paragon," she said wryly.

"Not that," he assured you. "I know you are made of flesh and blood, but I want you to feel free to let down your guard with me. To voice your feelings. Without fear that I will chastise you or belittle them."

Pulling back a little, she looked up into his handsome face. "You are such a good man," she told him before kissing him with all the affection he was feeling. "What a great bit of luck that our friends paired up and threw us together."

"I couldn't agree more," he said, hugging her to him as if he couldn't get enough.

Seventeen

$\mathcal{D}$espite Mrs. Dauntry's loudly voiced objection to the plan, Trent had decided that rather than a traditional wedding breakfast at the home of the bride, they would have a celebration of their vows at some later date when his own family was able to attend. His mother was staying with relatives in Scotland and his extended family was not in town. He'd consulted Ophelia about it and she agreed with alacrity, especially since she felt sure her mother would invite Lord Goring and his parents.

Thus it was that when the carriage came to a stop it was before Trent House in St. James's Square—where some of the older families in the *ton* still kept their town houses. Only the Lisles and Lord and Lady Mainwaring would be joining them for refreshments.

After he'd presented his new bride to the servants, who had lined up along the front hallway upon their arrival, Trent ushered Ophelia into the small sitting room where he'd instructed Wolfe to show their friends once they arrived.

"I hope that I will be up to the task of running such a large household," Ophelia said as they stepped into the room that Trent preferred to the formal drawing room which hadn't been redecorated since his grandparents' day. "I must admit that in the haste of our marriage plans, I didn't think of just how daunting a task it would be to fulfill my duties as your duchess. I believe there are more upstairs maids in this house than there are servants in my father's house."

But Trent was unwilling to let doubt creep into her thoughts. At least not so soon.

"I have every faith that you will be an excellent mistress to all my servants," he said, drawing her hand to his lips. "You are the most determined lady I've ever met. And I cannot for one moment imagine a little thing like keeping the housemaids in order would get the better of you."

"You're sweet," Ophelia said with a half smile, "but return to me in one month's time when your bed curtains are dusty and the chimney smokes."

Before Trent could reply, Wolfe entered the room.

"I beg your pardon, your grace," the butler said, looking troubled, "but a messenger has arrived and he said the matter is quite urgent."

Ophelia's eyes widened. "Maggie," she said, gripping Trent's arm. "Oh, please let someone have found her."

"It may just be the man I sent to look for George,"

he told her, clasping his hand over hers in comfort. "Why don't I go see to it while you chat with your guests? I promise if there is news I'll let you know."

She looked disappointed, but nodded. "All right. Go."

With a brisk nod, Trent followed Wolfe out of the sitting room and into the little chamber off the hall where he found not his investigator but a footman wearing familiar livery.

"Sir Michael Grayson asked me to bring this to you at once, your grace," said the young man, offering a folded missive.

Breaking the seal on the note, Trent read the hastily scrawled words three times before cursing and looking up at the footman. "Did he ask you to wait for a reply?"

"If you had one, your grace."

"Go downstairs and tell the cook to give you some refreshment while you wait," Trent told him. "I'll have my response for you within the hour."

When the servant was gone, Trent cursed again and pinched the bridge of his nose. He'd known that first afternoon that both Maggie and George disappeared that the husband had been in just as much danger as the wife.

The note from Sir Michael had been brief and to the point. He'd found George in a rooming house in Whitechapel suffering from a gunshot wound. It might have proven fatal, only the woman who ran the house had gone through his pockets and, thinking to gain some quick money, had sent for George's father. He was unable to speak just now and Sir

Michael said he'd let Trent know as soon as he was well enough to talk.

For George to have survived the war only to be almost killed by some miscreant bent on mischief was infuriating. And there was no guarantee he'd survive his wound, though his chances were better now that he was back in his father's care.

It would be both good news and bad for Ophelia, he reflected. Though now, at least, they could question George about Maggie's whereabouts.

Crossing to the writing desk in the corner of the room, he quickly wrote out a note to Sir Michael asking to be kept informed of any further developments and rang for Wolfe to take it to the messenger in the kitchen.

When he entered the sitting room again it was to find that Ophelia had been joined by their friends who were all laughing merrily over some nonsensical tale Freddy was in the middle of.

But as soon as Ophelia saw him, she gasped, putting an end to the frivolity.

"What is it?" she asked, rushing to his side.

"You look as if a cat walked over your grave," Mainwaring said.

"I've had some bad news, I'm afraid," Trent said as he allowed Ophelia to lead him over to an empty spot on the sofa.

Ophelia busied herself with pouring him a cup of tea and piling several sandwiches and biscuits onto a plate. The room was silent as the group watched her every move. Waiting.

Finally, unable to take it any longer, Trent reached out and touched her arm.

"Ophelia, please," he said softly. "I need to tell you this."

But it was clear that she didn't wish to hear it. Even so, she placed both his teacup and plate on the table and allowed him to pull her down to sit beside him.

"Perhaps we should go," Leonora said.

"Yes," Hermione agreed. "You need some privacy."

"No," Trent said, looking up at them. "I'd like you to be here."

"Maggie is dead, isn't she?" Ophelia said, not looking up from where she clasped her hands together in her lap.

"No," he said, placing his hand over hers. "It is George. He's been found. Shot. In a rooming house in Richmond."

"Is he alive?" Freddy asked, frowning.

"He is, thank God." Trent watched as Ophelia looked up at him, her gaze troubled.

"When can we talk to him?" she asked, looking determined. "We need to know what he knows."

"He's unable to speak just now," Trent said with a shake of his head. "Sir Michael will contact me as soon as he's well enough to do so."

Ophelia collapsed onto the sofa beside him. "I might have known. The first solid clue we've found and it is another dead end."

"Not yet, it isn't," he reassured her. "In fact, it

might be our most promising one yet. The fact that someone tried to get rid of him could mean that someone wanted him out of the way. Probably because he can prove definitively that he didn't sign Dr. Hayes's writ."

"And the good news is that Grayson is still alive," Mainwaring said with a nod.

"He's right," Trent said, taking a seat beside his wife and, despite her rigid posture, wrapping a comforting arm around her shoulders. "We must account this as a good thing. Though I know you are frustrated and want answers now."

A pall hung over the room as they all thought about what they could do next.

"Do you think this means that Maggie is lying somewhere injured, or worse?" Ophelia said in a shaky voice.

"I cannot know," Trent answered her honestly. "But we must assume that she is alive and then we need to work as fast as we can to find her."

"But where do we even begin?"

It was obvious to him that the week's events were finally catching up to Ophelia. Her usually optimistic disposition had been dimmed by the knowledge that there was no easy fix for any of this.

"I suggest that we let you get some rest, your grace," Leonora said after exchanging a speaking glance with her husband. "There's nothing any of us can do today, so why don't we agree to speak again tomorrow afternoon?"

"Oh but . . . I thought . . ."

It was clear to Trent that it had just dawned on

his new wife that once her friends left she'd be alone with him.

"An excellent idea, my dear," Freddy said, rising. "I believe we could all use an evening to ourselves."

Hermione kissed Ophelia on the cheek and whispered something to her that Trent was interested to see made Ophelia blush.

"Let me know if there's anything I can do," Mainwaring said as he clapped Trent on the back. "Tomorrow, of course. I have plans this evening."

"So would I if you lot would take yourselves off," Trent answered under his breath, sparking a guffaw from his friend.

For a moment he and Ophelia stood at the door. Then she broke away from him and wandered over to look out the window at the back garden.

He surveyed the elegant line of her back, from where dark curls kissed the back of her neck, down to the flare of her hips and the rounded swell of her bottom. All respectably covered by the deep blue she'd chosen to wear for the wedding. And yet, as enticing an ensemble as he'd ever seen.

Though that perhaps had more to do with the woman herself than the skill of her modiste.

When they reached the door to the duchess's rooms, Trent opened it and ushered her inside.

The pale green furnishings were old-fashioned, but had been aired out and thoroughly cleaned on his orders yesterday. And Ophelia's maid had already unpacked her things and made little changes that should make her feel more at home.

Once they were a little ways into the room.

Ophelia turned and straightened her spine. But before she could speak, he smiled and set his hands on her shoulders. "I thought perhaps I'd leave you to rest for a while."

She relaxed a bit, but her next words surprised him. "Perhaps you'll stay with me, and get some rest too?"

Her eyes were wide pools of blue, and he hadn't had a sweeter invitation in his life.

So he nodded, and after removing his shoes, and helping her out of her gown and stays, they climbed up onto the bed. And as if they'd been sleeping together for years, Ophelia tucked herself into the curve of his neck, and slid her arm round his waist, and fell asleep.

When Ophelia awoke some hours later, she was alone. And disoriented. Then it all came rushing back to her. The wedding, the news about George Grayson, and finally the sweet way Trent had curled up with her and gone to sleep.

A glance at the clock revealed she had nearly an hour until supper, so she rose and went to the bell-pull. Asking her maid to draw a bath, she set about preparing for the wedding night ahead.

Sometime later, feeling rather underdressed in a lovely but nearly transparent night rail and jacket that had been a wedding gift from Leonora and Hermione, Ophelia nearly jumped out of her skin at the knock on the connecting door to the duke's rooms.

"Come in," she called, standing casually before the fire.

When the door opened and Trent, newly shaved and bathed, and dressed again in black finery, stepped into the room, she gave a mental curse.

"I knew it would be odd for me to attend supper in my night rail," she said, mortified, "but Leonora and Hermione assured me that it was all the rage. But clearly you are expecting me in an evening gown. Give me just a few minutes, and I'll be dressed." As she spoke, she did not look up at him, simply scurried across the room toward the bellpull. But as soon as she lifted her hand to grasp it, she felt his hand on her arm.

"Do not," he said, "by all that is holy, change one thing about your attire and I will weep."

Arrested by the feel of him pulling her into his arms, she dared to peek up at his face and saw that he was dead serious.

"Are you just being polite?" she asked, frowning.

"My dear Ophelia," he said, his eyes intent, "I have never been more serious in my life. This is my favorite outfit you've ever worn in my presence, and if it were not likely to get me thrown into gaol, I'd demand that you wear nothing but this ensemble for the rest of our days together."

Something about the twinkle in his eye told her that he was only partly serious. "You're sure?" she asked. "For it does feel a little odd for me to be wearing so little while you are so well dressed."

"I do not wish you to feel odd," he said with a

half smile that revealed a single dimple. "Shall I take off some of my own clothes? Just for solidarity?"

"Now I know you're teasing me," she said, pushing away, but confident that he did not think her in breach of some sort of wedding night etiquette.

"Perhaps a little," he said, offering her his arm. "Now, let us go have some supper and you can tell me what else your friends told you about wedding nights. For I vow I am quite eager to hear what they had to say."

Unable to stop herself, she laughed, and allowed him to lead her through the connecting doors and their respective dressing rooms and into his bedchamber.

Whereas her own rooms were furnished in delicate pale greens and furniture clearly made for a lady, his bedchamber was quite masculine. The furniture was heavy and dark and the curtains and bedclothes were dark blue. And had been chosen sometime in the past half century.

"I'm afraid I haven't spent much time redecorating these rooms," he apologized, as he led her over to where a small table had been laid with a tablecloth and was covered with tureens and dishes filled with all sorts of delicacies.

"I'm afraid I'm too hungry to care," she said as he pulled out a chair for her, and to her dismay, her stomach gave a little growl.

"Then by all means, eat," he said with a chuckle as he took the seat opposite. "I am pleased to meet a lady who does not pick at her food like a bird."

"No danger there," she said as she bit into a bit of bread. "No danger at all."

He found Ophelia to be a lively conversationalist, and thanks to their shared circle of friends they were able to tell stories without needing to explain their various relationships to the players. Ophelia asked what it had been like for the quartet of Trent, Mainwaring, Freddy, and the now departed Jonathan Craven at school. And Trent was able to make her laugh over their boyhood scrapes and feats of derring-do. And she shared with him tales of her childhood in London, which despite her sister's presence, sounded a bit lonely to his ears. She'd had friends, of course, but having been kept home and educated by a governess, she and Mariah had had only themselves to rely on for most of their youth.

"Then at some point," she said wryly, "Mariah became the pretty one. It wasn't that I was considered to be particularly plain, you understand. Just that Mariah was so winsome—and quite able to use it to her advantage when necessary—that I faded into the background. It was galling to me at first. For every young lady longs to be the one who catches the gentlemen's eyes. But soon I found other ways to show my worth. My writing was one of them."

"How so?" he asked, fascinated by these tales of the young Ophelia. He found it hard to believe that she was ever seen as anything but lovely, but he supposed it was impossible to draw comparisons when two sisters were standing side by side.

Mariah was quite pretty, of course. But there was something rather vacant in her eyes that made him think that for all her looks she would not be nearly as entertaining a companion as her sister.

"You know how young people like to put on amateur theatricals and the like," she said with a smile. When he nodded she continued, "Well, I was often called upon to pen our little plays. Especially when my sister wished to take a starring role. So I would spend all night scribbling out the most dreadful plays. Truly awful things with melodrama and mysterious inheritances and the like. And Mariah would take the lead role, and naturally, the most handsome of our neighbors, or sometimes some schoolfriend he'd brought home, would play opposite her."

"So you were essentially playing matchmaker for your sister?" he asked with a laugh. He could think of few ladies who would so calmly hand over the best part to someone else. Even a sister.

"Sometimes." Ophelia shrugged. "But it wasn't as if I were pining for any of these gentlemen. As far as I was concerned they were just foolish boys who would make terrible husbands one day. I had no wish to find myself married off to one of them."

"And your sister?" he asked, genuinely curious. "Did she expect to marry one of them?"

"Hardly." Ophelia laughed. "She wanted them no more than I did. What she did want was their adoration, and their undying devotion. Mariah has always been remarkably practical when it comes to things like romance. She has no time for sentiment, does our Mariah."

Though she spoke wryly, Trent could sense that there was more to her confession than that. "What about you? Do you find any appeal in sentiment, Ophelia?"

The question hung in the air between them for a moment as he watched the candlelight dance across her lovely countenance. She really was the lovelier of the two sisters, he thought with a start. It wasn't that Mariah was ugly or unattractive. Far from it. But Ophelia had a quiet loveliness about her, something that took more than a glance to recognize. But once seen, it was impossible to miss again.

"I suppose I am as open to flattery as the next lady," Ophelia said now. "And sentiment has its place, does it not? I imagine the right words uttered at the right moment could make my heart beat quite fast. But I'm not one to be constantly bursting into tears over the way a sunset moves me, or waxing poetic over a flower's beauty."

Trent grinned at the image. "While you do not seem to be without feeling, I cannot imagine you are the sort of foolish creature who weeps over the delicacy of a bird wing either."

"Far from it," Ophelia confirmed. "Though I obviously appreciate bird wings as much as the next person."

Laughing, Trent reached across the table and clasped her hand in his."If you're finished with supper, I think it's time for bed."

Eighteen

Ophelia found herself less nervous about what was to come than she'd expected. The thing about it was, she trusted Trent, and from everything Leonora and Hermione had told her, the marriage bed could be quite pleasurable. Thinking back to the kisses and caresses they'd shared, which had been quite exciting, she thought he would make tonight just as intriguing.

Rising from her chair, she allowed him to take her by the hand and lead her to the enormous bed that dominated the room.

When they stopped just shy of the bed, he turned her in his arms and slid his hands over the gauzy fabric of her night rail. "I owe your friends considerable thanks for giving you this," he said as he reached up to untie the lace at her neck and slide off the thin robe.

She would have answered, but he stopped her with his mouth. And Ophelia wasn't sorry for the interruption. Of their own volition, her arms slipped around him and stroked over the hard muscles of his back, feeling the warm heat of him through the linen of his shirt.

His kiss was soft at first, a tentative caress that grew into something bolder as he opened his mouth and with a sure stroke of his tongue pushed into her. All the while holding her fast against him as if she were in danger of floating away.

Again and again he stroked, bit, caressed, and she gave it all back to him. Welcomed it when the soft fabric of her night rail added another dimension to the novelty of his touch.

When Trent's hand slipped between them to caress her breast, she gasped, startled by the pulse of feeling that ran from her nipple to her center. And even as he kissed his way over her chin and down to her exposed collarbone, he was untying the ribbons of her dressing gown at her neck.

"Let's get rid of this," he murmured against her chest, as he pushed the sleeves down and over her shoulders and down her arms. She drew back a little so that the gauze would fall to the floor. She watched his eyes darken more as he took in her nudity.

"I wondered how far that blush would run," he said aloud and, to her surprise, slid his arm beneath her knees and lifted her onto the bed.

In the dim light of the lamp at the bedside, she watched as he began to remove his clothes. First the cravat, which was gone far more quickly than she'd have imagined. Then the jacket, which he almost ripped in his desire to have it gone. Next, he untucked his shirt and pulled it off over his head.

Ophelia was unable to stop a gasp at the sight of his smooth bare skin. He was certainly a well-proportioned figure of a man, she thought, as she followed the trail of hair from between his nipples down until it disappeared into the dark fabric of his breeches with her eyes. And for a moment her gaze dwelled on where that blunt part of him that would make her his strained against its cloth prison.

When she dared to look up, Trent was smiling. "I can promise you there's no reason for alarm. I'm only a man. Just like any other."

"You're not like any other man," she responded with an answering smile. "And I'm glad for it. I certainly wouldn't welcome some other man into this bed to . . . to . . ."

"Have his wicked way with you?" he inquired as he began to unbutton his breeches. "Ravish you?"

"Have me," she said, and it was both a statement and an invitation.

And never letting his gaze leave hers, he stripped off his breeches and stood naked before her. Daring to look down, she saw that he was larger than she'd anticipated, but she was ready. And there was no more than a moment to stare before he was sliding beneath the covers with her and pressing his warm body against hers.

"That's better," he said against her hair, and soon she was falling into a dreamlike state as his big hands stroked over her bare skin with a gentleness that made her want to weep. "If you only knew how much I've wanted you," he whispered against her mouth before he scraped his teeth over her lower lip. "Since we first met, I think."

Her surprise was tempered by desire as he kissed his way down over her chin to her neck. As his fingers played over her sensitive nipples before he replaced them with his mouth. "You did?" she whimpered as he sucked her into his mouth. "Oh, my God."

"I did," he whispered as he moved to cherish the other side, first plucking at the peak, then covering it with his lips. "So sweet," he exhaled against her as Ophelia struggled to be still, but could not, and moved her hips as much as possible against him.

"Easy," he said, moving up to kiss her mouth again, even as he slipped a hand down over her abdomen and then farther, diving into the heart of her where his fingers stroked through her hair and over the wetness there.

She cried out at his touch and when he pulled away a little struggled to lift her hips and follow his hand. "Easy," he said again, stroking over her again, giving her what she had never known she needed before. "That's it," he soothed, pressing one finger inside her, nearly sending her over the edge even as he pressed his mouth to hers and she kissed him back.

It was impossible to remain still, and when his tongue and his finger began to work in unison, it was almost too much to bear. Unable to hold back any longer, she moved her hips. Again and again he pressed into her and she moved against his hand, chasing something she couldn't name.

"More, my darling?" he asked against her ear, even as he pressed a second finger inside her. She moaned, unable to remain silent. The striving of her body was all she knew, and when he abruptly moved away she almost cried out with frustration.

But soon enough he was back. Only this time, he slid his own legs between hers and braced himself on his hands over her. "This might hurt a bit," he whispered after a quick kiss, "but I hope not too much. And only the once."

And before she could reply, she felt his hand skate down to her knee, which he lifted over his hip. And she felt him pressing there, where his fingers had been. And the unfulfilled ache of the moment before became eagerness as he thrust inside her.

But instead of pain, she felt only relief.

Bit by bit, inch by inch, he pressed into her and slowly what had been relief became a pinch of discomfort.

She bit her lip. He'd said it would hurt, and he was right, she thought as he continued to press forward slowly, her body stretching to accommodate him. Until finally, he was fully seated within her. And there was no more pain. Only a curious fullness.

"Sorry," Trent said against her mouth, his voice hoarse as if he were in pain.

But she shook her head. "It's not that bad," she said, and to her surprise, it was the truth. He began to pull back and her body pulsed around him, which was also pleasure. And when he thrust in again, she gasped at the sensation.

Soon he was moving in a rhythm impossible for her to ignore, and she began to move with him.

"That's it," he said, sliding his hands under her, changing the angle and making her gasp. She was overwhelmed with the power of it. Of him, of how much her body ached to take him again and again.

And soon it was impossible to think at all, and when he moved to touch that sensitive part of her above where they were joined, she felt herself fly away into a fractured maelstrom of nothing but pure sensation. Her hearing dimmed and her vision darkened and she was at once herself and not herself. Somewhere far off she felt him speed up and then shout. And for a moment there was only this moment of sheer joy in her husband's arms.

When she came back to herself, Trent's weight upon her was heavy but pleasant. And at this moment, she felt well and truly wed. As if it had taken this between them to make things real.

As she stroked the soft hair at the nape of his neck, she realized in surprise that she loved him.

Not because of what they'd just done. That was remarkable, but not something that moved her heart, wonderful though it had been.

Instead it was small things. The way he'd responded when she burst into his home unannounced. His attempts to help her find Maggie. His obvious jealousy over Lord Goring. Even the sweet way he'd set her at ease tonight when she was embarrassed at being underdressed.

His friendship.

There was much to be said for the affection of

friendship in marriage. Add love into the mix, and it was very nearly perfect.

And she would own it.

To herself and to him if he ever asked.

When Trent came back to himself, he was startled to realize he'd collapsed like an inexperienced youth on his new wife.

"I am sorry," he said, moving to lie on his back. Pulling her into the circle of his arm, he lay still, catching his breath for a moment while enjoying the feeling of her soft warm body tucked against his.

There had been nothing ordinary about that, he thought as he stroked lightly over her bare arm. He might have guessed that the unconventional Miss Dauntry would prove to be as fiery in bed as out of it. For an untutored virgin, she was as eager and fearless as he could have hoped. Her response had almost been enough to rob him of control.

Perhaps there was something to be said for marriage between friends. He very much doubted he would have ended the night as satisfied had he chosen to wed some title-hungry debutante.

Beside him, Ophelia stirred a little, and he glanced down to see her frowning.

"What is it?" he asked, wondering if he'd been foolish in thinking things were rosy when there was a storm brewing.

She lowered her lashes and he was reminded of just how lovely she was. What was wrong with the men of London that they'd failed to notice? He knew he was lucky to have gotten her before they did, but still.

Looking up at him, she blushed but spoke anyway. "Is it always that . . . ?" She paused, clearly searching for a word to describe what they'd just done.

"Unbridled?" he asked with a raised brow. "Passionate?"

She pursed her lips. "I was going to say loud," she said with her own raised brow. "I am quite glad we were here and not at my father's house for I have no doubt they'd have heard me shrieking all the way in the servants' quarters."

"Wretch," he teased, kissing her lightly. "You had me thinking I'd changed your life entirely and all you are concerned with is whether anyone heard us."

She blushed. "You know very well just how good you are at . . ."—she gestured between them—"that."

He grinned and pulled her against him again. "I must admit to accounting myself as something of an expert at the business," he admitted. "But you acquitted yourself very well indeed. So much so that I almost forgot everything I know as soon as I had you in my arms."

She hid her face in his shoulder. "None of what my friends told me prepared me for the real thing."

"Some things have to be experienced to be believed," he said, kissing the top of her head. "Though one thing you may have noticed is that it can be quite exhausting."

As if the words had reminded her, she yawned.

"Perhaps we should get a bit of rest now," he said, resting his hand on her hip. "For I fear tomorrow will be quite busy."

Neither of them spoke about Maggie but they both knew that now George had been found, it couldn't be long before they discovered where his wife was too.

Ophelia awoke some hours later to the delicious sensation of Trent kissing his way down her stomach. She was still half asleep so she didn't quite realize what he was doing until she felt his hands on her knees as he pulled them apart and wedged his shoulders between them.

Her eyes flying open, she sat up a little. "What are you doing?" she demanded, placing her hand over her sex in a flimsy attempt at modesty.

But when he looked up at her, the intensity in his gaze made her take in a shaky breath. "Let me taste you, Fee," he said in a husky tone. Something about her nickname on his lips, coupled with the sincere passion in his eyes, made her swallow, then nod her acquiescence.

At her agreement, he returned to where he'd been, his hands on her knees as he gazed at the heart of her. Gently he removed her hand from where it hid her from view, and when he leaned forward to put his mouth where her hand had been, Ophelia couldn't bear to watch.

Closing her eyes, she laid her head back and gasped as his warm breath whispered over her. She gripped the sheet as she felt his tongue slide over her already wet cleft. Once, twice, he licked over her, drawing a gasp. When he dipped his tongue inside, Ophelia couldn't help but lift her hips. She'd never even imagined such a thing was possible, and when he stroked a finger inside her, she cried out.

As Trent licked at her and stroked with one hand, he used the other to find her breast, and thumbed over the sensitive skin of her nipple. "Easy, darling," he whispered against her aching flesh. Then with his hand still at her breast, he sucked at her hard. She cried out at the sensation and could not have kept still if her life depended on it.

Moving in rhythm with his thrusting fingers, she still was desperate for something more. Something to fill her up. To make her whole. "Ah, Trent," she gasped. "More, please. More."

And in answer, he pressed another finger into her.

Under his hands, she was undone. All semblance of self-control was lost in a storm of want and need and unfulfilled desire. But what she really wanted. What she needed, was him.

As if he had seen into her thoughts, he gave one last kiss to her center and made his way up her body to kiss her mouth. He tasted strange and, she realized, like her. When he guided his body into hers, she gasped in relief.

"Better?" he whispered against her ear as he thrust fully into her. And she was too overwhelmed to speak. But nodding, she kissed him hard, and following instinct, she moved her legs so that they were wrapped around his middle. Her feet locked around his lower back.

And when he began to move, Ophelia was struck once again by how right this felt. Being taken by this man, whose every touch could make her cry out with pleasure. Whose body fit into hers as if they were two halves of the same whole. With my body I thee worship, the marriage vows had said, and he'd done nothing but worship her with his body all night.

Soon they were moving again in what was becoming as familiar to her as breathing. Ophelia's body pulsed around him with every stroke. When the end came, they both cried out and Ophelia gasped as he scraped his teeth over her neck, as if he were an animal marking his mate.

It was wild and unbridled and utterly, utterly shattering.

Nineteen

Trent awoke the next morning feeling as sated and content as he'd ever been. He had suspected having Ophelia in his bed would bring them both pleasure, but the emotional connection between them had taken him by surprise. It was one thing to marry for convenience or propriety's sake, but there was something between them that went beyond mere convenience or friendly affection.

Even so, he was disappointed to find that his new bride was already up, and when he'd dressed and knocked on the connecting door, it was to find she was already downstairs at breakfast. Wasn't it supposed to be the other way around?

Quickly, he went downstairs and found her seated at the breakfast table, poring over a book.

"Good morning," she said when he leaned down to kiss her. "I hope you slept well."

"I did," he said with a wink.

When he had filled a plate and seated himself to

her left, he took a closer look at what she was reading.

"Is that Maggie's journal?" he asked, curious to know if she'd learned anything new.

"Yes," Ophelia said. "And there's a great deal more in here than just story notes. I feel rather bad about reading something so private, but if it will give me any clue to where we might find Maggie, I am prepared to do it."

"You're a good friend," he said, covering her hand with his own.

"I'd hope she'd do the same for me if our situations were reversed," Ophelia said simply. She made to close the book but when she moved the placeholder, it hung up on something. "That's odd," she said, reopening the leather-bound volume. He watched as she pulled at the endpaper where it was coming unglued from the cover. Sliding her finger beneath it she pulled something out.

"What?" Trent asked, pushing aside his plate. "What did you find?"

"I don't know," she said, pulling out a loose page covered on both sides with writing. "Perhaps Maggie's notes?"

He watched as she scanned the looping script. The gasped.

"Trent," Ophelia said, handing him the page. "Look at this."

Wordlessly he took it and read.

Another visit to see Mr. Daniel Swinton. He revealed that he is the cousin of Dr. Hayes.

But more curious, he told me that Mr. Car-
rington is also Swinton's cousin, being the
half brother of Dr. Hayes. How curious Edwin
made no mention of it when I showed him
my story. Perhaps they are estranged? Ask.

"If Edwin is Dr. Hayes's brother," Ophelia said,
her voice thrumming with excitement, "then that
might mean that Dr. Hayes would have no trouble
at all signing a writ on his word alone."

"And he'd claim the man who made the request
was the patient's husband instead of casting suspicion on his own brother," Trent said grimly.

"But why would Edwin do something like that?
Why would he want Maggie to be locked away?"
Ophelia shook her head. "It makes no sense."

"What if Edwin wanted Maggie to run away
with him?" Trent asked. "And what if Maggie said
no?"

Ophelia clapped a hand over her mouth. "Of
course. He was always making little jokes at George's
expense. I thought it was just teasing. Like brother
and sister. It never occurred to me that Mr.
Carrington might have some other reason for it.
That he might be secretly pining after her."

"Or secretly plotting against her," Trent said.
"There's something I need to tell you."

"What?" Ophelia asked, her eyes wide with
fear.

Quickly Trent told her about the broadsides that
Wrotham had brought to him the night before their
wedding.

"And you think Edwin might be responsible for that?" Ophelia asked. "Truly?"

"It would make sense if his goal was to convince Maggie that George Grayson and his club were responsible for any number of horrible things." Trent stood. "I think it's time I took a trip to the offices of the *Ladies' Gazette*."

"Don't you mean, *we*?" Ophelia asked, her hands on her hips. "Because I will not let you go confront him alone. He was my editor, my publisher. And if he is responsible for kidnapping my friend, then he will answer to me for it."

Trent bit back a curse. "I cannot allow you to go there when I have no idea what Carrington might do," he said. "He could do anything. We don't know what he's capable of. He's already almost killed George Grayson."

"Either I go," Ophelia said firmly, "or you don't."

"Ophelia," he said, feeling desperate. "Be reasonable."

"I am being reasonable," she said sharply. "I won't let you go there alone. And I won't let you go without me."

"Then I suppose we'd better just go," Trent said, exasperated. "Because the longer we wait, the longer your friend is in danger."

But when she and Trent stepped down from the curricle outside the offices of the *Ladies' Gazette*, it was to find that the door was locked, and no matter how many times they knocked no one answered the door.

"Do you know where he lives?" Trent asked, tearing down a broadside about the Lords of Anarchy that had been posted on the door.

"No," Ophelia said, taking the broadside from him and folding it in half. "It's not as if we were ever invited to his rooms or his house. He is a single man."

"The two of ye're looking for that Carrington fellow, eh?" asked the man who ran the green-grocer next door, as he swept the bit of street before his own doors. "He took off sometime this morning. Him and some pretty lady. In a carriage they were. Lots of bandboxes and the like. Think he might be gone for a while."

"Why would you say that?" Trent asked.

"Well, he asked me to look out for his offices," the man said with a shrug. "And that usually means he's going to be gone a while."

"Mr. Fellows," Ophelia said, stepping closer to the man, "you might know me. I'm Ophelia D . . . um, Hamilton, and I work for the *Ladies' Gazette*. Did he give any idea of what should happen with the paper?"

"Didn't say anything to me about it," Mr. Fellows said with a shake of his head. "Only took off."

Turning to her husband, Ophelia said, "Why don't you let me go inside and see if I can find some clue to where they went? And you can go get Freddy and maybe see if you can find out where Mr. Carrington lives."

Trent frowned. "I don't want to leave you here alone," he said. "He might come back."

"You heard Mr. Fellows," Ophelia argued, "he wouldn't have asked him to look after his offices if he were planning to be back anytime soon."

Shaking his head, Trent finally agreed. "But I'll be back in an hour. I'm just going to get Freddy. If you can't find anything in the newspaper office, then we'll figure out where he can have gone to."

"All right," she said, kissing him quickly on the lips, then she pulled out her key to the newspaper offices and slid it into the door. When it unlocked, she turned and waved Trent on his way and stepped inside, closing the door behind her.

There was no sign of Edwin or anyone else in the dark main room.

Lighting the lamp that was kept near the door for just such occasions, she held it high as she wended her way toward the back of the office near where both her and Maggie's desks were situated.

A quick glance over the two desks showed that nothing had been disturbed since her visit earlier in the week with Trent. And despite the eerie quiet of the rooms, she pulled out Maggie's chair and, setting the lamp down, began to scan through the stacks of letters and notes and half-finished pages that were stacked on top of the desk's surface.

Nothing new had appeared in the main stack since her visit a few days ago, however, and she quickly set it aside to open the drawers. Though she'd been in these offices dozens of times before without the least bit of unease, today there was something about the lack of good lighting and company that made it feel especially eerie. Or perhaps it was simply the knowledge that the man she'd worked with for nearly a year was responsible for her dear friend's disappearance.

She'd just begun to flip through the stack of books that had been hastily hidden away in the top drawer when she heard a heavy footfall on the floor.

Gasping, she turned and stared out into the darkness that was broken only by a sliver of light from the front door.

"Hello?" she called out into the darkness. "Trent? Is that you? Why are you back so soon?"

When there were more noises, as if more than one person were crossing the room, she stood. "Trent. This isn't funny. Please make yourself known."

But she knew somewhere in the pit of her stomach that it wasn't Trent.

"I simply do not understand why you find it so difficult to mind your own bloody business, infernal woman!" Edwin's voice rang out from the shadows, like an alarm bell, stripped of the even-tempered façade he must have cultivated with his newspaper staff to hide what he really was. To hide the monster beneath.

Mr. Fellows must have been wrong about him leaving town. She hoped against hope he was also wrong about Maggie being gone too. If she was still nearby there was a chance she'd be found.

Swallowing, she decided to act as if she'd not noticed the change in his manner. As if she didn't suspect he'd done something unspeakable to her dear friend. "Edwin, you almost gave me a fright. I was

here looking for some further clue as to where
Maggie might be held."

"Ophelia," Edwin said as if he were speaking to
a naughty child. "I might have known that you'd
not be content with simply letting your husband
look into the matter. Always sticking your nose
where it doesn't belong, aren't you?"

His face grew clearer as he stepped farther into
the light. And so did his hand, which held a pistol
pointed right at her.

Not allowing him to see how startled she was by
it, she stood and held her hands up, as if to placate
him.

"If you mean I always look after my friends,"
she asked calmly, "then yes, I do agree that I am
nosy. How could I not be when Maggie is still
missing? I had hoped that you would help me.
But of course, you have no need to look for her.
You know well enough where she is. Don't you,
Edwin?"

His smile was as handsome as always, but the
coldness in his eyes rendered it chilling. "I do know
where she is, yes," he agreed with a nod. "As well
as where the three ladies Maggie was searching for
are. She was quite busy, your friend."

Perhaps if she could convince Edwin that she
was entirely clueless about his crimes then he would
let her go. "Three ladies? I don't know who you
mean. Maggie and I didn't share everything."

"Of course, I forgot I'd removed that page from
her notebook," Edwin said with a rueful shake of
his head. "It's difficult to keep track of everything,

Ophelia. You have no idea how much I've got going on up here." He tapped lightly on his temple, and Ophelia swallowed. If what she suspected of him was true, then she couldn't begin to imagine what horrors he held in his mind.

As if they were merely chatting, Edwin continued, "They are just the three latest women who dared to rebuff my advances. I couldn't let Maggie find them and bring them back out into the world." He shuddered delicately. "She stumbled upon them quite by accident while working on that asinine story about the home for unwed mothers. First she learned that Dr. Hayes is my half brother, then that he'd taken care of the other three for me when they became too—unhappy, shall we say? It's too bad really that Maggie learned about all of it when she did, because I had other plans for her. But alas it wasn't to be."

If she could only keep him talking, Ophelia reasoned, then perhaps Trent would return in time to help her gain the upper hand over him. Because despite her belief in her own abilities, she knew without a doubt that Edwin would not hesitate to use his superior strength to do whatever it took to keep her silent.

"And so that morning after we'd both turned in our stories you sent your men after us," Ophelia said aloud. It was a statement not a question.

"Indeed," he said with a smile, as if proud of a bright pupil. "I could hardly allow Maggie to keep prying into my affairs. And she wouldn't take my rejection of her story as the final word. Her sort never does. She was going to take it to some other paper. Which would not do at all. So, I had Hayes prepare the writ and keep his men at the ready, waiting for my signal. My brother dislikes these tasks but he dislikes questions into his methods more."

"I'm surprised it took me so long to figure out the relationship between the two of you," Ophelia said, trying to keep him talking. "I mean it was all right there. You are both concerned with women's issues—his of the medical variety and yours with more mundane matters. And of course there is one glaring similarity between the two of you."

She let the words hang in the air, as if daring him to ask for more.

And he did.

"That would be?" Edwin asked, sounding annoyed that she would claim to know anything about him at all.

"You both like to have others do your dirty work for you," she said grimly as two hulking men stepped up behind him.

His teeth flashed white in the darkness. "Well done, Miss Dauntry. Or should I say, your grace. How sad I was to learn you'd allowed that beast to wed you. And to take you into his bed. I had supposed I'd reunite you with Maggie. But I'm afraid since you have become so damned risky for me to make disappear, I will need to be cleverer than I was with your friend."

Staring, she tried to gauge how she could possibly get past the three of them. Her only chance was to put her head down and burst past them before they realized what happened.

But when she tried, it was only to find herself held fast by each arm, the impact of going from a fast run to a dead stop making her head spin.

"Tsk-tsk," chided Edwin with a wagging finger. "You know better than to think you can get past these two fellows. Why, they might have done you some serious harm."

It was clear from his tone that he'd not have minded.

"What are you going to do with me?" Ophelia demanded. If Trent would only return she might be able to get out of this mess. Alone she was no match for the three of them. No matter how hard she fought. "Perhaps you can just let me go," she coaxed. "I am a duchess now, you know. That means that people will be looking for me soon."

"Will they?" Edwin asked, with a cold smile. "I think not. Your dear husband has better things to do than search for the likes of you. And your parents and sister are relieved not to have to deal with you themselves anymore. Face it, my dear, you are in my tender care for the time being and here you shall remain."

Turning to the two men behind him, he snapped, "Take her upstairs, both of you. And be sure not to wake the other one. I have a headache and cannot endure another screaming fit like last night's. It's easy enough to silence her, but then she's out for too long to be any fun."

And before Ophelia could think about the

implications of that little speech, the two hulking men were dragging her along the floor and toward the back where the stairs leading to the apartment upstairs were located.

"Wait," she shouted. "You don't have to do this!" Turning to her captors, she continued to shout. "Please, sirs, my husband is a duke, a very wealthy man, and he will quite happily pay you whatever sum you ask for. Only send for him and find out!"

"They are impervious to your charms," Edwin said with a dismissive wave. "Now, get her out of here and come back at once. I have some other tasks for you."

And unable to break away from the viselike grips, Ophelia allowed the men to pull her along through the house and up the back stairs to the apartment above.

When they opened the door, she narrowed her eyes against the brightness. For up here, there were dozens of lamps lit. And huddled in one corner of the room, on a filthy mattress of straw, lay Maggie Grayson.

And Ophelia very much feared she might be dead.

Twenty

When Trent stopped his curricle before the offices of the *Ladies' Gazette*, he was disappointed to see that there were no lights coming from within. Perhaps Ophelia was working in the back, where her light wouldn't show.

"I thought you said Ophelia was here," Freddy said, leaping to the ground while Trent handed the reins to yet another loitering urchin.

"I did," Trent responded, stepping up to the door and hammering on it. But no one responded. Turning, he saw that the greengrocer next door was peering out the window. Gesturing for the man to come out, he and Freddy waited while he did just that.

"Do you remember me from earlier? I was here with my wife and we asked about the man who owns the newspaper next door."

"Aye," the man said with a nod. Then looking sheepish, he said, "I didn't tell ye the whole truth before."

A chill crept down Trent's spine. "What do you mean?"

"Only that the fellow next door paid me to say he was gone. But the truth is he's there right now."

"What?" Trent's voice cut the air like glass. "You lied to me?"

"He said you were looking for him for running off with yer wife. Only I knowed that couldn't be true if the lass that were with you was yer wife."

"Then why didn't you tell me before?" Trent suppressed the urge to throttle the older man. If he'd known Carrington were anywhere near the newspaper offices he'd not have left Ophelia within a mile of them. "You could plainly see that she was my wife."

"How was I to know you weren't lyin'?" the grocer said with a shrug. "And Carrington did give me some coin."

Trent bit back a curse and pulled a handful of coins from his purse. "Now, what do you know? About the man next door. Everything."

The man pocketed the coins before admitting, "That's all I know. Though I did hear some shouting over there a bit ago. Quiet now though."

Before Trent could demand his coin back, Freddy pulled him aside. "Calm down. I have an idea."

To the greengrocer, he said sharply, "You strike me as a man who doesn't miss much. Do you know if there is another key to Carrington's place next door? Perhaps he gave you one for safekeeping or maybe hides one somewhere, nearby?"

When the man looked as if he were about to ask for more money, Trent bared his teeth. And looking slightly taken aback, Mr. Fellows nodded. "He gave me this when he first moved in. I wouldn't be surprised if he'd forgot all about it."

He proffered a large ring of keys with the right one separated out.

Not bothering to take it off the ring, Trent turned to Freddy. Reaching into his greatcoat, he handed his friend one dueling pistol and then pulled out another for himself.

As they crossed to the door of the newspaper office, he said in a low voice, "As soon as the lock is opened, we'll go in on the count of three."

As soon as the door shut behind her, Ophelia hurried over to where Maggie lay still on the lumpy mattress. Falling to her knees, she reached down to feel her friend's neck for a pulse and almost wept with relief when she found one. It was weak, but it was there.

"Maggie, my dear friend, what's happened to you?" she said in a low voice as she examined the other woman's body for injuries. It was on her head that she found the likely cause of her unconsciousness. A large lump was visible on the back of her head.

Ophelia wondered if it had happened before she was taken into this shabby little room, or perhaps during an attempt at escape. There was no way of knowing.

All she was sure of now was that Edwin was a monster and was likely responsible for the disappearances of three more women in addition to Maggie. Why hadn't she insisted on going with Trent? Together they would have been able to extricate themselves from Edwin's clutches. But alone, with an injured Maggie to protect, she had only her wits to use against him.

But first, she needed to see about Maggie.

Scanning the room, she saw that on the dresser there was a pitcher of water along with a glass. Perhaps some water would revive her friend. At the very least she could dampen her handkerchief and wipe down the poor girl's face.

Soon she'd poured a small glass and placed the damp cloth on Maggie's head. But though she swallowed a bit of the water, she didn't awaken. It was perhaps for the best, Ophelia thought grimly. She certainly wasn't enjoying her time here in captivity. Let Maggie remain oblivious while she could.

Standing, she raised the shade of the window and found it faced the street below. She wondered if it would do any good to try to catch the attention of someone down there. Edwin would likely fob off anyone who came in response with some nonsense story about a mad sister or the like. He was familiar enough with the way everyday people responded to the suggestion of madness. They steered as far away as they could.

As if it were catching.

Still, she scanned the street below to see if anyone was looking in their direction. But all she saw was a lad holding the reins of a red-and-blue-trimmed curricle. Which looked quite familiar.

Gasping, she covered her mouth with her hand. Trent had returned for her. But her relief was coupled with the fear of what Edwin might do to her husband when he came looking for her. Because if she knew anything about Trent it was that he'd never take no for an answer.

Trent had fought against the French for years. He was skilled at strategy and combat in a way that Edwin couldn't possibly understand. He'd likely dismiss her husband as a soft nobleman with more familiarity with the cut of his coat than how to defend himself against thugs.

But she'd seen him still sweaty from swordplay, and had noted that instead of being winded he was invigorated. He could hold his own against someone of Edwin's ilk. And he'd know how to handle the brute force of Edwin's henchmen as well.

And she would do her own part, by letting him know that she and Maggie were upstairs, and alive.

Fortunately, Maggie's captors hadn't bothered to remove everything from her prison that might be used as a weapon. Or a means to signal for help.

There before the hearth were two andirons, perhaps so familiar they'd not even registered with the kidnappers. Ophelia didn't want to consider what it meant about Maggie's likely state of unconsciousness for the duration of her captivity that she hadn't tried to use them herself. Or maybe she had and her current injury was the result.

Clenching her teeth to suppress her anger, she

slowly hoisted one of the andirons as far up as she could and dropped it on the bare floor just outside the edge of the carpet. Then, not content with that one loud sound, she did it again. And again. Until her arms were weak with fatigue.

If nothing else, she thought with a determined grin, at least Edwin's head would ache worse now.

"What the devil is this?" Edwin Carrington cried out as Trent and Freddy burst into his office with pistols drawn. "I have a good mind to call the watch on both of you. You have no right to come in here like this."

"It's funny you should talk about rights, Carrington," Trent said calmly, "when you are even as we speak holding both my wife and her friend Mrs. Margaret Grayson against their will."

"I have no idea what you're talking about, Trent," snapped Carrington, as if he weren't being held at gunpoint. "I haven't seen Ophelia since she came here two days ago with you. And as for Maggie—"

"It's her grace, the Duchess of Trent to you," Trent spat out. "And don't try to cozen me with your lies and tales of unrequited love. We both know quite well how you dispose of those ladies who don't return your twisted affections."

"If you're going to speak in riddles," Carrington said with a shrug, "then you should at the very least allow me to have a drink to go along with it."

He stood and stepped toward the decanter of brandy on the end of his desk.

But Trent, noting it was made of heavy crystal,

shook his head and moved the decanter out of reach. "I don't think so."

"A nice try, however," Freddy said with a nod of encouragement. "But amateurish at best."

"You'd better sit back down, Carrington, and tell me where you're keeping my wife and her friend."

"I don't know who's been telling you these tales," Carrington said, sitting back down, "but they are very much mistaken, I can assure you."

"Even your own brother?" Trent asked, his pistol never wavering. He knew they'd not gotten a confession from Dr. Hayes yet, but the lie might be enough to make Carrington tell him where Ophelia was. At least that's what he hoped.

"What has he been saying?" Carrington demanded, going pale. "What's the high-and-mighty Dr. Hayes been saying to slander me now?"

Trent noticed with pleasure that the newspaperman's eye was twitching.

"Only that you've used him as a means of getting rid of some of your more unsatisfactory lady friends. The ones who don't return your affection, I mean. What must it be like to find oneself rejected again and again by the opposite sex? I wonder."

"He doesn't know what he's talking about," Carrington snapped. "He gets confused. He's not as young as he used to be, you understand."

"Oh, I think he was quite lucid about the matter," Trent said, resting his shoulder against the wall. "He recalled very well the names of the women. As well as how he wrote out writs declaring them to be insane. It was really quite clever of you to get rid of them in that way. I must say. Very clever indeed."

"Don't patronize me, you ass," Carrington snarled. "You think it was easy for me to persuade him to do that? My whole life I'd had to beg for crumbs from him. While he grew richer and richer off the monies he collected from the families of those miserable madmen he treats. It's only right that I get something back from him. Especially when he hasn't given a penny to our poor mother."

"Ah, sibling affection," Freddy said dryly. "It fair brings a tear to my eye."

"Why don't you tell me what you've done with Maggie Grayson," Trent said grimly. "It was obvious to me the other day that you held her in some affection, though I mistakenly thought you were thinking only of doing away with her husband. I might have known you'd choose to punish the woman who rejected you, too. Can't let her get away with that, can you?"

Even Trent's quick reflexes were no match for the anger of a madman.

And as if he were an arrow let loose from a bowstring, Carrington leaped forward to clutch Trent by the cravat with one hand. In his other, he had a knife, which Trent felt pressed hard against his neck.

"Put the pistol down," Carrington said coldly, and pressed the knife harder. Carefully Trent lowered the gun to the surface of the desk. It would do Ophelia no good if he got himself killed by this madman before he was able to find her.

Out of the corner of his eye, he saw Freddy lift his own pistol to point directly at Carrington's head. Catching his friend's gaze, he gave a subtle shake of his head. Even so, Freddy gave Carrington a hard look before he lowered his weapon and placed it next to Trent's.

"A wise choice, Lord Frederick," Carrington said smugly. "If you kill me you'll never know where Ophelia and Maggie are, will you? Though I fear they'll both be dead before you get to them."

"Just tell us where they are, Carrington," Trent snarled, "and we'll let you go without any sort of retribution."

"I fear you've got it backward, your grace," Carrington said silkily, picking up and pocketing Freddy's pistol and then taking Trent's in his free hand and training it at Freddy. "I have all the weapons here."

"Just go," Freddy bit out. "You can't possibly think you can get away with kidnapping a duke and a duchess."

"Why shouldn't I get away with it?" Carrington said scornfully, moving from behind the desk so that he could more easily train the pistol on them both. "I've made four women disappear without a trace And I was able to shoot George Grayson right beneath the nose of your cronies in the Lords of Anarchy. Once I'm finished with you lot, Maggie and I are leaving for France. So, there won't be any question of there being consequences for anything I've done."

"You're madder than anyone your brother has

deemed insane, Carrington," Trent said through clenched teeth. "If you do not let me go find my wife right now, then I guarantee you'll face the consequences of all your crimes. It's now or never."

Just then, a loud crash sounded from above them. And in the split second it took for Carrington to react, Trent twisted out of his grasp, kicked the pistol out of his hand, and twisted the other man's wrist until he dropped the knife.

Quickly, Freddy scrabbled to pick up the knife and the pistol.

"Where are they, you bastard?" Trent demanded as he shoved Carrington's elbow behind his back.

"You think you're so smart, Trent." The editor sneered. "Let's see if you and your noble friend can figure it out."

More than anything in the world, Trent wanted to wipe that smirk off the kidnapper's face, but now was not the time to give in to his brute desires. He needed to go find out what that crash upstairs had been. Ophelia might be in trouble.

Pressing the editor's face down onto the desk, he turned to Freddy and let his friend grab Carrington by the elbows. "Tie him up. I'm going to find Ophelia."

Trusting Freddy to take care of Carrington, Trent scanned the dark room until finally he saw the outline of a door in the rear wall. He pushed through it and was relieved to see a set of stairs leading upward.

Taking them two at a time, he raced toward

where the loud crashes continued to sound. Until he stopped before a closed door on the second landing. For a moment the noise stopped. And not waiting to see if it would begin again, Trent threw himself against the door. It was three times before it gave, but when he fell into the room it was to see Ophelia hoisting an enormous andiron over her head.

On seeing him, however, she gave a shout of joy, and dropped the heavy fireplace ornament to the floor, which shook with the impact.

"I've never been happier to see anyone in all my life," she shouted as she threw her arms around his neck.

"What happened?" he demanded. "I suppose it was Carrington who brought you here?"

"Him and his two henchmen," she said against his shoulder. "Only look, Trent, Maggie is here, and she's not well."

Pulling away from him, she led him over to where Maggie lay still on a dirty mattress. But as Ophelia went to her knees beside her friend, Maggie's eyelids fluttered open.

"Maggie, dear," Ophelia said, smoothing a hand over the other woman's cheek. "It's Ophelia, I'm here."

"I know," Maggie said without opening her eyes. "You were making an awful enough racket to wake the dead."

"She was quite possibly saving your life, my dear Mrs. Grayson," said Freddy from the doorway where he dragged Edwin—his hands tied behind him with what looked like his own cravat—forward. Just for good measure, Freddy also held a dueling pistol on the other man. "Now, I don't know if the three of you are overly attached to this awful place. But I for one should very much like to get rid of this miscreant and go home."

Looking up at Trent, who had still not let her go, Ophelia smiled at Freddy. "I think that is an excellent idea."

"Freddy," Trent said to his friend, "will you please take Carrington to the nearest magistrate while Ophelia and I see that Mrs. Grayson is transported to our home so we can get her some proper treatment?"

"Perfectly fine by me," Freddy said grimly. "Come along, Carrington, I find myself quite hungry and wishing for my supper."

Before his friend could get far, however, Trent called after him. "By the way, old fellow. Thanks for your help. I could have done it alone, but not without a couple of nasty knife wounds, I fear."

Over his shoulder, his friend grinned. "What are friends for?"

With his captive protesting all the way, Freddy led Carrington away.

Pulling her away from where her friend lay on the floor, Trent held Ophelia against him, unable to let her go as all the things that might have happened if he hadn't returned to find her went through his mind.

"My God, he might have killed you, Ophelia," he

breathed against her hair. "Or worse. He's kept her here for days, likely without food or water. How much worse would he have treated you when this is what he did to the woman he loved!"

"But you came back," she assured him, stroking a comforting hand over his back. "You came back and you are here now and we are both fine. And so is Maggie."

Quickly she explained to him how as soon as he'd left she'd begun searching Maggie's desk and then had been interrupted by Carrington. "He was raving like a madman, Trent. You should have heard him. None of it made sense."

"I should be horsewhipped for leaving you here," Trent said, his mouth tight. If things had gone a different way he might now be cradling her broken body instead of her very live one. "I should have known there was some trick. I might have lost you."

"But you didn't," she assured him. "And when I saw that Maggie was here and alive, I was as relieved as I could be because I knew you would come back. Then I saw your curricle out the window and decided to attract your attention since you had to be downstairs. Though I wasn't sure Edwin was still there. But I used the andirons to make as much noise as I possibly could. And they did the trick."

Laughing, Trent pulled her against him again. "I love you, you stubborn, intrepid girl. I love you to distraction."

"You do?" she asked in a soft voice. "You don't know how relieved I am to hear you say it. For I very much fear I've been falling in love with you for weeks now."

"Then it's a good thing we're married," Trent growled in her ear. "Because there are some very naughty ways I'd like to show you my love just as soon as we get back home."

"An excellent idea," Ophelia said, kissing him quite thoroughly. "Now, you'd best go get help so that we can set that plan in motion."

"Your wish is my command, your grace," Trent said, bowing low over her hand before he disappeared down the stairs.

"He's a lovely man, your husband," Maggie said weakly, surprising Ophelia from her besotted staring after Trent.

"Maggie!" she gasped, rushing over to her friend's side. "I hope you didn't hear all of that!"

"Enough," Maggie said with a grin. "But your secret is safe with me. After all, you're married so there's no shame in it."

"I was so afraid I'd never see you again," Ophelia told her friend. "Thank goodness we found you before Edwin could do his worst."

"I'm not really sure what he intended," Maggie said, frowning as she struggled to sit up. "All I know is that he wanted to keep me away from George. Because he saw him as a rival of some sort."

"Do you love him?" Ophelia asked softly. "George, I mean?"

"Of course I do, my dear," Maggie said with a smile. "Just because we fight does not mean that we don't love each other."

"I suppose that's true," Ophelia said thoughtfully.

"Marriage is not about always agreeing," Maggie said wearily. "It's about knowing that even as you fight there's no one you'd rather be with."

Maggie needed to know that George was recuperating too, Ophelia thought. But that would come later. For now, she needed to rest herself.

Just then Trent returned, the two hulking brutes who'd attacked them on either side of him.

Ophelia's eyes grew wide, "No! Those are the men who—"

"It's all right, my dear," her husband said as he put an arm around her. "I know who they are. But for now, they work for me. When they've finished removing Mrs. Grayson to the carriage, I've got the watch downstairs to take them away."

"If you're sure," Ophelia said, watching the two men like a hawk as they gently lifted Maggie onto a litter.

Slowly they walked behind the two men and their burden as they went down the stairs, and out the door to the waiting carriage.

"You care very much for those you love, don't you?" Trent asked as they watched the two men who normally wielded manacles get manacled themselves.

"Of course I do," Ophelia said, kissing him lightly on the lips. "And you wouldn't have me any other way."

Which was the honest truth.

Epilogue

"How much longer?" Trent asked Ophelia, who was seated, along with Mainwaring and Hermione, in the drawing room of Craven House.

"Five minutes more than the last time you asked," his wife responded with a smile. "Babies are notoriously bad at punctuality, my dear," she assured him with a rub on his back.

The four had descended upon Freddy and Leonora's residence after Leonora had been overcome with labor pains at the belated celebration of the Duke and Duchess of Trent's marriage. Beside himself with nerves, Freddy had carried her from the ducal mansion himself and deposited her carefully in their carriage with orders for a footman to summon the physician.

Unable to leave immediately thanks to the hundreds of guests in their ballroom, Trent and Ophelia had finally been able to get away two hours later. They'd come into Craven House expecting to find that the baby had arrived, but Hermione and

Mainwaring had greeted them with the news that there was no news.

"Bad form," Trent grumbled. "Though I should expect nothing less from any child of Freddy's. He's always enjoyed making a grand entrance."

"Too right," said Mainwaring from where he sat with Hermione perched most scandalously on his knee. "Been that way since our school days. Though it would serve him right if the child turned out to be as stiff rumped as Freddy's eldest brother. In fact, I think that would be splendid. Imagine the fireworks!"

"It's quite rude of the two of you to speak ill of Freddy when he was so devoted to Leonora as to breach the sanctity of the birthing room," Ophelia said with a sniff. "How many husbands do you know who care so much about their wives that they would demand to be there for the birth of their child?"

But that didn't seem to make a difference to the men.

Trent made a rude noise, and Mainwaring openly scoffed.

"There is no great valor in going where he has no business going," Mainwaring said with a scowl. "All he's doing is making things more difficult for the rest of us. Now wives all over London will be demanding that their husbands be there to hold their hands while they are . . . well, you know."

"The husbands did have a role in creating the child," Ophelia argued. "It's the least they can do to be there for the pain of birthing them."

"Fee," Hermione said apologetically, "I'm afraid

I'm with the gentlemen on this one. There is no way I will allow Jasper anywhere near me during the birth of our child. I would sooner invite all the members of Brooks's and their wives. It is a private business, and as much as I love you, Jasper, I do not wish for you to see me like that."

"You needn't fear on that score, darling," said Jasper, kissing her hand. "I promise to stay far away smoking and drinking while you're bringing our babe into the world."

Ophelia narrowed her eyes at the other couple. Exchanging a glance with Trent, who had also heard something in their words, she spoke up. "Is there something you two would like to tell us?"

Smiling at each other, like two lovebirds caught kissing, the Mainwarings turned to face their accuser.

"I was waiting until the celebrations for your wedding and the arrival of Baby Lisle died down," Hermione said with a grin. "But if you'll keep it to yourselves, then yes, we are expecting a happy event."

With a squeal, Ophelia launched herself across the room and pulled her friend up in a hug.

At a more decorous pace, Trent followed and clapped Mainwaring on the back and kissed Hermione on the cheek.

"Wonderful news," Trent pronounced, pulling Ophelia against his side. "And not too far after this one to keep them from being friends."

"Just what I said." Mainwaring grinned. "I'd like to see them all at Eton together. Like we were, only more popular."

"And better looking," Trent said with a wink.

"Hard to be better looking than this," Mainwaring said, gesturing from his head to his toes. "Though I daresay there is godlike. I've never quite achieved that."

"Only in your mind, dearest," Hermione said with an elbow to his ribs.

"Better get busy, the two of you," Mainwaring said with a pointed look in the direction of the Duke and Duchess of Trent.

"It's not for want of trying," Trent said just before Ophelia jabbed *him* in the ribs with an elbow. "That is to say, we are quite looking forward to the time when we can announce our own blessed event."

"Better," Ophelia said with a scowl.

He was saved from replying by the sound of the door being thrown open.

They all looked up and saw Freddy, in his shirtsleeves, looking disheveled but brimming with happiness in the doorway.

"It's a girl!" he said with a grin. "Mama and baby are doing well. And can I be the first to say that my daughter has the best set of lungs in England!"

The quartet of onlookers shouted a huzzah and rushed over to hug and congratulate the new father, who quickly ushered them upstairs to Leonora's sitting room.

Inside, they found a nursemaid cradling the newest little Lisle, who was demonstrating her excellent lung capacity.

"Lads," Freddy told the other two men, as Ophelia and Hermione rushed over to see the baby, "I don't think you know what love is until you've watched your own child being born. I don't know why every man doesn't demand it."

"Lord Frederick," said Dr. Simpson, London's most celebrated *accoucheur,* as he entered the sitting room, "I hope you will not go about preaching this nonsense to your fellow *ton* husbands. For if every man were as intrusive in the birthing chamber I'd be forced to leave my profession."

"Have no fear, Dr. Simpson," Hermione assured him after a pointed look in her husband's direction. "I do not think the ladies of the *ton* will be quite so keen to invite their husbands in as Leonora was."

"Whatever you wish, my dear," said Mainwaring, exchanging a relieved look with Trent. "I will follow your wishes in these matters since you are the one who will be doing the hard work."

"Leonora is well, Dr. Simpson?" asked Ophelia from where she was holding the new baby, who had stopped crying just as soon as Ophelia picked her up, against her chest.

"She is indeed, your grace." Dr. Simpson beamed. "Indeed, were it not for the unusual circumstance of Lord Frederick insisting upon being there for the birth, it would have been a routine matter."

"She likes you," Trent said, stepping up beside Ophelia to look down at the impossibly tiny thing in her arms. "You've got a natural talent, it would seem."

Ophelia beamed up at him. "I hope so, for I mean to have a passel of these."

"That many, eh?"

"Well, perhaps just a plethora."

Unable to stop himself, Trent leaned down and kissed her.

"Don't do that in front of my child," Freddy chided, coming forward to take the baby away from Ophelia. "Come, Leonora should be ready for visitors now."

After ascertaining that it was indeed the case, he ushered the others into his wife's bedroom.

"Congratulations," Ophelia said, moving to the bedside to take Leonora's hand.

She was pleased to see that her friend looked exhausted but overjoyed. And when she took the baby from Freddy, something about seeing their little trio together brought tears to Ophelia's eyes.

"Isn't she the most beautiful baby you've ever seen?" Leonora asked, beaming.

"By far," Mainwaring said with a nod.

"In all my years," agreed Trent.

"But not quite as beautiful as her mama," Freddy said with a grin.

"I just wish Jonny were here to meet her," Leonora said, tears springing to her eyes. Kissing the child on her tiny nose, she said, "He would have loved to meet you, my dear girl."

"He'd have been proud," Hermione said with a watery smile. "And surprised to find us all married off. But not disappointed, I think."

"No," Freddy agreed, exchanging a look with Mainwaring and Trent, who stood with their arms around their wives, in a semicircle around Leonora's bed.

"He'd have been happy," Trent said with a grin. "Damned happy."

Author's Note

In 1829, Freeman Anderton's lawsuit against prominent alienist (psychiatrist in 19th-century speak) Dr. George Man Burrows for wrongful confinement (which Anderton won) revealed something to the British public that had not hitherto been common knowledge. Namely, that it was a common practice of many alienists to use unofficial "letters de cachet" to lend legitimacy to their attendants when they came to take away the person in question, solely to prevent those around the "lunatic" from interfering.

And, perhaps more disturbing, was the fact that these declarations of a person's lunacy were most often made without the physician ever having examined the patient.

In his defense against Anderton's suit, Burrows argued that it was often necessary for a physician to rely on the word of family members or close friends to determine a person's state of mind because "procrastination could end up in suicide or homicide in an urgent case" (Suzuki 53).

It doesn't take a devious mind to see the possibilities for corruption of this practice, and it's one of those possibilities that I write about in *Good Dukes Wear Black*. While there don't seem to be any cases similar to the one I describe in the book, where Dr. Hayes is persuaded to have women confined on the word of his own brother, it does seem to me to have been possible. And from there I wove my story.

If you'd like to read more about the treatment of madness in the 19th century and the ways in which alienists navigated the waters between the public and the domestic, I highly recommend *Madness at Home: The Psychiatrist, the Patient, and the Family in England, 1820–1860,* University of California Press, (2006) by Akihito Suzuki.

Coming soon. . .

Look for the next novel in Manda Collins's
Lords of Anarchy series

READY SET ROGUE

Available in January 2017
from St. Martin's Paperbacks